Petra's BIKERS

ROYAL BASTARDS MC

USA TODAY BESTSELLING AUTHOR

MISTY WALKER

To all the fans of this series who waited so patiently for Moto, Sly, and Petra to get it on. I hope I did you justice.

ROYAL BASTARDS CODE

PROTECT: The club and your brothers come before anything else, and must be protected at all costs. **CLUB** is **FAMILY**.

RESPECT: Earn it & Give it. Respect club law. Respect the patch. Respect your brothers. Disrespect a member and there will be hell to pay.

HONOR: Being patched in is an honor, not a right. Your colors are sacred, not to be left alone, and **NEVER** let them touch the ground.

OL' LADIES: Never disrespect a member's or brother's Ol'Lady. **PERIOD.**

CHURCH is **MANDATORY.**

LOYALTY: Takes precedence over all, including well-being.

HONESTY: Never **LIE, CHEAT,** or **STEAL** from another member or the club.

TERRITORY: You are to respect your brother's property and follow their Chapter's club rules.

TRUST: Years to earn it …seconds to lose it.

NEVER RIDE OFF: Brothers do not abandon their family.

ROYAL BASTARDS MC SERIES
FOURTH RUN

Royal Bastards MC Facebook Group
www.facebook.com/groups/royalbastardsmc

Website
www.royalbastardsmc.com

Five years ago, she took a piece of me.
Now it's time to collect.

From USA Today bestselling author Misty Walker comes a secret baby, age gap, dark MC romance.

It was supposed to be a one-night stand. A quick release before Coyote went back to his nomad lifestyle with the Royal Bastards MC.

But it's been five years, and he's still searching for the girl with the owl eyes who disappeared into the night. And not just because she stole his leather cut. He can't seem to get her out of his head.

Until one day, she pops back up out of nowhere. Instead of breaking down her door and confronting her, Coyote does what he does best. He hides in the shadows, watches from a distance, and learns everything he can.

Turns out Riley Renna isn't who he thought at all. Somehow, she's involved with a rival MC—the Sons of Erebus—and has a kid. A little girl who looks suspiciously like Coyote.

When the president of the Sons starts moving in on his family, Coyote knows the time for just watching is up. It's time to step into the light and claim what's his.

Daddy's home, Little Owl.

Petra's BIKERS

PROLOGUE

Petra

The club's music pounds a steady beat that flows through my body as I move. The people dancing around me are just as lost to the music as I am, and our combined energy is nearly palpable. God, it feels good to let everything go and pretend I'm a carefree twenty-something like almost everyone else here.

I close my eyes and lift my hands in the air, letting every ounce of stress I felt earlier go. I feed off the smell of perfume, sweat, and alcohol, a combination that equates to freedom and joy.

As a third-year resident at UMC, I'm surrounded by so much death and sickness. I need this reminder that people are thriving in this world. Some of them are even happy.

"Let's go get some water," Mia yells next to my ear.

My eyes open, and I find my best friend and co-worker at my side. She grabs my hand and tugs me toward the bar, where we find one open stool. She takes it, and I slide between her and the man in the next seat.

"The vibe is amazing tonight," I say as I wave to get the

bartender's attention. She gives me a nod and finishes the drink she's pouring before making her way over to us.

"It really is." Mia tugs on the neckline of her sparkly, champagne-colored top. She's a true ginger, so she wears every emotion on her skin. And right now, her bright red cheeks tell me she's overheated.

"Two waters, please," I say.

"You got it." The busty bartender grabs two plastic bottles and sets them on the bar.

I set a ten-dollar bill in front of her and smile. "Keep the change."

"Thanks, babe. Let me know if you need anything else."

Both Mia and I twist the caps off the bottles and chug. The cool liquid re-energizes me, and by the time I reach the bottom, I'm already scouring the dance floor for the crowd that looks like they're having the most fun.

I catch the eye of a tall man with long hair, a beard, and dark, sultry eyes. Just my type. I send him a flirtatious smile that he returns right back to me.

"Oh, he's hot," Mia says.

"Delicious." I bite into my lower lip, my gaze still firmly on him. When he walks toward me, I grab Mia's hand and lean into her. "Oh my God, he's coming this way."

"Get it, girl. He looks like he'll be fun to grind up against for the night."

As he struts his way to the bar, he drags a hand through his hair in a montage moment usually reserved for movies.

Yes, this is what exactly I need tonight.

As the crowd parts, his body comes into view, and it's every bit as tantalizing as the top half of him. He has on low-slung jeans and a gray, acid wash T-shirt that somehow looks both trendy and casual.

I straighten my slinky tank top and tug on the hem of my corset-style leather skirt. Since my day-to-day uniform is a pair of scrubs, I go all out when I get a night off. I even shaved. Everywhere.

Not that I plan to go home with someone, but something about my silky panties rubbing against bare flesh makes me feel bold.

"Hey," he says, tucking his hands into his pockets. "Can I buy you a drink?"

"You sure can," Mia chimes in, hopping off the stool. "I was just leaving. Take my seat."

"I don't want to break up the party."

"Not at all. I need to pee." She pats the stranger on the arm as she brushes past him. "She likes tequila."

"Noted." He offers me the stool, but I decline, so he sits down. "I'm Tyler. What's your name?"

"Cameron." I shake his hand, noting his callouses. Definitely not a doctor like the last three men I dated. "Nice to meet you, Tyler."

"It's *really* nice to meet you, Cameron." He flags down the bartender and orders us tequila shooters. I don't drink often, but I have a day off tomorrow and nothing better to do than recover from a hangover.

"Cheers." I tap my shot glass with his and toss the liquid down. It burns, and my face screws up, but Tyler is right there holding a lime to my lips. I smile and bite down, letting the sour flavor erase the liquor.

"Thanks."

"No problem." He runs his thumb along the bottom of my lip. "Lime juice."

My cheeks heat, but I shake the nerves off. I'm not about to be bashful. "What do you do for a living, Tyler?"

"I'm an acquirer of goods."

My brows knit. "What does that mean?"

"Wealthy people hire me to find very specific merchandise." He rests an elbow on the bar. "What do you do?"

I could be honest, tell him I spend a hundred hours a week at the hospital where I don't even have time to pee, let alone shower, but that feels like too much. I'm not that girl tonight. Nope.

"I'm a go-go dancer at a club downtown."

"Really?" He flashes me a wolfish grin. "I need to see those moves in action."

Standing, he takes my hand and leads me out to the dance floor, where I show off my best moves. The liquid courage helps, but so does this fine as hell man watching me like I'm giving him a private show.

"You're fucking beautiful," he shouts over the music, gripping me by the hips and tugging me into him.

"Thanks." I toss him a wink and wrap my arms around his neck. He smells expensive, like citrus and oak. His clients must pay him well.

After another shot of tequila and a full hour on the dance floor, I'm parched. The twelve-hour day I had before getting ready to go out is catching up with me. Tyler probably thinks I'll be going home with him tonight, but I need to have a connection with someone before I'm comfortable enough to get naked. If he wants to see me again, I'm down for that, but otherwise, this is where it will end.

I hook a thumb over my shoulder. "I should go find my friend, but I had an amazing time with you."

"Party's over, huh?" He pouts, but there's no pressure behind the statement, which I appreciate. But there's also no offer to give me his number.

That's disappointing.

"I'm afraid so." I search through the crowd, trying to find Mia, but since the club doesn't close for another three hours, it's still popping.

"Can I give you and your friend a ride home?"

"You've been drinking," I remind him. I've seen too many

people come through the ER busted up or even dead from drunk driving accidents. There's no way I'll let that be me, or worse, Mia.

"I'd never drive drunk," he says solemnly. "I have a driver in the lot waiting for me."

"A driver? Maybe I'm in the wrong business."

"I do okay." His confident smirk is all-telling. This guy is loaded.

"Let me find Mia, and I'll ask her what she thinks."

"Okay. I'll be at the bar." He leans down and kisses me on the cheek. "Whatever you decide, I hope I'll leave with at least your phone number."

Finally, the offer I was hoping for. My insides do a happy dance. "Only if you plan to use it."

"Oh, I'll use it. This isn't the last time you'll see my face."

I walk the perimeter of the club twice, not finding Mia, and send a ridiculous number of texts, all of them unanswered. The buzz I had fades quickly, and an uneasiness settles over me. This isn't like her. At all.

I find Tyler right where he said he'd be. He's on his phone and nursing a glass of brown liquor.

"She's not here," I say.

He tucks his phone away. "Is this something she does often?"

"Never. We always come together and leave together."

"Did you try to call her?" he asks.

"I texted her. All of them are sitting at delivered." My shoulders sag.

"How about this? I'll have my driver swing us by her house so you can see if she made it home. If she's not there, I'll help you call hospitals or the cops, whatever you decide." His genuine concern puts me at ease.

I could take an Uber to her house, but it would take an hour to get a car on a Saturday night in downtown Vegas. And with the way I'm feeling right now, this can't wait.

"Okay. Thank you."

He places a hand on the small of my back, leading me outside. A black, tinted-out limo pulls up the second we step up to the curb.

"This is me," he says, opening the back door.

Looking back, I'll see all the signs I missed, all the red flags flying right in front of my face. But at this moment, I'm too worried about my friend to pick up on any of them.

I duck into the car, sliding along the buttery leather. The last things I remember are Mia, duct tape across her mouth and hands tied on the seat in front of me, and the sharp sting of a needle being pushed into my neck by someone who was waiting for me inside.

I wake up with my head pounding, my tongue thick, and every muscle in my body aching. Whatever I'm lying on is hard, cold, and unforgiving. As my brain registers everything that happened, I bolt upright.

I'm in a pitch-black room. No, not a room. A metal box, maybe?

A grunting noise comes from my right. Judging by the tone, I know it's a woman. I blink, adjusting to the dark but can't see shit. Feeling around, I find a cold, bare foot. Someone else is in here, and they're not okay.

I crawl that way, my knees scraping against the steel as I go. She grunts again, and I recognize the voice. It's Mia. My hands skim up her shoulders until I reach her face and feel the slick duct tape stuck across her mouth.

"Oh my God, Mia." I grimace as I rip off the duct tape. "What happened?"

The second she can, she lets out a pained sob. I hug her to me while she collects herself.

"There was a-a-a guy," she stutters, her body trembling. "We were dancing, and he asked if I wanted to go smoke a joint in his car."

"Mia," I scold.

"Don't *Mia* me. You're here too." Her voice cracks at the end.

I sigh. "Fair point. What then?"

"He took me to that limo, and as soon as I was inside, he attacked me. Oh my God, Cam. Where are we? What's going on?"

I fall back on my ass. "I don't know. I couldn't find you at the club. Tyler, the guy I met, offered to help me find you. Then I saw you and"—my hand flies to my neck where I feel the sore spot from whatever I was injected with—"another man drugged me."

"They drove us to the middle of fucking nowhere, Cam. Seriously. Nowhere. Then they put us in here without saying a word."

"Give me your hands. Let's find a way out." I work the tape off her wrists, and we hug for a long moment. "How did this happen?"

"I have no idea. I thought we were smarter than this," she says.

"Apparently, we aren't, but let's be smart now. Come on. Feel around for a latch or something."

Right as we stand, a loud clattering comes from the far end of the container, and artificial light spills in. Two shadowy figures walk inside. I know from the silhouette that one of them is Tyler. I spent all night admiring his frame and beautiful, flowing hair that I freed from its elastic while we were on the dance floor.

"You're awake," Tyler says.

"What the fuck, Tyler? What is this?" Venom drips from my words.

He ignores me, turning to the other man. "Go take a look. You'll be happy."

A flashlight clicks on, and he aims it at us. I wrap my arms around Mia and squint at the bright light.

"Very nice," an accented voice says. French, maybe?

"I told you. Doubt they're virgins, but they're pretty enough to make up for it." Tyler tucks his hands in his pockets casually, like this is normal. Is it normal for him? When he said he acquired goods, did he mean—oh, God. He meant women. He acquires women.

The man I don't know walks closer and caresses the side of my face with the back of his hand. I flinch and jerk away. "Don't touch me, asshole."

He ignores my outburst and glances over his shoulder at Tyler. "Very nice. I'll give you twenty for the meek one and forty for the feisty one."

Mia whimpers, her hold on me tightening, but my mind is stuck on what he said. Twenty? Forty? Is he talking dollars?

"She's worth fifty, at least. She's a dancer."

Why did I make up that stupid lie? Would it have made a difference?

The stranger's attention returns to me. "A dancer, huh? Okay, then. Fifty. She'll be fun to break."

Tyler claps his hands. "Great. Let's go finish our business, and then they're all yours."

"What are you talking about? You can't sell us. We're human fucking beings," I spit out.

The stranger clucks his tongue, not at all bothered by my outburst. "That's where you're wrong, sweetness. Your country, your constitution, your government make you think you have inherent rights. But all those things mean shit when you cross the path of men who have enough money and power to override your freedom. Men who have money, like me? We're the ones who are free. We have no laws, no rules, no one to tell us what we can or can't do."

I squeeze Mia's shoulder, drop my arm, and grab her hand,

hoping she'll follow my lead. With no plan other than to run, I knock the flashlight from his grip and run, dragging Mia behind me.

Tyler blocks our exit, but I've taken self-defense classes. I shove the base of my palm into his nose. A sickening crunch echoes off the steel walls, and he grunts in pain. It's enough to get me past him but not enough to save Mia. He grabs her wrist and yanks her backward, out of my hold.

I pause, looking out at the empty parking lot we're in and then back to Mia, who's full-on sobbing now.

"Even if you get away, and that's a big *if* because we will catch you, you'll never see your friend again. I'll make sure she pays for your mistake." Tyler ignores the blood trickling down his face.

What do I do? Try to run for help? Or go back and wait for another chance? Really, there's no choice. I can't leave Mia here to fight alone.

I double over and scream out my frustrations.

"Good choice." The man with the accent approaches and jerks me upright with a tight grasp on my upper arm.

With the light from the streetlamps overhead, I get my first look at him. His face is littered with pockmarks, his nose is round like a drooping balloon, and his eyes are dark as night. It's July in Vegas, so the temperature is sweltering, yet a chill runs up my spine.

"What do you want from me?" I whisper.

"Do you want the truth?" he asks, his tone playful and light.

"Yes."

"Everything. I want to use you up until that fire behind your eyes is extinguished."

"What then?" I don't want the answer, but I need it.

He fists my hair and jerks it back so I'm looking him square in the eye. "Then I'll kill you, and this will all be over."

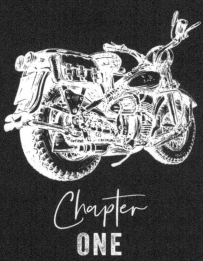

Chapter
ONE

Four and a half years later ...
Petra

"There's nothing more we can do for her," Marcia says from the hallway. "Right now, she's clean and wants to stay sober. Which is an amazing feat."

I wonder if they know I can hear them. I'm in Marcia's office, but they didn't close the door when Sly demanded to speak with her in the hall, and I'm not deaf. Though for the last few years, I wish I had been. Then my memory wouldn't be full of vile voices echoing through the chambers of my mind.

"But she's still ... well, you know." There's an edge of irritation to Sly's tone.

"She refuses to discuss what she's been through, and if we can't get her to talk, there's no reason for her to stay. Her memories will come back when she's healthy enough to handle them."

On top of the drug and alcohol addiction that got me sent here, I also have no memory of my life before the day I was taken, and even those memories are sketchy. Marcia calls it dissociative amnesia. I blocked out who I was, and now, it's tucked away in a part of my brain I can't reach, no matter how hard I try.

"Can't you hypnotize her or some shit?" Moto asks.

"Hypnotherapy can be a useful tool if the participant is willing. Petra is not."

"Let me get this straight. She's been here a month, and you still haven't found out who she is or what she's been through?" Sly thinks he wants to know. But he doesn't. Some horrors are better left unsaid.

"I assure you, getting clean after God knows how many years of drug and alcohol abuse is no easy task. Petra exceeded all my expectations." Marcia leads the men back into her office, where she plucks a card from her desk and hands it to Sly. "She's always welcome back when she's ready to heal the emotional wounds."

I'm right here. You don't have to talk about me like I'm not.

"Fine." Moto crouches in front of me. "You ready to go, Dove?"

Dove. It's what both he and Sly have taken to calling me, outright refusing to use the name given to me by my captors. Petra. I remember the day the pock-marked man, who demanded I call him Sir, took me to his home and gave me that name. He promised when he was done with me, he'd kill me.

He lied, and sometimes I wish he followed through.

Instead, after he had his fill, he gifted me to Anthony, who forced me into marriage after his previous wife died. I suffered even more physical and sexual abuse from him but was also introduced to Xanax and hydrocodone and got access to alcohol. It's how he kept me docile enough to do whatever disgusting thing he wanted.

Until one day, everything changed.

The Royal Bastards are heroes in disguise. They didn't mean to save me. Matter of fact, they wanted to use me as bait to get to Anthony, assuming I meant something to him. Too bad my husband didn't care if I lived or died. But it didn't deter the Royal Bastards. They still killed him and his soulless son.

Good riddance.

The Bastards could've dropped me back off at Anthony's mansion. Let me continue to self-medicate myself to death. But they didn't. They took me in, cared for me, and when it became clear my addiction was something I couldn't kick on my own, they sent me here.

"Dove?" Moto asks again, and I blink, snapping out it.

I nod and stand, keeping my eyes trained on the ground with my hands linked at the base of my spine. Both of my owners required this submissive posture, and it's a hard habit to break after years of being forced to take this stance or risk being tortured.

Sly practically growls. "Do you see this? You were supposed to fix her."

That stings a little. I know I have work to do so I can reintegrate into society, but it's only been a few months since they pulled me from my hellish life.

What if they don't want a timid, meek drain on their resources hanging around? Where will you go?

That thought has me releasing my hands and tipping my chin up in a way I know will please them.

See? I can do better.

"Mr. Sly—"

"Ain't no mister, doc," Sly corrects.

Marcia nods. "Sly, she's not broken. She needs time and safety. Two things I trust you can give her?"

"Can't get any safer than with us," Moto says, taking my hand.

My gaze flicks to where we're joined. My fingers—thin and so pale I can trace the path of the blue-green veins running up and down their length—are a stark contrast to his darker ones, with black grease crusted into their dry cracks from working on bike engines.

"Petra, are you leaving here willingly?" Marcia asks.

"Yes," I say with all the confidence I can muster.

"And do you feel safe?"

"Yes."

It's true. While I don't remember who I am or where I came from, I remember my life before the Royal Bastards and know with every fiber of my being that I'm more than safe with them. I'm protected.

Though I don't know why. I'm nobody.

"Okay. If you ever need me, you have my card. I put my cellphone on the back in case you can't reach me here." Turning her attention to Sly, she adds, "Please find her a psychiatrist as soon as you get her home."

He nods, and Moto snags my backpack before tugging me down the hall and out into the desert sun. Tilting my face to the sky, I close my eyes and trust Moto to lead me in the right direction while I bask in the fresh air and warmth.

Before I was rescued, I would go months without stepping foot outside. Now that I'm free of that life, I relish every chance I get to be outdoors. It's a gift most people take for granted until it's no longer available to you.

Sly walks backward, both middle fingers in the air directed at The Healing Ranch, and shouts, "Fuck you for nothing!"

I understand his frustration. After trying to fix me on their own, it became clear I needed professional help. I wasn't really talking. I was sneaking alcohol and weed, things readily available in a biker's clubhouse, and having panic attacks and nightmares.

They thought sending me here would be a cure-all, that I'd walk out a normal woman, memories intact. That obviously didn't happen.

Sly's anger is misdirected. I'm the one he should blame because Marcia was right. While I lapped up all treatments to get me off the drugs and alcohol, everything else was off-limits.

When Moto stops short, I open my eyes and see two black Harley-Davidsons. My mouth gapes. When they brought me here, it was in a white van. I've never ridden on one of these intimidating beasts, or maybe I have. I don't know.

"Thought you'd like to ride home in style." Moto flashes me a smile that both warms and frightens me. While all the Royal Bastards have been kind, patient, and accepting, there's always that niggle in my mind warning me not to get too comfortable. That men can't be trusted. That their true colors will come out eventually.

Sly hands over the smaller of two large helmets hanging on the handlebars of his bike.

"Got you this." Setting the matte black helmet on my head, he flips down the visor, then carefully clips the buckle in place and tightens the straps. It's heavy, and since I'm still weak and recovering from malnourishment, my neck feels like a wet noodle being pushed to the ground. "You'll get used to it."

"I get her first," Moto says.

"I'm the one who brought the helmet," Sly protests.

"You snooze, you lose." Moto tosses my backpack at Sly, who shoulders it.

I'm used to their constant bickering. It's been that way since day one. They're competitive and enjoy challenging each other over everything, even stupid things, like me.

Moto hops on his bike, throws on his blacked-out helmet topped with small devil horns, and motions for me to come close. After a quick tutorial on how to ride bitch—his words, not mine—I climb on.

Panic starts at my stomach and climbs up to my throat when I'm forced to place my hands on Moto's midsection. I went too many years not having a say in who touched me and who I touched that now, I'd rather have an impenetrable bubble around me.

That's not realistic, though. Plus, Moto and Sly haven't done anything to make me think they want to take advantage of me, and they've worked hard to earn my confidence since I've been in their care.

The engine comes to life in a deafening roar that's soon quieted by rock music playing in my ears.

As my head swivels to look at Sly in question, the volume of the music mutes, and his voice—clear as day—asks, "Didn't think we'd leave you without a way to communicate, did you?"

"Do I need to push a button to talk?" I feel around the helmet.

"Nope. All three mics are paired, and you can speak whenever you want."

"Pretty cool, huh?" Moto asks.

"Yeah." It warms my heart that they'd think to do this and makes me feel better knowing I have a way of asking them to stop if I need a bathroom break.

"We usually wear domes that don't have the face shield and all this gadgetry, but it's a long ride, so we thought this was best," Sly says.

"Hang on tight, Dove." Moto presses my hands into the soft leather of his cut, encouraging me to tighten my grip.

He gasses it, and I nearly fly off the back at the force. Not feeling like the loose leather vest is a good place to hold, I worm my hands under his cut and feel his hard abs tense through his T-shirt. I wonder if I made a mistake but then his hand is on mine, his rough thumb stroking back and forth twice before moving back to the handlebar.

We hit the freeway, and the increased speed sends a *zing* of excitement through me. It doesn't take me long to loosen up a little and take in my surroundings. On my right, I see the Vegas Strip, and for a second, I think I recognize it. The bright lights, tall casinos, and busy streets all look vaguely familiar. But I brush it off, knowing most people have been to Vegas. It's likely I did in my previous life too.

A life I know existed but can't quite reach.

Back at the ranch, I tried to remember who I was before I became a human pet, but in order to do so, I'd have to backtrack from the day I was taken. But I can't go there. The one time I did, perched on a couch in Marcia's therapy room, I had such a severe panic attack that I was convinced I was dying. My chest constricted so hard that I couldn't breathe, and eventually, I passed out.

I think it's better this way. Whoever I was doesn't matter. I'm more worried about who I'll become now. Now that I'm not drowning my pain in drugs and alcohol.

I'm sober now, and I plan to stay that way. I don't know what the future holds, but I know Moto and Sly will always make sure I'm okay.

"You all right?" Sly's voice comes over the speaker in my ear.

"Yeah."

"We'll stop in an hour to fuel up but let us know if you need a bathroom break before then."

"Okay."

The music returns, and before long, I lose myself to it. Music is another luxury I haven't had access to for a long time, and I realize I like it. My body aches to move to the steady rock tempo. When we get back to the clubhouse, maybe I'll ask the guys if there's a way for me to have music in my room. Judging from experience, I know they'll comply.

My heart soars, and again, my appreciation grows for the two men who have given me so much in such a short amount of time.

Ever since I was brought to the clubhouse, they've been there for me. They took it upon themselves to make sure I had what I needed and felt safe. It was a scary time for me, and I was certain they only took me to use me the way so many others have.

I was wrong.

When they saw how frightened I was, they sat me down

and laid it out for me. I was there to heal and find my way. Under no circumstances would anyone there take something I wasn't giving freely.

I struck the jackpot the day they came into my life.

Though, in the dark shadows of my mind, I can't help but wonder, for how long? When will they tire of me? When will they expect me to leave the comfort and safety of the clubhouse? I see the curious way the club president, Loki, watches the way Sly and Moto dote on me. I know he's wondering what Sly and Moto get out of it because I wonder that too.

I know they want more from me, even though they'd never push for it. But sometimes, I catch their heated gaze, or their touch feels more than friendly. It scares me because I like it. I like them. And that thought is terrifying.

My thoughts keep me busy until Moto steers the bike off onto an exit and pulls into a gas station. I stay on the bike until Sly comes to my side and helps me off. Even standing on solid ground, my body continues to vibrate.

"Need the restroom?" he asks, and I nod after he removes my helmet. "Gas us both up; I'll take Dove inside."

"I can go alone," I insist.

"Not happening." Sly takes my hand and leads me inside and to the women's room. "I'll wait right here."

"Don't you need to go?"

"I will after I hand you off to Moto."

I tilt my head, wondering what he thinks will happen to me in the bathroom.

He reads my expression and says, "The business the club deals in sometimes creates enemies. Enemies that might be watching and looking to take advantage of the people in our lives. Better we're safe than sorry."

I gulp and scan the nearly empty gas station. "Should I be worried?"

Sly flashes me a cocky grin. "You think I'd let anything happen to you?"

Deciding that he wouldn't, I step inside the grimy restroom and do my business. After washing my hands, I find Moto waiting for me.

"You good? Need a snack or something?"

"Maybe some water?"

"Got you covered back at my bike. Sly should be out in just a second." He nods to the men's room, and as if summoned, Sly walks out.

"Ready?"

Back at the bikes, I drink water from a thermal tumbler Moto had stashed in his saddlebag. Handing it back to him, I say, "Thanks."

Then we're on the road again. This time, I'm on the back of Sly's bike with my arms around his middle. He's trimmer than Moto but just as muscled. His riding style is different too. Moto rode straight and true, but Sly veers side to side as we fly down the freeway.

I giggle with nervous energy, not sure if I enjoy it or not.

After seven hours, we finally pull up to tall steel gates with the Royal Bastards insignia welded to the front. The gate parts, and we park in the gravel lot. I'm tired and road-weary as Sly pulls off my helmet, and along with Moto, we walk inside.

I'm home.

Chapter
TWO

Sly

"I don't like that we both have to leave." I climb onto Moto's bed, where he's already resting. Rolling to my side, I prop my head up on a hand.

"I don't either, but everyone else is tied up." He turns on his side, mimicking my position.

He's the sexiest man I've ever laid eyes on. His face is angular, with a straight nose, high brows, and a sharp jawline. His long, stick-straight black hair is tied back in a low ponytail, perfect for fisting when—

"I asked Goblin to keep an eye on her." He interrupts my dirty thoughts. "Still doesn't feel right. One or both of us have been with her since the beginning."

From the first time I saw her, I felt a pull toward her. She had nobody, and since I know what that feels like, I became her somebody. There wasn't anything sexual about it. I just wanted her to know somebody cared, so I spent time with her. Even if she wasn't talking and lost in her demons, I was there.

Moto saw how much time I was spending with her, and when something's important to me, it's important to him, so he started hanging around too. He saw how special she was. Truly fuckin' special.

That's when things started clicking into place, and we realized we wanted her for more. But that can't happen until she's well.

"Still don't like it. She just got back, and we haven't found her a therapist yet."

"I got some names, but I want you to do a deep dive into their history and make sure they can be trusted." He places a hand on my hip.

"Sure. Just email me the list." I lean in and give him a chaste kiss. Though I want to deepen it, we need to leave soon.

"Does she know?"

I flop onto my back. "I told her this morning."

"Was she okay with it?"

"Yeah. She said she'll probably catch up on sleep and stay in her room. She asked for a speaker, so I set her up with a smart speaker. You'd think I gave her a diamond ring with how excited she was."

"Good. Prez said he'll keep away the hangarounds and patch pussy." He combs his fingers through the curls on top of my head, and I close my eyes. I love these quiet moments where it's just him and me.

To everyone outside these doors, I'm the one who's good with money, can hack my way into any system, and has sniper-level shooting skills. Moto handles our schedules, making sure our gun shipments are delivered on time, and when he's not doing that, he's in the garage, fixing up our bikes.

But in here, we're just us. Two men who connected on a level most wouldn't understand.

"That's good," I drawl sleepily, and he traces a line down my cheek. His touch relaxes me, always has. He's my best friend, and though we don't talk labels, he's much more than that.

What started out as us tag-teaming bitches, slowly

progressed into us fuckin' them at the same time. Then one night, the chick we were with wanted us both in her cunt, something neither of us hesitated to do. It turned me on to feel his cock sliding along mine, and I came so fucking hard.

After that, there were no boundaries between us, and when there weren't any women around, we found out we liked fuckin' each other, too.

It's not just the sex, though. We love each other as brothers, roommates, lovers, and partners.

We don't get into it with our club brothers. It's none of their damn business. Pretty sure they know anyway; it's just not something we sit around the fire pit and talk about. Same way we don't sit around and discuss everyone else's relationships. We're club brothers—a bond stronger than any blood—but we're not big on feelings.

"I guess you haven't found anything else on Dove?" he asks.

"No. I've combed through pages and pages of missing person reports, but none of them are her. It's like she just appeared out of nowhere."

"I can't believe she spent a month at that place, and she still doesn't have her memory."

"Me neither." I sigh when he smooths the lines that formed between my eyes at the thought of Dove.

"But if she did, what would we do? Take her home and walk away?"

"We'd have to."

That thought makes me frown. Ever since we landed eyes on the scared girl, we've both experienced the same pull to her that we do with each other. It's protective, sure, but it's so much more.

The asshole she was married to was a giant prick, and finding out she was given to him as a present made us want to bring him back to life just so we could kill him again.

The day we found her, she was drugged out on pills, high as a motherfucking kite, and curled into a ball on Anthony

Corsetti's bed. We thought she'd be the perfect bait to get Roch's girl, Truly, back after Anthony's son, Max, took her. When Anthony told us to go ahead and kill her, something broke in me. No one should be that disposable.

I should know. I grew up disposable.

But I found my family, and Dove can too. Only time will tell whether that'll be with her blood relatives or here with us. Not so secretly, I hope it's with us. And someday, I hope she'll see us as more than her caretakers and maybe open up to the idea of being with us.

Not that we've ever done something like that before. We're used to one night of pleasure before sending the chick on her way. We've never had an inkling to start a triad relationship. Until Dove. Now that's all we want. But her mind is all screwed up from God knows how many years of abuse. We don't know if she'll ever come around, but we're willing to wait it out.

Our threesomes have even stopped. That's how serious we are about this.

"You think we're wasting our time?" he asks.

"If we were, would you do anything differently?" Leave it to Moto to bring up the deeper questions. Introspection is his superpower.

"I don't think I would. Would you?" I meet his gaze. The sun is shining directly into his eyes. It's the only time you can tell they're brown. In any other lighting, they're pitch black.

"No. I want to be there for her when she finds her way."

I fist his ponytail and bring him in for a kiss. Our tongues tangle, and our breaths come faster. I wish we had time for more but duty calls.

I pull away. "We'll finish this later in the hotel."

"Fuckin' better after a kiss like that."

We get out of bed, both of us shifting things in our pants around to make room for our hard dicks. "Ready?"

"Let's do it."

It's late when we drive up the dirt road to the house where we're delivering the guns. Miguel, our supplier, ensured us these guys are solid and that there won't be problems. But when the house comes into view, we spot at least twenty men, guns aimed at us, and Neo Nazi flags hanging in the front window.

One of the newer patch-ins, Ford, slows the van and glances over at me, unsure how to proceed. We're outnumbered and under-armed, but I'm trusting Miguel, so I jerk my head for him to continue.

The second I'm off my bike, my gun is in my hand and aimed in front of me. Glancing at Moto and Bullet through my periphery, I see they've done the same, aiming at men on either side, covering us the best they can from all angles.

"What the fuck is this?" I call out.

A man with a large gut, an Aryan tattoo on his bald head, and wearing suspenders comes out of the shadows. "Just a precaution. Ain't never done business with you before."

Fucking backwoods hillbilly. I hate Central Oregon for this very reason. Too many racist assholes and too much space to congregate together where no one is looking for them.

"This deal is over before it's begun if you don't get your men to lower their weapons," I say.

His jaw ticks as he sizes me up, gauging how serious I am. Whatever he reads from my expression has him holding his arms out to the side and slowly lowering them, a sign for his men to put away their guns, which they do. Well, all but one. An asshole to my left keeps his aim on Moto.

It's not an accident. I'm sure of that. Moto is Japanese, and these motherfuckers have scrambled up brains. Yet Moto holds his stance, not even a slight shake in his hands. He's got nerves of steel.

"Him too." I point at the fucker with a shotgun pointed at the most important person in the world to me.

"Todd," the ignorant bastard of a leader says. "Put that gun down now."

Todd doesn't listen. He remains frozen in place, his face hidden by his weapon.

"Todd," the bald asshole scolds again.

Todd huffs, then tucks the gun under his arm.

"There. All better. I'm Stan." The leader holds his hand out for me to shake, but I just stare at it. No way I'm touching his level of filth. "It's like that, huh?"

"Yeah, it's fucking like that," I spit out. "Let's get this over with."

I walk around to the back of the van and open it up, revealing three wooden crates packed full of submachine guns. Whatever they're using them for, I don't wanna know. I don't need that shit on my conscience.

"Can I test the merchandise?" Stan asks.

"Be my guest." I get in and crowbar open one of the crates, revealing the MP5s. I hand one over to him and hop down, making room for Stan's men to unload them.

I follow him up to the house, where the porch lights flood the front yard in a white glow. He inspects the weapon before calling for one of his men. "Grab me some rounds for this, would ya?"

A dude with no shirt and suspenders removes the magazine from his weapon and hands it over to Stan, who snaps it in place and sets his aim on a beer can sitting on their dilapidated fence. He fires a couple rounds, sending the can flying.

"All good?" I ask.

"Yeah." He whistles to two other men and motions for them

to come over. One holds a giant black duffel bag and hands it over to me before helping carry the crates up to the house.

Setting the bag on the hood of the van, I unzip it and flip through the stacks of bills. There's always a risk. I can't count and inspect each bill, but if they short us or deliver fake bills, they'll answer to Miguel and his crew. I've heard rumors of how brutal they can be, so they'd be stupid to fuck him over.

Stan spits a black string of saliva to the ground through his two front missing teeth. "Get gone now."

"Don't have to ask me twice, asshole," I grumble quietly so only Moto can hear me. Except Stan apparently has super hearing.

"What was that?" he asks, an edge in his tone.

"I said, you don't have to ask me twice." I straighten my spine and lift my chin.

"Ford, pack up. We're out of here." Moto storms over to his bike.

Ford tosses the duffel of cash in the back of the van and slams the loading doors closed before jogging to the driver's side and sliding behind the wheel.

"I don't like to be disrespected on my property," Stan calls out.

"Then don't say dumb shit," I say.

Through my periphery, I see Moto's head fall back on his shoulders and rest there for a split second before he reaches behind him to pull out the Glock he keeps tucked in his waistband. He hates it when I antagonize people, but these backwoods racists don't get to insult Moto and get away with it.

"What did you say?" Stan inches closer, his hands on his sides.

"Sly, let's get out of here." Moto grips the back of my cut and tugs, but I'm not budging.

"Listen to your *friend* over there." He's in my face now, close enough I smell the putrid chewing tobacco on his breath. But my rage is too bright to focus on it.

I shove him in the chest, and everyone goes quiet. After that last remark, Moto is now at my side. He's done with these pricks too.

"You've got gusto. I'll give you that." Stan turns his head and spits, a line of drool getting caught on his chin. "Since I'm feeling generous, I'll also give you five seconds to get off my fuckin' property."

Moto leans in. "There are at least twenty of them and three of us. Let's go."

I stare Stan down, neither of us breaking eye contact for two of those five seconds before I turn and hop on my bike, Moto doing the same. The van's engine comes to life, and Moto leads us, turning around and driving back down the dirt road. Before we can get to the end of the drive, though, a blast sounds.

At first, I think it's a warning shot. Their last attempt at showing us who's boss. But then I see Moto's shoulder jerk forward, and he swerves. Those fuckers shot him.

Everything happens in slow motion after that. Moto goes down hard in a ditch near the end of the drive. I pull up next to him, throwing down my kickstand, and Ford parks the van behind us, shielding us from any more fire.

In seconds, I'm next to Moto. He's wincing in pain, grabbing his shoulder, and there's blood. So much fucking blood.

"Help me get him in the van," I yell.

With Ford's help—and a whole lot of cursing from Moto— we get him through the side door and lay him flat in the back of the vehicle. Since the van's used for cargo, there aren't seats back here, just thick moving blankets and tools we always take on a run in case one of our bikes has problems.

Once inside, I stand to flip on the interior light. Moto clutches his shoulder, his face screwed up in pain. Blood is everywhere, already pooling underneath him.

"Drive," I tell Ford, who nods and gets behind the wheel.

"Our bikes," Moto says. Sweat has gathered along his brow, and his chest is heaving.

"Fuck the bikes. We need to get the fuck out of here." The second those words leave my lips, gunfire breaks out, and I hear the ting of the bullets hitting the van.

It would be so easy to give in to the panic I feel over Moto getting hurt, but I can't. Not now. He needs me to be strong and quickly get us out of this situation.

I take the passenger seat, grab the rifle Ford had sitting on the console, and unroll the window, leaning out to shoot. Five or six of the shitheads are lined up across the top of the drive, firing at us. I take aim at Todd and press down on the trigger, rejoicing in the way blood blooms on the front of his white shirt.

It's enough to take the heat off us, and Ford peels out, sending gravel spraying behind us. Once I'm certain we're not being tailed, my focus shifts to Moto. I climb into the back, grabbing some clean shop rags and a blanket.

"Sorry about this," I say, gently removing his cut and T-shirt. He howls in pain until both are gone, and he's left bare-chested, blood bubbling out of a wound on his deltoid. That's good. For one thing, it's a through and through. For another, pretty sure no bones were hit.

I quickly cover him with a blanket and use the rags to staunch the bleeding. He fights me when I press firmly onto the wound, but I bat his hand away.

"We have to stop the bleeding," I say.

"Hurts like a bitch."

"I know. I'm sorry. Just hang on."

"Where am I going?" Ford asks.

It's a tricky question, one without a good answer. An ER will be forced to report a gunshot. Even though we weren't at fault, getting the police involved is never a good thing and will tie us up for months, if not years. Reno is nearly six hours away, and it could be a deadly call to make without knowing how much damage has been done.

"Clubhouse," Moto grits out.

"I don't know if you'll make it that long." I pull the rag away and see the bleeding has mostly subsided.

"I'm fine. You see it for yourself. Bullet went right through me. Nothing a few stitches won't cure," Moto says.

The part of me that loves this man and can't imagine a life without him screams to get him to the nearest hospital, but the club member part of me knows he's right.

"Gotta put the safety of the club first." Moto meets my gaze. "You know it, and I know it."

It's the life we signed up for. When we patched in, we accepted that our lives were at risk every day. We can't operate our business, legal or otherwise, with the cops breathing down our necks.

"Fine, but only if you remain stable. Things start going downhill, and we're going to the hospital, club be damned," I say, bending down to place a kiss on his temple.

I feel eyes on us and sit up to find Ford looking back through the rearview. I put on a stoic expression, daring him to say anything, but he gives nothing away, turning his attention back to the road. If he had any doubt about my and Moto's relationship, I just cleared it up for him.

But some things are more important, and keeping Moto alive and well is one of them.

Chapter
THREE

Moto

I've been shot before. Few years back, a gun deal went bad, and I got clipped on my side. This hurts worse.

"How are you holding up?" Sly carefully wedges himself underneath me so my head is resting on his lap. Sharp, stabbing pain radiates down my arm in this position, but I don't say shit about it. He's a fixer, a problem solver, and I know it's stressing him out that he can't heal a gunshot.

"Fine. Barely hurts." I lie, wincing when he removes the rag to look at the entrance wound before lifting me up to check the exit.

"The bleeding has almost stopped. That's a good sign, but I need to keep the pressure on it."

"Did you text Roch?" I ask.

Roch, our Sergeant at Arms, has a girl named Truly, whose mom is a veterinarian. Occasionally, she helps us out when we've needed patching up. It's not ideal, but it's all we got.

Would it kill one of my brothers to hook up with a doctor or a nurse?

But no. Khan, our VP, is with the club's lawyer, Bexley.

Loki, our Prez, is married to Birdie, who is in culinary school. Truly's having a baby in the next few months and is in veterinarian school. Coyote, our nomad turned patched member, is with Riley. Then there's Goblin, who—in a weird turn of events—is Riley's dad and hooking up with Riley's mom, who's some sort of wine heiress or some shit.

Then there's Sly and me, lusting after a girl with amnesia after getting fucked up by two men who kept her hostage.

Petra.

I wonder who she was in her past life. She could've been anyone and lived anywhere. We have no idea, and the only man who could give us any clues is dead out in the middle of the Great Basin Desert, getting his bones picked clean by wildlife.

"Yeah." He drags his lower lip through his teeth. "Aiyana's off at some fucking conference for vets or some shit. But Truly'll be at the clubhouse to help."

Fucking perfect.

I close my eyes as dizziness kicks in. I've lost too much blood, information I keep to myself. Last thing I need is for Sly's blood pressure to skyrocket any more than it is already.

I swallow thickly. "That'll do just fine. I'm sure she's learned sutures by now."

"This is so fucked. Please let me take you to the ER. We can make up some bullshit story about an accident. We're far enough away from where we dropped those guns that even if the hospital reports it, they won't be able to connect us to Todd's shooting."

"No point in risking it when it's not life-threatening."

He thunks his head on the metal side of the van, cursing at my stubbornness, but we both know he'd make the same choice. Putting the club at risk over this is unnecessary.

Ford hits a pothole, and I don't have time to bite down my reaction before crying out.

"Sorry," he calls back to us.

"Fucking do better, dipshit," Sly shouts.

"Yeah, dipshit." I smirk and earn myself the slightest up-turn of Sly's lips.

"You're an asshole."

"And you're freaking the fuck out. I'm fine."

"Don't patronize me. It wasn't that long ago I was the one who got shot, and you were doting on me like you were my fucking mom." His brows raise, daring me to argue, but I can't. A few months back, while the guys were on a run, he took a hit to the leg. I'll never forget what it felt like to see him hurt. It's probably what he's going through now, though feeding into this downward spiral will get us nowhere.

"Whatever. You milked that shit for weeks." My voice is gravelly, and my throat is dry.

Ignoring my dig, he carefully reaches for a bottle of water and tips it to my lips. More water dribbles out of the side of my mouth than makes it in, but the cool liquid feels good going down.

Sly's phone chirps, and he caps the water before pulling it out and putting it on speaker. "Yeah?"

"What the fuck happened?" Loki booms. Our president doesn't like it when things go wrong, and in our line of business, a lot of things go wrong.

"Miguel had us delivering to some douchebags with shit for brains. There were twenty or more of them, all armed and looking for a reason to shoot." Sly saws on his lower lip.

Even pissed off, he makes my cock twitch. He has a straight jawline and strong chin covered in a short scruff, long curls in a messy pile on his head with a short fade on the side, a thick neck that leads to broad shoulders, and eyes that change color depending on what he's wearing. Right now, he has on black, so they're smokey gray.

He glances down at me, and whatever he sees in my

expression must give me away because he flashes me a two-second grin before his lips flatten again.

"Shit. Okay. I'll call Miguel and find out what the fuck he was thinking selling to those pricks." Loki sighs. "And Moto? Is he okay?"

"I'll live, Prez," I say.

"Good. Now get the hell back here before something else happens."

"Will do." Sly ends the call.

For the next couple of hours, I drift off, only waking when the searing pain in my shoulder intensifies. Each time I rouse, Sly's eyes are on me, narrowed, with his jaw ticking. He must be sore from sitting on the hard floor for hours on end—I know I am—but not once does he complain, his only concern being me.

"We're pulling into Reno now," Ford calls back.

"Fucking finally." I shift slightly and grimace.

Sly pulls off a blood-soaked rag and presses a clean one back on my shoulder. "Hardly bleeding anymore."

"That's good."

"Think Truly will leave you with a cool scar?" One dark brow quirks.

"No clue. Why?"

"Well, I already know you're tough since I saw you take the bullet, but Dove doesn't know. A cool scar might impress her."

I roll my eyes. "You're an idiot."

When I hear gravel crunching under the tires, I know we're home. It's only daybreak, so I don't expect the crowd of bikers and ol' ladies standing out front, awaiting our return. But when the side door slides open, there they are. Our family.

Dove avoids crowds like no one else, so the real kicker is seeing her standing to the side, hands on her hips, and a distressed look on her face. I cock my head and study her because she looks different in a way I can't pinpoint. Like her eyes are clearer, her body language more confident.

Did something happen while we were gone?

Sly helps me sit so he can slide out from under me and hop out of the van. I use my non-injured arm to push myself to the edge where Khan, the big fucker, is waiting to help me out.

To everyone's surprise, Dove pushes to the front of the crowd, jaw set firm, lips pursed, and holding a strong posture. I've never seen her like this, and I flick my gaze to Sly, who looks just as confused as I am.

I mouth, "What the fuck?"

He shrugs and returns his attention to her.

"Get him inside and flat on a table. I need to look at the wound. Do any of you have access to some Betadine, lidocaine, sutures, gauze, that kind of stuff?" she asks no one in particular. Even her voice has changed from timid and soft-spoken to take charge and assertive.

"Yeah. I brought all of that with me," Truly says, confused as hell and for good reason. "It's inside."

"Perfect." Dove lifts the blood-soaked rags covering my wounds and inspects them with a trained eye. "What about antibiotics? Who knows what kind of contaminants this has been exposed to."

"Dove?" I keep my tone calm and even. But inside, I'm overwhelmed with a whole lot of, *what the fuck?*

It's as if she doesn't hear a damn word I say, returning the rag to the wound and looking up to Khan. "Well? Get him inside and on a table. Now."

Khan snaps to attention, throwing my arm over his shoulder to take some of my weight, which I'm grateful for because even though the pain is dulled from the confusing situation, I'm weak. Once inside the clubhouse, Sly and Khan help me up onto a table in the large dining area.

"Truly, where are the supplies?" Dove is in a zone, rushing behind the bar and scrubbing her hands with soap.

She looks like herself, long black hair shielding most of her face. She's wearing one of my RBMC T-shirts that drowns her frame and Sly's sweatpants, rolled up at the top—her standard outfit since moving in. But she's not the same woman we've come to know over the last few months.

"Should we be concerned?" Khan says, wringing his beard.

"No fuckin' clue, bro." Sly folds his arms across his chest.

"Okay, everyone clear out. I need some space." As if this is a goddamn operating room, Dove holds her hands out and Truly, somehow knowing what she wants, slides latex gloves over them.

The guys hesitantly disperse to the other side of the room where the bar is. Our three newly patched-in members fall into their old roles as nomads and serve us coffee.

Without the crowd to overhear, I decide to poke around at the elephant in the room. "Dove, let's pause for a minute to—"

"Not now," she says in a hushed tone, but her eyes don't leave my shoulder.

I shut up, and for the next half hour, Truly and Dove work seamlessly, poking me with needles, commenting about how things look and stitching me up. I have no idea what the fuck is going on, but since they're confidently moving forward, I swallow the pain and let them do whatever they want to me.

"I'd feel better if we could get an X-ray to make sure there aren't any bullet fragments." Dove sighs, snapping her gloves off and setting them in the pile of bloody gauze next to me.

"Let's take him over to the clinic," Truly suggests.

"No, no, no." I place a hand over my bandaged shoulder and sit up. "You bitches have fussed over me enough."

"Moto, you could get an infection or even lead poisoning. It'll just take a second," Truly says.

"All I need is some sleep and a shot of tequila." I hold two fingers in the air at Miles, who nods and pours me the shot. That's not all I need, though, because my mind is still spinning with how the fuck Dove knew how to fix me up, and I'm fucking desperate to know. After throwing down the liquor, I lay my eyes on her and watch while she busies herself getting everything picked up. "Can you help me to bed?"

Her hands pause. "I need to finish cleaning up."

"Truly, you got this?" I ask.

"Of course." She sets a hand on Dove's arm. "Go on. I'll get this."

Dove nods, and Sly, wanting in on the conversation, rushes over and helps me up. "Come on, tough guy."

Trailing behind us, I feel Dove's unease coming off her in waves. My mind reels with possibilities. Maybe she remembers who she is, maybe this one part of her came out subconsciously, maybe she fuckin' knew this whole time and has been playing us.

Sly kicks open the door to my room and helps me settle in bed. Dove's never been in here. I've never invited her, thinking it might trigger her. You know, going into a man's personal space. I don't know. It felt safer talking to her in her own room where her own shit is. Like it would comfort her or something.

I follow her path around the room as she takes it all in—and there's a lot to take in. Framed pictures of my years with the club line the walls, along with some posters of shiny, souped-up engines and my dream bikes. Three stacked shelves hold my Marvel comic figurines and a fat stack of comics.

Sly takes a seat on the leather chair in the corner and leans back, resting his hands behind his head. He's tired too. It was a long-ass night, and we could both use some shut-eye.

"You like toys," she says, and Sly chuckles. The guys have always given me shit about my comic addiction, but I don't give a fuck. Those comics saved me when I was a kid.

"They're not toys. They're figurines."

She smiles softly, but her light brown eyes don't leave the contents of my shelves, hands clasped behind her back. I fucking hate it when she does that because I know it's a posture she was made to keep while she was owned. At least her head is high and not bowed. I see red when she does that shit.

"Dove," Sly says. "Take a seat. We need to talk."

She takes a resigned breath, and Sly moves from the chair to the other side of my bed, offering the chair to her. She sits, drawing her knees to her chest and wrapping her arms around them. Her blue-black hair forms a curtain around her body and covers most of her face, only letting a sliver of her brown eyes shine through.

"So, when did your memory come back?" Sly asks, not beating around the bush.

Her gaze flicks between us before she opens her mouth and shocks us both.

Chapter
FOUR

Petra

My heart thumps so loudly in my chest that I'm certain Moto and Sly can hear it. My stomach roils, and my skin turns to ice, goosebumps spreading along every inch of my body.

I don't want to tell them. I'm confused and terrified. Terrified they'll make me go home, terrified they won't make me go home. And, oh my God, I know who I was before all this happened. It's overwhelming. Too overwhelming. The only thing I want to do is curl up in bed and put all the pieces together.

But the two pairs of eyes on me are demanding an explanation, and I already know they won't stop until I give them what they want.

"I don't know exactly." All my confidence from minutes earlier when I was in my element disappears.

"Not good enough," Sly says. "Was it today, yesterday, the entire time we've known you?"

"No. It was today. When I saw you get out of the van. I think." I chew on the inside of my mouth until I taste blood.

"What do you mean, you think?" Sly narrows his eyes on me.

"We're just trying to understand." Moto shifts on the bed, his face scrunching for the briefest of seconds. I imagine he's in a great deal of pain. The local anesthetic wasn't adequate.

I wish we had access to something stronger. Maybe Truly can get ahold of something from her mom's clinic.

"Dove," Sly says, bringing me out of my thoughts.

"There was no big rush of memories. I saw Moto and knew what needed to be done. It wasn't until I was stitching him up that I realized I knew a lot more." My lip quivers. I need space and time to figure out what I should and shouldn't tell them. Before making any decisions, I need to know what I want to happen. "I'm tired. Can I go back to my room now?"

"No." Sly's clipped tone startles me because it's out of character. Although both have been nothing but kind, Moto demands more from me and doesn't let me hide the way Sly does.

"He just means, we've been waiting for your memories to return, and now they have. It's exciting, Dove. I'm sure you have people who would love to hear from you," Moto coaxes.

"I don't. There's no one. I'm no one." I rush out of the room, slamming the door behind me.

Instantly, I feel guilty for causing a scene, and for a minute, I wonder if they'll punish me for it. Fear seizes my mind, and I run to my room as if someone is chasing me, closing and locking the door. Then deciding that's not good enough, I push my nightstand in front of it.

But no one comes.

You're not a prisoner anymore, Cameron. Sly and Moto aren't your jailers. They're . . . I don't even know.

And Cameron? Am I Cameron anymore? No. It doesn't feel right. I'm Petra.

I close the blinds, bathing my room in darkness, then climb into bed, drawing the down comforter over my head. My body relaxes the smallest amount, but it's enough that I can unclench my jaw and breathe without feeling like there's a fifty-pound weight on my chest.

With the world blocked out, I can work through this because I honestly don't know when it all came back. One second, I was standing outside, waiting for Moto to return, worried to death his injuries were worse than what they were telling me. Then I saw him, and I snapped into action without thinking.

It wasn't until I was throwing sutures that I realized I shouldn't know how to do this. It's not something a woman like me knows. Except, I did. Because I'm Cameron Bixby.

Was. I was Cameron Bixby.

I go through my memories slowly, working backward from the night I met Tyler. I was a third-year resident. I lived in Las Vegas. My parents, Lori and Savannah, lived close by in Henderson. Oh my God, my moms. They must've been destroyed when I went missing.

The panic returns, this time bringing tears along for the ride.

I had grandparents. Aunts and uncles too. An entire close-knit family. My disappearance had to have been devastating. I wonder if they're still looking or if they think I'm dead. I need to call them. I need to tell them I'm okay.

The desire to get up, do something, and fix all this suddenly hits me, but it's gone just as fast.

It's been more than four years. What if they had a funeral? What if they already grieved for me? Returning might do more harm than good. They'll be disappointed in me. I was stupid that night and way too trusting of a handsome face. It's embarrassing.

I turn to my side, tucking my legs to my chest.

Then I remember something else. Someone else. Mia. A nurse at the hospital I was working at. My best friend and the person I was out with the night *it* happened. The last time I saw her, she was being held by Tyler. The pock-marked man decided not to take her after all. He said he'd have his hands full with me.

Where did she end up? I swallow hard. Is she still alive?

My head throbs, and I'd kill for a drink. Or a Vicodin. Or even a Xanax.

Sly warned me my room had been cleaned of all liquor before I came home from the ranch and that everyone had been instructed not to give me anything. But did he find all my hiding spots? I doubt it.

I throw off the blanket and scramble to the ground, reaching under the bed. Nothing there but that was an easy find. Jumping to my feet, I check all my drawers, not surprised to find them alcohol-free. But I'm not done. I stashed mini bottles all over my closet.

The guys insisted on providing me with an entire wardrobe, but I haven't worn most of it in favor of their baggy T-shirts and sweatpants. I dig into the pockets of jackets, button-downs, and pants hanging neatly. Nothing. I rip shirts, sweaters, and cardigans off the built-in shelves, coming up empty.

That's fine. I'll just sneak some from the bar. Everyone was up all night worried about Moto and dealing with their supplier, so I doubt anyone is still hanging around.

I press my ear to the door, not hearing a sound when there's almost always music playing or the TV on if someone's awake. I push the nightstand out of the way and open the door a crack, just enough to peer down the hall. It's quiet.

Slinking out of the room, I tiptoe to the main area. It's one long room that spans the entire length of the house but is divided into zones by furniture. The game area where there are pool tables, dart boards, an oversized couch, and a massive TV, the bar with a long wooden counter lined with stools, and the dining area where there are enough tables for everyone to sit down for meals.

I head straight for the bar, ducking under the pass-through so I don't accidentally wake someone with the latch. It's then I notice the open glass shelves that house all the liquor bottles are now fully encased in glass cabinets. I pull the handle on the first one I come to. Locked. I check each one, and all of them are locked.

When did this happen? I remember some banging around yesterday, but Khan's always fixing or building something, so I didn't think anything of it. Maybe they're tired of the hanga-rounds drinking all their booze. I don't know.

I'm not deterred because there's still the beer fridge. Except it has a padlock on it.

Did they do this because of me?

Shame burns crimson on my cheeks. They don't trust me, apparently for good reason. I lean over the bar, resting my fore-head on my arms, my breaths coming fast and hard.

What the hell am I doing?

I've been home from rehab for a couple days, and I'm al-ready trying to break my sobriety? I squeeze my eyes closed, tears popping free. I'm a failure. A complete and utter failure.

"Dove?"

I wipe my face across my arm before tipping my head up to see Sly standing on the other side of the bar, arms folded, dis-appointment written all over his handsome face.

"What are you doing?" he asks.

"I don't know."

"I see you found our additions." He flips the latch on the pass-through and approaches me nonchalantly, but it's for show. He yanks on the first cabinet. "Khan did a good job, don't you think?"

"I wasn't . . . that's not . . ."

"Don't lie to me."

A sob breaks free, and I let out a growl of frustration. I'm ir-ritated at myself, at my situation, at my inability to sort through all the mess in my head.

"I'm sorry," I cry.

Sly scoops me up like I weigh nothing, and I tuck my face

into the crook of his neck. He smells clean, like he just showered, and I relish knowing that even though he's manhandling me, I don't feel unsafe. All the damage the men before them did is being healed by two men who show me nothing but kindness and respect.

He carries me down the hall, and I'm not sure whose room he'll deposit me in until Moto's scent hits my nose. The distinct musky aroma mixed with a slight tinge of gas and oil, something that shouldn't smell as good as it does. But I associate that scent with one of the men who gave me hope when I thought that was something I'd never feel again.

Setting me down on the bed, I peer over at Moto. He's halfway sitting up, his nearly black eyes on me with a questioning look on his face.

If beautiful could describe a man, that's how I could describe him. His long lashes, high cheekbones, and smooth complexion is combined with a strong brow and straight jaw to be uniquely masculine and feminine.

"What's going on?" he asks.

"That's what I brought her in to find out." Sly moves to climb in next to me, and I scoot closer to Moto to accommodate his size. "You've had some time to think, Dove. Now it's time to talk."

"I don't know where to start," I say, weaving my fingers together and squeezing so hard my knuckles turn white.

"Start with telling us your name." Moto sets a hand on my joined ones, and I loosen my grip.

Long seconds pass, knowing that once Sly has that information, he'll find everything else out. Being a hacker, his first instinct isn't to ask questions; it's getting on his computer and digging until he has the answers. He doesn't trust people. He trusts his laptop.

"Dove," Sly urges, cupping my cheek and turning my head to face him. "What's your real name?"

"Cameron Bixby." There's no point in being obtuse. They'll get it out of me eventually. Now I must trust they'll let me decide what happens next, even if I don't know what I want to happen next.

Sly releases me and jumps to his feet, his fingers twitching. Just as I expected. He's itching to research.

"Don't," I beg, not wanting him to discover my life through words on a screen.

"Why?"

"I'm not a homework project. I'm a person."

"That's not why, and you know it. I only want to help."

"Do you remember everything?" Moto asks.

"I think so, but it's hard to tell."

"And what you remembered had you wanting to drink?" Sly returns to his spot next to me.

"You drank?" Moto's tone is almost accusing and all the guilt from moments ago returns.

"No. Remembering everything from the day I was taken made me want to forget again."

Until now, my memories from that time were spotty at best. I remembered the faces of the men who took me, but I didn't remember the details, and I didn't remember Mia. Seeing her terrified face through the window of the limo as we drove away is a memory I wish I didn't have.

"What did you remember?" Moto asks.

"I wasn't alone when I was taken. My best friend, Mia, was with me. We need to find her."

Chapter
FIVE

Sly

The urge to go to my room and plant my ass in front of my computer is so strong that my legs bounce. But she asked me not to, so I won't. Yet.

"What's her last name?" I ask, storing away every detail she can provide until I can convince her that she needs my help.

"Garcia. She was a nurse at the hospital I worked at. The man—Tyler was his name—was supposed to take us both, but I fought back and tried to run, and he changed his mind." Her eyes go cold, and her face blanches. "He said I was handful enough."

"Fuck me," I mutter, scraping a hand down my face. She's never gone into detail about what happened to her, but I've been around men who like to own women, so I have a pretty good idea.

"You were a nurse?" Moto asks, not pressing her for more details about her time as a prisoner. We've tried that route before, and it always ended with her in a full panic that took days to recover from.

"A doctor. A third-year resident, actually. I wanted to work in emergency medicine."

"Thank fuck you were." Moto traces the professional-looking bandage across his bare shoulder. Truly might've been able to handle it, but I'm certain Dove's experience helped.

"A doctor, huh? I always knew you were too special to be hanging out with the likes of us." My joke falls flat because Dove balls her fists and inhales deeply.

"No," she says on an exhale. "I'm not her anymore. I don't even recognize the person I used to be."

"Come here." Moto lifts his uninjured arm, and she curls into him willingly. It must be bad if she's allowing him to physically comfort her. Ever since she came here, she's been very hands-off. It's why we haven't pursued her. If she can't stand to be touched by one man, imagine her reaction to two.

"I wish I didn't remember. It's too much. I don't know how to handle it."

"That's why we're here. Let us help." I inch closer, watching for any signs of distress, but when there are none, I turn on my side and cup her hip while Moto snakes his hand under my neck, joining the three of us together.

My whole life, I never fit in. Not until I became a Royal Bastard. Clicking with Moto made me feel even less like an outsider, and now, being here with him and Dove feels special. Like something that was always meant to be.

But I'm not a fuckin' idiot. This isn't the right time to talk about any of that.

"How can we help?" I ask.

Dove peers over her shoulder and, with fire in her eyes, says, "I want to find her. Make sure she's okay."

My gaze shifts from her to Moto, who nods solemnly. Of course he fucking does because we'd give this woman anything she asked for.

"We can do that, but we're gonna need you to tell us everything you know," I say.

"Okay." She sits up cross-legged and tucks her hands

between her legs. She looks so young like this, drowning in our clothes. But you don't have to look any further than her eyes to see she's been through some shit.

This time, she doesn't stop me when I get up to grab my laptop. I return and sit down in the chair, nodding for her to continue. For the next hour, she recalls every detail from that night. I take notes of places and distinguishing factors. I don't let myself process her words. I listen with a clinical ear so my emotions don't muddy the facts.

Moto, however, doesn't. Each time I look over at him, he grows more and more pissed off. I can feel the rage coming off him in waves.

Neither of us are known for our murderous tendencies. We save that for Khan and Loki. But we all have kills under our belt, and I can tell with a hundred percent certainty that our hands are about to get real fucking dirty.

"Anything else?" I ask.

"I don't think so." Dove looks exhausted. Moto too. Not me, though. I'm teed up, ready to get digging.

"Do you feel comfortable staying here with Moto? I have some shit to do, but I don't want to leave him alone." Mostly the truth. The man just got shot and could use someone to look after him. But even more than that, if Dove's with Moto, she can't be looking around for an escape to her issues.

"Of course." She flashes me her first real smile of the day, and it's like staring at the sun. Blinding and intensely powerful but beautiful, nonetheless.

Feeling bold with all the adrenaline running through my veins, I give her a kiss on the head before moving to the other side of the room and doing the same to Moto, who's half-asleep. Dove watches the interaction, and a curious blush creeps across her pale skin.

I've never shown Moto any kind of affection in front of her before, but if this were a test, she passed.

"I'll check in on you guys in a bit." Before closing the bedroom door behind me, I catch Dove snuggling into Moto's side and closing her eyes. Most men would feel jealousy at seeing the object of their attraction with another person, but that's not what I feel at all. I'm content as shit knowing they're getting closer and bonding. It's a step in the right direction for us.

Before heading to my room, I swing by the bar to see if Sissy and Tabitha have put out any food. Both started out as club whores, but things have changed, and now, they're our house mice.

Not that long ago, we were a group of single men who worked hard and partied harder. Sissy and Tabs took care of *all* of our needs, and I'm embarrassed to say it now, but most all the brothers took advantage of their proximity.

Now that most of us have somewhat settled down, Tabs and Sissy stick with cleaning up and cooking for us in exchange for housing, food, and some pocket change. They're as much a part of the club as patched-in members, and I'd be sad if either of them decided to leave.

"Hey, honey. How are you doin'?" Tabitha asks, setting down some turkey sandwiches on croissant rolls. "Wasn't sure who would be awake after being up all night, so I threw a few of these together."

"I'm all right. Thanks for this." I snag a sandwich.

"What about Moto? I heard you guys ran into some problems."

"You're not going to believe this, but Dove got her memories back. Turns out she's an MD. Patched Moto up real nice."

Tabitha's eyes go wide. "Legit? That's crazy."

"For real." I take a bite and chew slowly, still trying to wrap my head around the turn of events.

"So, what does that mean for her? Does she have family?"

"She's not talking about any of that yet. When she was

taken, she was with a friend. So far, that's the only thing she's talking about."

"How does that make you feel? I know you and Moto are sweet on the girl." Her head tilts, and her eyes soften.

I shrug. "Dunno. If she wants to leave, we'll let her. But kinda hoping she sticks around. Guess we'll find out."

"And you're going to help her find her friend?" she asks.

"Yeah. Heading to my room now to start digging around."

"Let me know if you need anything."

"Thanks." I grab another sandwich and add it to my plate. I'll need the fuel. "Save two of these for Moto and Dove when they wake up?"

"Sure thing, honey." She lifts two off the tray and sets them on a paper plate.

I give her a wave and head back down the hall to my room. My king-size bed is front and center and pushed up against the far wall, calling my name.

I love sleep. Matter of fact, I could take three naps a day, get eight hours at night, and it still wouldn't be enough. But that'll have to wait.

I stride over to my messy work area and sit at my desk. On both sides are bookshelves that hold computer parts, towers, and laptops instead of books. My supply of burner phones and gadgets is in the cabinets underneath the bookshelves.

This is my happy place. I've been fascinated by tech since I was a kid, but growing up dirt poor, I didn't have access to much. Now I have everything I could ever want, and it still blows my mind.

I open my laptop and set it to the side. The kind of research I need to do requires the software I have built into my desktop.

I want my first search to be on Cameron Bixby. I'm itching to know every detail about her. A bigger part of me wants to hear about her past from her lips, and I know that's what she wants too, so instead, I type in Mia Garcia.

The preliminary results take me to news articles about two friends who went missing four years ago. My eye catches on a photo, and I click on it. It was clearly taken in a hospital next to a nurse's station. A tall, pretty girl with curly red hair and freckles beams at the camera, but I barely see her. My eyes are glued on the shorter girl with long, black hair and a creamy complexion.

There are similarities to the person sleeping in Moto's bed right now. The height, hair, and size all match up. But the girl in the picture is light and carefree, while the Dove we know now is weighed down by all the shit she's been through. Smiles are few and far between, and the confidence the girl in the picture is exhibiting? I've never seen it once.

I skim through the article, knowing there'll be nothing useful. It was July, and the two girls were at a dance club in Vegas where they lived. No one saw them leave, and the bartender said they had minimal drinks. The only thing I find worth noting is that Dove—Cameron—was seen dancing with a man. I can only assume this is the man that took her. It's common for traffickers to drug their victims and lead them out of the club under the guise of taking home their drunk girlfriend.

I close out of the article and scroll through twenty or so more before starting the real work. Within an hour, I'm logged into the LVMPD computer system and looking at the police report for Mia. Her parents reported her missing when she didn't answer their calls the morning after the abduction.

The police intentionally withheld a witness report that says they saw Mia walk outside with a short, muscled man. She was visibly intoxicated but was going willingly, so no one thought anything of it. I make note of that, but otherwise, the cops have jack shit to go off, and the case has gone cold.

This is when I should log out of the system and move on to different methods of finding Mia, yet my fingers hover over the keyboard. I type Cameron Bixby and delete it four times before hitting the search button, telling myself the more I know about that night, the closer I can get to answers.

Cameron's moms reported her missing at the same time Mia's parents did, making me wonder if they checked in with each other before contacting the police. It seems like throwaway information, but it tells me a lot. Dove was close enough with her parents to make sure they had access to her friend and her friend's parents. That means she's loved, missed, and most likely has people looking for her.

While her case is still open, it's gone cold like Mia's. There are pages of notes for each time one of Dove's moms called in to check on the progress, of which there's little. Nevada is a trafficker's dream, and it ranks tenth in the nation for total trafficking cases. While they don't know that's what happened, it fits the criteria.

I log out of the system and decide to take a break. It's been a couple hours, and I need to check on Moto and Dove. After a stop in the kitchen to grab the plastic-wrapped sandwiches and a couple bottles of water, I step inside Moto's room. Dove's still asleep, but Moto's awake, absently playing with Dove's long hair.

I give him a chin lift and set the plate on the nightstand next to him, unscrewing the lid from the bottle of water and handing it to him. Taking my previous spot on the bed, I turn on my side to see both of them.

"How are you?" I ask in a hushed tone.

"Better. Fucking hurts like a bitch, but I'll be okay."

"Good. I'll go grab you some painkillers in a minute." I close my eyes, the events of the last twenty-four hours finally catching up to me.

"What did you find out?"

"Not a whole lot. Cops don't have leads. They probably assume she was trafficked and won't ever be seen again." I yawn.

"She have family?"

"Yeah. Two moms. Sounds like they were crushed when she was taken."

"They were?" Dove turns to face me, her eyes sleep swollen.

I cup her cheek and swipe away a rogue eyelash with my thumb. "They were."

"I'm sure they'll freak out when they find out you're alive and well," Moto says, and Dove freezes.

"I'm not going back there." Her words brook no argument.

"You want them to go on thinking you're out there being tortured or worse, dead?" I ask.

"It's been years. I'm sure they've moved on. Going back there would just upset them."

I hear what she's saying but disagree. I think it would be the happiest day of their fuckin' lives. I'm not about to argue this with her, though. She's a grown woman who can make her own life choices.

"Let's table that for now and work on finding Mia." I point over Moto's shoulder. "I brought some food. You need to eat."

"Thank you. I'm starved." She leans over Moto's body, careful not to hurt him.

Her position puts her small but round ass right in Moto's face. His eyes lock on it before flashing over to me. My brows lift, and we share a look of appreciation.

She plops back down, plate in hand, grinning. "This looks amazing."

Watching her eat is a treat. For the first month or so, we could barely get her to drink protein shakes, let alone eat food. She was malnourished, and the bones in her body protruded unhealthily. The drugs and alcohol stole her appetite, but now that they're flushed from her system, she's eating regularly and gaining weight.

Now that I've seen a picture of how she was before, I realize she has a way to go. But every day is progress.

We make small talk while they eat lunch, my eyes feeling heavier with each passing minute.

"Can we stay in bed all day?" Dove stretches her arms above her head. "I'm so comfy, and honestly, I'm not ready for everyone's questions."

"You don't owe anyone jack shit," I say.

"You guys rescued me, gave me a safe home, sent me to rehab, clothed and fed me. Of course I owe an explanation."

"Fuck that. They can come to Moto or me if they have questions."

"I can't put that on you." Her head shakes almost imperceptibly.

"Sure you can. That's what we're here for. To be a wall of protection for you," Moto says.

"You have been, and I'm thankful."

"But to answer your question, yeah. We can stay in bed. At least you guys can. I promised Coyote I'd take a shift at the club so he can take Riley on a date or some shit." I close my eyes. "I have two hours until I have to be there."

"The strip club?" Dove asks.

"Yeah."

"I'll come," Moto offers.

My eyes pop open. "Bro, you just got shot. Take a night off."

"You know me. I can't be kept down."

"Can I come too?" Dove pushes her hair off her face.

"You want to come to the strip club with us?" I ask incredulously.

Royal Treatment is a new investment business for us. Not only do we wash our illegal money through it, but it also provides a steady source of income for the club. Khan and his construction company, another business used to wash, just finished renovating the place, and we opened last week. Since Coyote and his ol' lady, Riley, have been working endless hours to get it up and running, he's due a night off.

"Why not?"

"No reason. You can come," Moto says.

"But first, can we sleep a little?" I yawn again and roll onto my back, surprised when Dove wraps up the uneaten portion of her meal and settles her head on my chest. Damn, it feels good. It seems remembering her identity is helping her open up a little, and I'm here for it. I'm so fuckin' here for it.

Chapter SIX

Moto

Bringing Dove here feels fuckin' wrong. She's easily frightened and doesn't like new situations. Though I'm beginning to think we never knew her at all.

It's early in the night still, so when we walk through the door, it's dead. One girl's on stage, and only two or three customers are sitting at the bar. But that's it.

"Oh wow." Dove spins in a circle, her eyes going in every direction.

I don't blame her; it's fuckin' epic. The ceiling is made of twelve-by-twelve mirrors, reflecting bouncing green and pink strobe lights, and pink LED strips line every table and the floor. There are three stages—the main stage is bigger and in the center of the room—with black leather smoking chairs placed around each one. If the customers don't want tits and ass directly in their face, there are elevated booths around the perimeter that have small tables in the middle to set your drink on but also give the dancers enough room for a lap dance.

In each corner, silver, human-sized birdcages with plexiglass floors are suspended from the ceiling, so you can see the girls dancing no matter where you sit. A DJ booth sits next to a bar that offers well drinks and top-shelf liquor. It's as classy as a strip joint gets.

"You like it?" Sly places a hand on the middle of her back and leads her to where the new office, security room, and dressing rooms are.

"I don't know." She shrinks in on herself a bit.

"Want me to take you back home?" I ask. We ended up driving the cage here since I can't ride one-handed, and our bikes are still fuck knows where.

After Loki called Miguel to tell him about the redneck's hospitality, he promised to make it right. I hope our bikes will be delivered back to us in one piece.

"No. I'm okay." She looks down her body, tugging on the loose fabric of her sweats. "I wasn't thinking. I should've changed."

If she only knew that she's sexier in my hoodie and Sly's sweatpants than any of the strippers dressed in nothing but a thong are.

"You don't need to worry about that. We'll be in the back." Sly places his finger on the scanner and unlocks the door. While Loki, Khan, and Coyote designed the aesthetics of this place, Sly oversaw security, so of course, everything is state of the art. He gets a hard-on for anything tech, and when Loki gave him the green light, he went hog wild.

The first door we come to is the dressing room. Wanting to give Dove the full tour, we stop by there first. Two rows of lockers make up the middle of the room. There's a wall of lighted mirrors and vanities on one end and a small kitchen with a fridge, microwave, and a couple small tables for eating on the other. This is where Riley works. She's the house mom and takes care of everything the women need.

Four or five girls are milling about, getting ready for the night. They light up like the Fourth of July when they see Moto and me. The asshole who owned this joint before us was apparently a piece of shit, so the girls who stuck with us through the renovation are thrilled as hell to have decent bosses.

"Hey, boys." One of the dancers, Roxy, steps up to us. She's sweet and one of our highest earners.

"How's it going?" I ask, allowing her to give me a hug but keep it brief. I don't want to give Dove any reason to question my loyalty to her.

"Who's this?" she asks, sidling up to Dove.

"Petra, this is Roxy," Sly introduces. "Roxy hires the talent for the club and also dances."

Dove smiles timidly. "Nice to meet you."

"Petra, huh? That would make a damn good stage name. You dance?"

"Oh, no." Her hands wave frantically in front of her.

Roxy studies Petra. "That's too bad. You have that innocent, *Sleeping Beauty* vibe the men would eat up."

The rest of the girls take notice of Dove now and come to get a look for themselves. It's making her wildly uncomfortable, but I know she'll be embarrassed if we bail.

Dove's eyes hit the floor. "Thank you."

"Should we go hang out in the security room?" Sly asks, giving her an out.

"Why don't you leave Petra here with us while you go do manly things?" Roxy grabs Dove's hand.

"It's up to her," I say.

"Come on. It'll be fun," another of the dancers, Navaeh, says.

"It's slow, and we're bored. We can do a makeover," Roxy adds.

I take Dove in, looking for any sign of distress, but instead, I find a small smile on her naturally ruby lips.

Nope, we don't really know this girl at all because the Dove from last week would've been hiding behind us or curled up in a ball by now. We'll need to relearn everything about this new version of her, and I gotta say, I'm not mad at it. Just confused.

"Okay." Dove allows herself to be pulled away from us and over to the costume area.

"We're just down the hall if you need anything," Sly says, but the women wave us off.

We share a look before leaving for the security room. Once inside, we kick out the bouncer tasked with keeping an eye on things until we got here and take a seat in front of the many screens showing every angle of the club.

"You think she's okay in there?" I ask.

"I don't fuckin' know. It's been a wild twenty-four hours." Sly kicks his feet out, hands on the back of his head, the chain connecting his wallet to his belt buckle clinking on the metal of the chair. His casual sexiness gets me every damn time, and when he catches the hungry way I'm staring at him, he smirks with all the arrogance in the world. "You okay over there?"

"Asshole." I shift my gaze to the monitors. "I'm fine."

He glances at my arm that's been fitted into a sling. "Think Loki will let us blow up that hillbilly compound?"

"Doubt it. But it wouldn't hurt to ask." I chuckle, then change the subject. "Anything else interesting turn up?"

"No. But I need to look into this Tyler guy. I think Loki knows of a few traffickers. I'll ask him about that."

"Bad company to keep." I move to put my hair back in a ponytail but realize I no longer have access to both hands.

Sly stands and takes the hairband off my wrist, moving behind me and gathering the long strands in his hands. He's never done this before, and he struggles to smooth it out but keeps working at it. Tingles race down my spine when his rough fingers graze the back of my neck.

"You know, we could always cage Dove like Loki did with Birdie. Worked out well for him." He gets the band on, but it's too loose and slides down the ponytail. "How the hell does this work?"

"After you get it around the hair, you have to twist it and loop it again."

"Is that a no about caging her?" he asks, trying the ponytail again and failing.

"I think she's been caged enough."

"Probably right." He sighs. "Guess we'll have to rely on our charm to make her stick around."

"It doesn't even sound like she wants to go in the first place."

"She will. It's hard right now. Too much shit going on in her head. Once she gets it sorted, she'll want to."

"Then I guess we have a small window." I reach behind me and give his wrist a squeeze.

"I did it," he says, pride in his voice and his hands resting on the back of my neck. I don't know how it looks, probably a lumpy mess, but I don't care.

"Thanks."

He dips down and kisses my jaw, nuzzling his nose against my earlobe, humming. "We never had our night in the hotel. Why'd you have to go and get shot?"

"Sorry," I deadpan.

"Are you in pain?"

"A little. It's not bad."

"I think I know how to make you feel better." He spins my chair and sinks to his knees.

Nothing in the world makes me feel more powerful than having this alpha male, masculine biker kneeling in front of me. Fuckin' nothing. This man has killed people, he's on the FBI's Most Wanted List for his hacking, he shoots with sniper fuckin' precision, and he's on his knees, undoing my belt and pulling out my cock that is hard as stone for him.

"Shit, yeah," I say as his tongue drags up the sensitive underside of my length, eyes locked on mine.

Leaning back in my chair, I widen my legs, giving him more room to work. I moan when he wraps his lips around me and bobs up and down. Fuckin' ecstasy.

He makes quick work of the blowjob, doing things to me he knows drive me wild. We've pleasured each other for years and fucked women together for longer than that, so we know each other's bodies very well.

My balls tighten, and I come to life, an orgasm tearing through me, causing me to forget everything except how he's making me feel. I come in his mouth, and he swallows every fucking drop before kissing the tip and tucking me away.

"Better?" he asks, standing.

"So much." I notice he's hard and wonder if I can pull off returning the favor without jarring my injury. His cock is fuckin' amazing—long, veiny, and uncut. It makes my mouth water just thinking about it.

"Don't get any ideas. All sexual favors will be one-sided until you heal up." He bends over and kisses me hard, thrusting his tongue in my mouth so I can taste my own cum. It only makes me want more. "That's all you get for now. But I'm keeping tally. You'll have a lot of making up to do."

"Gladly."

"Should we go check on our girl?"

Our girl. I wonder if that'll ever be true. While Sly and I have a good sex life, we've yet to make things official. No real reason for it; we just haven't. Whether it's because of our own hang-ups or because we've grown comfortable with how things are. If Dove decides she wants to be with us, it'll give us the push to take things one step further. Make things legit as fuck.

"Let's go." I stand. "But can you help with my belt first?"

He grins and fastens the leather and metal. "You're awfully needy."

"Shut up."

There's more action going on in the dressing room than

earlier. The dancers are coming in and out, all in full costume—
if that's what you can call a G-string and pasties. The one thing
missing is Dove.

"Roxy," Sly shouts.

"Over here," she calls out from the other side of the first
row of lockers.

We find Dove standing in front of a full-length mirror, hair
done up in two French braids so you can see her whole beautiful face. If that wasn't a big enough change, her outfit sends
me over the edge.

Two silky strips of fabric cover each breast, then crisscross
over the top of her chest and tie in a bow around her neck.
Connected to that fabric, just under her breasts, is tight, see-
through lace from around her torso to just above her belly button. She's also wearing black booty shorts with a garter belt
around each thigh. It's sexy even though she's the most cov-
ered-up woman in the room.

"Goddamn, Dove," Sly says, his eyes comically wide.

Her cheeks color a beautiful shade of red as she turns away
from the mirror to face us. She's stiff, and her hands are at her
sides, but she's not trying to hide her body.

"You look beautiful." I notice she has on makeup too.
Eyeliner that does a swoopy thing off the corner of her eye,
and her lips—already a light shade of red—are made more so
with shiny lipstick. I can't believe this is the same girl.

"This is something I would've worn out before . . . you
know." She toys with the ends of her braids. "But that was a
long time ago, and it's probably not age-appropriate now."

I realize I've never asked her age. I assume late twenties, but
sometimes I think she could be even younger than that. Sly is
thirty-seven, and I'm thirty-four, so we've never felt too old for
her. Not like fuckin' Loki who's robbing the cradle with Birdie.
He's nearly twice her age.

"I don't know how old you are, but I can say with confidence that you're not too old to be wearing that." Sly gestures with a hand.

"I'm thirty-one," she says.

"Girl, I'm twenty-three, and I don't look this good in this outfit." Roxy checks her out from head to toe.

Dove kicks a leg up behind her, displaying her black platform stilettos. "Though I probably wouldn't have worn these back then."

"Those are fuck hot," I say.

She moves to tuck her hair behind her ears, then realizes it's not there and drops her hand. "Thank you."

"So, what do you say?" Roxy asks. "Wanna take a twirl out on stage?"

"Oh, no," she refuses adamantly. "It's been a long time since I've danced and never professionally."

"Why not? An ass like that should be twerking every chance you get." Roxy points two fingers toward Dove's pert, round behind that I want to sink my fucking teeth into.

"Actually, the last time I danced, I met a guy, and he abducted me before he sold me into a sex trafficking ring."

Roxy's smile freezes in place, then her mouth drops open as this information churns in her brain. I shoot my gaze over to Sly, who appears dumbfounded by the nonchalant way she dropped that atomic bomb. Which is exactly how I feel.

"Are you kidding?" she asks.

"No. I was used by two men before the Royal Bastards saved me, and dancing wasn't one of the things they wanted from me." Dove could be talking about the weather or a fuckin' football game and have the same tone she's using now.

"Goddamn. I'm so sorry." Roxy takes both Dove's hands in hers. "You're tough as shit, and now that it's behind you, I think you should dance every chance you get."

"Thanks. Maybe I will."

Chapter
SEVEN

Petra

The ride home is a bit awkward. I think I said too much, but it was all true. Now that I know who I am, I don't want to hide. Pretending it didn't happen won't make me feel better. And so what if it makes other people uncomfortable?

I recognize the shift in my attitude is probably giving Sly and Moto whiplash, but the second I remembered who I used to be—strong, confident, smart, valuable—it's like a light went on in my head. I want to get back to being that person.

For that to happen, it only makes sense for me to not put on a false front. I'm proud of everything I've been through because it means I survived.

I'm stronger and smarter, and I value myself so much more now that I've lived through hell. The confidence will return in time, and when Roxy asked if I danced, an idea popped into my head that might help with the last part of me that was squashed into a pile of rubble.

I just need to get the guys to agree. Not because I need their permission, but because it feels like we're a unit now. When they check in with me about what they're doing, it makes me feel important and special, and I hope by reciprocating, they feel the same way. Maybe that's co-dependent and needy of me, but with everything that's happened, having them there to back me up means everything.

"Did you have fun?" Moto asks from the back seat.

"Yeah. I haven't been around that many women in a long time. I forgot what it felt like to put on makeup and a cute outfit."

"Is that something you did a lot back in Vegas?" Sly's arm is draped casually across the steering wheel. I think that's what I like most about him. He's always calm and cool. Things need to be really messed up for him to even bat an eye.

"In college, yes. Once I got to med school, I slowed down, then when I entered my residency, it was rare for me to go out."

"How crazy is it that you're a doctor?" Moto's tone is full of awe.

"Was a doctor," I correct, turning to look at him.

"You could be one again if you wanted."

"I don't know what I want anymore."

Sly reaches a hand over and sets it on my knee. His thumb strokes lazily back and forth, his touch sending prickles of awareness throughout my body. "We'll support you no matter what you want to do."

"What if I want to lie around the clubhouse and not do anything for the rest of my life?" I am happiest when I'm there. Maybe because it was the first place in a long time I felt safe, or maybe it's because that's where my guys are. I don't know, but the idea of staying with them forever appeals to me. But that could be because I'm scared.

"If that's what you want, you know we're okay with it," Moto says.

I chew on the inside of my mouth as I try to wrap my head around everything I've lost and gained since being taken.

More than four years of my life are gone, but now that I have my memory, I can get it back. Is that what I want? To go back to Vegas and reclaim what was once mine? But then I would lose Moto and Sly, and that thought makes me physically ill.

Or I could forget who I was and stay here, work on building a new life from the ground up. I've done a good job so far, and I'm happy here with my guys.

Except that doesn't feel right either. Cameron is a part of me, too, and it'd be impossible to forget.

Moto and Sly will force me to make decisions soon. But not tonight, so I push it all away. It's too devastating right now. Like a big, messy pile of laundry was dumped into my lap. It'll take some time to organize it and put everything in the right place.

We park and get out of the van. It's late or, depending on how you look at it, early, so the clubhouse is quiet and peaceful when we walk inside. Our rooms are all next to each other, so we head down the hall, stopping when we reach the first room, which is mine.

"Thanks for taking me tonight," I say, remembering Moto got shot yesterday. "Actually, I'd like to take a look at your wound and rebandage it, if that's okay?"

"Sure." Moto shrugs.

"I guess I'll see you both tomorrow then?" Sly asks, walking backward to his room.

"Yep," I say and follow Moto inside the second door.

Finding the basket of supplies Truly left, I dig through and pick out what I need while Moto takes a seat on his bed and removes the sling.

"Can you help me?" He lifts up one side of his heather gray tee but struggles to get it off.

"Sure." I sit next to him and lean across his body to carefully take the shirt off.

Yesterday, when he was bleeding and injured, I hadn't paid any attention to his body. But now that I'm not in an emergency situation, I take notice. His skin is pale with a gold undertone and silky smooth. His pecs and abs are defined, and his waist is tapered with a clearly defined V leading below his worn, black jeans.

I'm shocked when my core clenches at how hot this man is. It's something I never thought I'd feel again, and I'm taken aback. It's not that I didn't think he was good-looking before because I'm not blind. But my body just stopped reacting physically after I was taken. Sex quickly became torture, something I had to do to survive another day.

I shake it off and get to work. That's not why I'm here, and besides that, he doesn't think of me that way. Like a sister? Yes. Like a desirable woman? No.

"How is it feeling?" I kneel before him, pulling on a pair of gloves and slowly peeling off the tape keeping the gauze in place.

"Not too bad. I can take it." He winks and flexes his pecs, one at a time.

I purse my lips and shake my head, rolling my eyes. "You're ridiculous." I inspect the sutures. It wasn't my best work, but I'm out of practice. "No signs of infection, but you'll definitely scar. Sorry about that. I used to be really good at this."

"Sly said if I scarred, you'd know how tough I am." He chuckles.

"Getting yourself shot doesn't earn you a badge of honor. That was scary." I cover his wound up with a clean bandage and tape it down. Yanking off the gloves, I realize he didn't make a retort. Our eyes meet, and there's so much going on behind his dark orbs that I can't read.

"You were scared for me?" he asks in a husky tone.

"Well, yeah. I mean, you and Sly are my best friends. I don't know what I would do without you."

He playfully yanks on one of my braids. "Best friends, huh?"

"We are, aren't we?" It's a throwaway term these days and juvenile for how much I care for him, but it's the only descriptor I can come up with.

He studies me for a long minute, and I can't read what he's thinking. Heat creeps up my neck and onto my cheeks. Maybe I'm not that important to him. Maybe I'm more of a hassle than anything. That, I could believe, considering everything he's done for me with no reciprocation. But I thought he was fond of me, at least a little.

Finally, his smile returns and his normal demeanor takes over. "Yeah, Dove. You and Sly are my people. Don't ever question that."

I breathe out a sigh of relief. A lot has been unspoken between us, probably because they think I'm fragile, so they keep things light.

But I have a feeling all that's going to change soon.

"Can I help?" I ask Sissy who's preparing dinner for the guys.

"Sure, darlin'. Get on in here. There's a whole bowl of veggies that need to be chopped up," she says as she stirs a pot of something that smells delicious on the stove. "Gotta say, I love having you around more."

It's been a week since my memory has returned, and things have changed drastically. Before now, I was confused and scared. I hid away in my room, only coming out when necessary, and even when I did, I avoided everyone. But as little pieces of who I was return, I no longer feel the need to hide away completely, and sometimes, like now, I purposely seek out interaction.

I don't miss the look of shock on everyone's faces when they see me out and about, but I don't draw attention to their reactions; I just go about the day like I've always been this way.

"Me too." I go to the sink and wash my hands before getting to work.

The kitchen looks like it belongs in a restaurant. There's

one long, stainless-steel counter down the center with utensils and pots hanging from a shelf above. Across from that are an industrial-sized stove, refrigerator, and two dishwashers next to a huge stainless-steel sink.

Sissy hums as she moves through the kitchen, taking the veggies as I cut them up. I try not to think about Sly and Moto having sex with her or Tabitha because it makes me uneasy. Looking over at her, I can't help the intrusive thoughts. She's sexy in an obvious way with her big boobs, small waist, and skimpy clothes. I can see the appeal, but I don't want to.

I'd hate her if she wasn't so darn nice and caring. Her and Tabitha's roles in the club have shifted since most of the patched-in members have old ladies now, except the newbies. But by the time Duncan, Ford, and Miles patched in, Tabitha and Sissy had already closed their legs to the guys for good. Now the two of them are a couple, which makes me feel better about future trysts with the two men who stay on my mind every day.

"What are you making?" I ask.

"A stew. The stormy weather has me wanting some comfort food."

"It smells amazing. How did you learn to cook?"

"Trial and error. I knew there'd come a time when our other services wouldn't be needed, and I wanted to make myself handy so they'd never ask me to leave." She's so blasé about the whole sex thing.

If I think about it, I can see the similarities between her and me. She slept with the guys for room and board while I slept with my masters so they wouldn't kill me. The stakes were higher for me, but the same basic concept.

"Why do you want to stay? Don't you want to have your own life?" I ask.

She stops in her tracks and scowls at me, making my chin dip to my chest and my shoulders hunch. What did I say wrong?

"This is my life." She motions around the room. "I came here when I didn't have a friend in the world or a penny to my name. Those men out there gave me somewhere to go and a family to belong to. Now I know your story, and I'm real sorry about everything you've been through, but we're not the same. There's no gun to my head. If I wanted to go, I'd go."

"I'm sorry. I didn't mean anything by it."

She relaxes and gives me a sympathetic smile. "I know you didn't. I just get worked up when people think me and Tabitha are being taken advantage of, you know?"

I think about it for a minute and realize I was comparing them with the wrong period of my life. "I do, and I guess our current situations are more similar. After all, I'm still here when I don't have to be."

"Exactly. Now give me those potatoes." She playfully shoulders me out of the way and scoops up the baby reds.

Once I finish with all the jobs Sissy has for me, I seek out Moto and do a wound check on him. Or at least that'll be my excuse for just wanting to see him. After that intense moment we shared in his room, I have the urge to be around them all the time.

But before I step foot into the main room, I hear a voice that doesn't belong to any of the club members.

Despite how much I've come out of my shell, men I don't know still frighten me. I pause to listen at the swinging door before going through it. The voice I hear is vaguely familiar, though I can't quite place it. The hairs on my arm stand on end, and I get the compulsion to flee.

But why?

"You heading out, honey?" Sissy asks, taking note of where I'm perched with both hands and my ear on the door.

"Someone's out there."

"If it were an important meeting, they'd be in the Chapel. You can go out there. It's okay."

I know she's right. Whenever they're conducting club

business, they go inside the windowless, soundproof room and close the door. Only patched-in members are allowed in, and the only rule I've been given is not to disturb them when they're in there. So, if they're at the bar or in the game room, I'm allowed to go out there.

I steel my spine, telling myself I'm brave now, and the guys won't let anything bad happen to me. Pushing the door open, I take a couple steps out into the area behind the bar. Since everyone's to my far left in the dining area, no one notices my entrance. Which is good. I can slink by them without anyone the wiser. I'm halfway to the hallway, keeping my eyes forward when I stop.

That voice. I know it.

Slowly glancing over, I see the man who has haunted my nightmares for years. The men who kept me prisoner were assholes, but that's nothing compared to my feelings toward Tyler—if that's even his real name.

That man sweet-talked me, charmed me into thinking he was a good guy trying to help me find Mia that night at the club. His intentions were much more sinister, and I wouldn't have been sold if he hadn't taken me.

His handsome face and kind eyes haunt me, and he's currently sitting at a round table, sandwiched between Sly and Moto.

No. No. No. No.

What is happening? Did he find me, and he's here to drag me back?

Sly laughs at something Tyler says, and my stomach turns. Did they set me up? Were they only holding me here until they could find out who took me, and now they're selling me back?

Adrenaline floods my system and what used to be a fight or flight instinct turns into crippling anxiety rooting me in place. I need to run, but I can't. My legs don't work, and if I don't get ahold of myself soon, I'll drop to the floor like a sack of potatoes.

None of this makes sense.

I'm going to pass out, but they'll notice me if I do. I can't let that happen. I need to run, and fast. Yet every time I try to move forward, I feel myself slipping away.

At the ranch, they taught me how to talk myself down from a panic attack. I try to think of five things I can see, but blackness starts to fill my vision. I try to think of four things right now that I can feel, but all that comes to mind are Tyler's rough hands forcing me into the limo with the pock-marked man. I try to think of three things I can hear, but Tyler's voice is on repeat in my mind. I try to think of two things I can smell, but only Tyler's cologne fills my nostrils.

Before I can attempt to find one thing I can taste, my body grows heavy, sinking into the ground, while my mind floats higher and higher. Darkness takes over, and I pass out cold.

Chapter
EIGHT

Sly

"I'm telling you guys, the money isn't in guns like it used to be. It's in women. And the younger, the better." Cal leans back, kicking his feet out. He's far too relaxed to be talking about human trafficking.

I nod, smiling at the fucker despite my growing urge to put a bullet in his brain right here in the dining room. He has two men with him standing guard, but I trust my brothers could take care of them.

Before I can do that, a thud sounds from near the bar, gaining all our attention.

Shooting to my feet, I see Dove in a heap on the ground. I run to her side and fall to my knees. "Dove?"

Moto rushes over and joins me on the ground while Loki, Khan, Goblin, and Cal crowd around us.

"Give us some space," I bite out, shooting a look to Loki, who gets my meaning. None of us want this asshole's eyes on our women. He's dangerous.

"Just one of the club whores. Why don't we go back to the table while they clean this up?" Loki leads them back to the dining room. I don't care if my brothers see her like this, but I sure as shit don't want Cal anywhere near her.

Moto places his ear near her mouth and two fingers on her neck. "She's breathing, but her heart is fuckin' racing."

"Let's get her to her room," I whisper to Moto and lift her up in my arms. It's not hard to do since she's still trying to get to a healthy weight.

We hurry down the hall, and I lay her down before brushing her hair away from her face. She's pale on a good day, but right now, she looks ghostly, with no color on her cheeks at all.

"Dove, wake up." I lightly slap her cheek a couple times. She startles awake, sitting up so fast I don't have a chance to move before she slams her forehead into mine. "Shit."

"Are you okay?" Moto asks, sitting down next to her.

Her eyes are wide as saucers, and she looks ready to run. What the fuck is going on?

"Get the hell away from me." She tries to slip past me and roll off the bed, but I catch her and pin her down by the shoulders.

"Dove, it's okay. You're safe."

"Please, don't do this," she begs, absolute terror in her eyes. "I'll leave. You'll never see me again. Just don't do it."

Moto glances over at me, his brows knitted, and mouths, "What the fuck?"

I shake my head because I'm as clueless as he is. Maybe she's having some kind of psychotic break? Maybe she found some drugs or alcohol lying around? We did our best to clean it up, but this is a biker clubhouse. There's no way we can catch everything.

"Calm down and tell us what the fuck is happening with you." My voice comes out stern and louder than I meant, proven when she cowers away from me. I blow out a breath and soften my tone. "We're confused, Dove. Just tell us what's going on, and we'll take care of it, okay? You can trust us."

She shoves at me, the tendons in her neck popping out, and she bares her teeth. "Trust? I don't trust you. I don't trust any of you."

This isn't her. She might not be the most open book, but she's told us over and over how good it feels to be able to sleep at night knowing she has her two protectors. None of this makes any fuckin' sense.

"Listen, we promise to let you go after you tell us what happened," Moto reasons.

She makes one last attempt to leave before she sinks back to the mattress and covers her face with both hands. Pitiful, angry sobs come straight from her chest in a roar. Whatever she's feeling is big, and we need to get to the bottom of it before we lose her forever.

"Shh, Dove. It's okay. We're not here to hurt you, but you gotta explain all this." I loosen my hold on her shoulders but keep them in place, just in case.

Her hands fall away from her face, revealing mottled cheeks and damp eyes. "Why is he here if you're not going to hurt me? Huh?"

I tilt my head. "Who?"

"*Him*. Tyler. If you're not giving me back to him, why is he here?"

"Tyler," Moto says, curling his lip. "You mean the fucker who took you? He's not here."

"Yes, he is." She turns her attention to me and scoffs. "You were laughing with him."

"You mean Cal? Dove, that's not Ty—" It all clicks into place. "Shit."

"What? I don't get it," Moto says.

"Cal is Tyler. He must've given her a fake name, or we have the fake name. Either way, it's him."

Moto jumps to his feet. "I'll fuckin' kill him."

"Wait. We need to be smart about this. We can't bust in there, guns blazing, or we'll never find Dove's friend."

"What are you guys talking about?" Dove asks, seeming to relax a little now that it's clear we had no idea who we invited here.

I stand up and pace the room. "I've been on a hunt to find Mia, like you asked. I talked to Loki about it, and he mentioned he knew a guy who's always trying to get the club to help out with protection for his *shipments*. He extended an invitation to talk to us about it, not because we're interested, but because he might have some information since he works out of Vegas." Sitting back down, I take Dove's hands in mine. "If I'd known he was the same damn guy, I never would've asked him here. You gotta believe me."

"So, you're not giving me back?"

"Fuck no. I swear to God, Dove, that world will never fuckin' touch you again. You hear me?"

Moto steals one of her hands. "We'd rather die than see you go back to that."

Her shoulders slump, and all the fight, all the emotion, all the fear leave her body. "I believe you, and I'm sorry. I just saw him, and I didn't know what to think. I panicked."

"Understandable," Moto says.

"Do you think he recognized her?" I ask.

"I don't know. I wasn't paying any attention to him."

"If he did, there's no way he'll want her walking around, knowing who he is and what he does." I run a hand through my hair. "We need to go back out there. I'll keep asking questions, see what he has to say. After he leaves, we'll have a sit down with Loki."

"I can't sit next to that fucker and not kill him," Moto growls.

"You have to. For Dove's sake. If he recognized her, she's in danger. And even if he didn't, we still need to find her friend."

Dove's eyes ping pong between us, listening to the conversation.

"Sly, I'm telling you. I will stab a screwdriver through his eyeball the second he talks about taking other women. I can't do it." The manic look on his face is proof of the fury he's feeling, and if he doesn't trust himself right now, I can't trust him to be who I need him to be.

"Fine. Stay here. It'll make me feel better knowing Dove's protected anyway." I stand but dip down and kiss Dove's cheek before I leave. I've kissed her forehead, crown, even kissed her hand once, but this is the first time I've gotten this close to her mouth. It's intimate, and I let my lips linger longer than what's appropriate before pulling away. "I'll be back."

"Be careful," she whispers.

"I will." Steeling my spine and wiping away all emotion— something I've trained myself to do—I walk back into the dining room like fuck all just went down.

"Everything okay?" Cal asks, one brow raised.

"Just another slut who can't handle her liquor. Puked a few times, and now she's passed out." The words taste like acid on my tongue, but I can't give anything away.

"What's her name?" he asks with way too much interest.

"Who asks a whore what their name is?" I playfully slap his arm with the back of my hand. "Am I right? Doesn't matter anyway. I got her taken care of. Now, where were we?" I sit back down next to the asshole who changed Dove's life forever.

"I was just telling Loki how I'm expanding and could use some muscle from guys who know the discreet West Coast routes. From what I understand, that's you."

Loki chuckles, but his fingers squeeze his cigarette butt so tight that he's flattened it. He knows something's up, and for a man with control issues, it's driving him insane. Good thing he's a professional at keeping his wits about him under pressure.

He flicks ashes into the tray. "We have our ways."

"That's good."

Now that I know who Cal really is, this conversation went from me gaining knowledge of the business as a whole to me gaining knowledge of *his* business. It changes everything.

"Walk me through it. How does this all work?" I ask.

"Two ways. For our more discernible clients, my team will scout specific *products*." He steeples his fingers, elbows on the table. "That's the real money maker. But those situations take time and effort, so in the meantime, we collect a wide range of products. That's what we need help with. Once we have a group of them in a secure location, we need to be able to transport them to the clients who tend to go through the products more quickly, so they aren't as particular about the quality."

My blood boils. He's not talking about antique furniture. He's talking about girls. Girls that will be used, abused, then tossed away like trash. Since Dove's still alive, I'm assuming she was purchased for a specific client. While I know she was gifted to Anthony at some point, I'd love to know who that original asshole was.

"Do you keep a client list or a log?" I ask, earning a frown from Loki. I'm pushing too hard, but this man is standing between me getting the information I need before I can rip him limb from limb.

His gaze shifts from me to Loki and back, jaw ticking. "Our system is proprietary. You'll excuse me for not divulging too much of it."

"Of course," Loki butts in. "How much money are you talking about for our services?"

There's no amount Cal could offer that would get Loki to accept, but this change of topic will keep him off our scent, so I'm thankful for the diversion.

"Fifty Gs per delivered package." He shrugs. "It's a decent amount for a day's worth of work."

"But a lot of risk. If we got caught with a truckload of your product, it'd earn us a hefty sentence." Loki stamps out his cig.

"Sure, but I trust you have your routes in place because they're safe. And there's no way you're earning that much running guns."

"Not quite," I say. "Are you the boss, or do you work for someone?" When Loki scowls at me, I add, "We just want to make sure this is a legit offer."

"I answer to someone but run my own crew. My client doesn't like to be bogged down with details. He prefers to sit back and collect the money."

That's interesting, and I know my next step will be finding out who this client is.

I fold my arms on the table, leaning into him. "What happens if a girl escapes?"

His brows lift, and he chuckles, but it's not humorous. My digging is out of line, and it's irritating him. "You mean while the package is being transported?"

"Or after they're delivered to your customers," I say.

This time Khan elbows me in the side, and I glare back at him. I have no fucks to give at this point. I need answers.

"I'd be trusting you to keep track of our products." He narrows his eyes on me. "As for after they're delivered, their owners wouldn't allow them to escape. For obvious reasons. And if they did, it would be a security breach that would need to be handled."

That's all the answer I need. He doesn't want to get caught, and Dove is a liability. Does he know she was gifted to someone else? And if so, does he know what happened to Anthony? Is she already on his radar to get "handled"? I have no clue, but it makes me uneasy.

"We'll think about it and be in touch." Loki stands, and everyone follows suit.

As Cal is walking out, he stops abruptly and pins me with a look. "What did you say your whore's name was?"

I widen my stance. "I didn't."

"Just asking because I thought she looked like someone I used to know. Though your whore's a lot skinnier, and her hair is longer." He purses his lips and looks to the ceiling as though he's thinking hard. "Other than that, they look similar. Just can't remember her name . . ." His piercing gaze lands on me. "It was Cameron. Is that chick's name Cameron?"

"Nope. Don't think so," I deadpan.

"Hm, all right then." He holds a hand out for Loki to shake. "We'll talk soon."

Loki reluctantly obliges. "Sure, man."

Chapter
NINE

Moto

Dove curls into me, head on my chest and her body trembling, while we wait for Sly to return. I don't know what to say other than to tell her it's going to be okay and reassure her we'll protect her with our lives.

"You wanna talk it out?" I ask.

She's quiet for a minute before speaking softly. "Every day of those four years was horrible, but the day he took me was the worst." Her head pops up, and those mesmerizing brown eyes peer up at me. "I broke his nose, you know."

It's not what I expected her to say, and a laugh bubbles out. "Seriously?"

She smiles. It's small, but it's there. "Yeah. I almost got away." She rests back on my chest. "But I didn't know where we were, and I couldn't leave Mia behind."

"It was brave to go back for your friend."

"A lot of good it did. The guy, I don't know what the hell to call him because the only name he ever gave was Sir, and I really don't want to call him that ever again—"

"Fuckwad," I suggest.

"Yeah, okay. I was angry at myself for fighting back because if I hadn't, Fuckwad would've taken us both. I could've protected her."

"What happened after that?" I prod because speaking things out loud lessens the power it has over you.

"You don't want to know."

"If you want to tell me, I want to know." I settle a hand on her hip and wait for her to show any signs of discomfort, but nothing comes. She feels good in my arms, technically arm, since my left arm is in this goddamn sling.

"It was bad at first, probably because I fought back, and he wanted a submissive pet. He hit me, punched me, burned me, and he raped me every single day. It got better when I gave up trying to get away and accepted it. After that, he left me alone during the day, and I was free to swim and read books. Then nighttime would come and . . ." Her voice cracks.

Every muscle in my body tightens with each word she speaks, and I vow to find every single person who ever wronged her and make them eat their own shit.

"I'm so sorry, Dove."

"After a couple years, he was tired of me. By that time, I was nearly catatonic when he came to my room, and he wanted someone with more spark. So, he gave me to Anthony, who was better than Fuckwad, probably because he drugged me and gave me access to alcohol. I don't remember half of what he did to me."

"He was cruel too?"

"Yeah."

"I'm glad he's fuckin' dead, though I wish I'd been the one to kill him."

She props her head up on the hand resting on my chest. "You're serious when you say things like that, aren't you?"

"As a fuckin' heart attack."

I study her as she processes that. Any other woman would

be terrified by my words and scramble to get away from someone who could take a life without losing sleep. But not our Dove.

"I like that you want to protect me." Her tongue peeks out to wet her lips. Lips I want to kiss, devour, own. If she were any other girl, I would've by now. Hell, Sly and I would have fucked her two ways from Sunday by now if she wasn't coming out of the most horrific experiences a person can go through.

"Always."

Her hand reaches up and settles on my cheek. "You're a good man, Moto."

It's not true, but the fact that she thinks I am has me feeling like the fuckin' king of the world. That's the power she has over me.

"You're a good woman." We stare at each other for a long minute, not saying anything. I've almost mustered up the courage to tell her how I've been feeling when her hand withdraws, and she lies back down.

"Where did you grow up?"

"California."

"Do you have family?"

I guess it's time for fifty questions, but if it makes her feel like she knows me better, then so be it.

"I do. They're still in Cali."

"Do you speak with them?"

"Sometimes. They're not exactly happy about my life choices. My mom cries at least once every time I call, so I try not to do it too often."

"Why?"

"I grew up in a traditional household. The fact that I didn't go to college, get a real job, and settle down with a wife to pop out babies is disappointing."

"They're missing out," she says.

"I don't think they'd agree but thank you."

The door opens, and Sly walks in, huffing like the Incredible

Hulk. It breaks the moment, and Dove sits up ramrod straight, eyes wide.

"What happened?" she asks.

Sly doesn't answer, just paces back and forth, one hand fisted in his dark curls and the other planted on his hip. I'm nervous as hell watching him.

When I can't take it anymore, I say, "Sly. What the fuck happened?"

"He recognized Dove. He didn't outright say it at first, but he dropped her name when he was leaving."

Dove's on her feet in an instant. "No, no, no."

"He saw your face when you passed out and knew who you were."

"I need to go." She opens her closet and rips clothes off hangers, chucking them on top of me on the bed.

"Hold up. You're not thinking clearly," I say.

"He'll come back for me. I'm not useful anymore. I'm too old, so he'll kill me. I know it."

"We won't let that happen." Sly walks over to her, but she isn't listening. He grips her wrists, stopping her from making any bigger of a mess. She struggles, trying to yank free, but he holds tight as she screams at him to let her go. He doesn't. Eventually, the fight leaves her, and she rests her forehead on his chest. "Listen to me. We won't fuckin' let that happen."

He releases her wrists, and they immediately go around his waist. She whispers, "I'm scared."

He wraps his arms around her, one hand settling on the back of her head. "I know, but we got you. The whole damn club has your back."

She blows out a breath. "Okay."

"Good girl," he says, and despite the situation, those two words stir life into my cock. I can't help it. It's a visceral reaction from all the times he's said it in the past while we're balls deep in a woman. I shake it off.

Read the room, asshole.

She sniffles and pulls away, realizing the disaster she created. Laughing, she says, "I threw a bit of a tantrum, huh?"

"Just a little." I hold out a hand, gesturing to the clothes I'm buried under.

"I'm sorry." She pushes the fabric off me and onto the floor to be dealt with later.

"No worries."

"So, what do we do?" she asks.

"Not sure yet. Church is in fifteen." Sly nods to me.

"Got it."

"Can I come since this has to do with me?"

"Not happening, Dove. But I promise we'll let you know what we decide to do." Sly, the brazen fucker, cups her cheeks and stares her dead in the eyes. "He won't get near you. Understand me?"

She melts into his touch, gripping his wrists while his hands stay glued to her face. They share a moment much like the one I had with her minutes ago.

Maybe I'm reading too much into this, or maybe my senses are right on, but something's happening. She's coming around. She's feeling a pull for both of us.

Time will tell if she moves toward it or pushes it away.

"Every time one of us finds a bitch, we go to war with someone. Can things be fuckin' easy for once?" Loki pinches the bridge of his nose.

"You're one to speak," Khan mutters under his breath.

"At least with me, we made some fuckin' money. How many of you can say that?" Loki asks. Birdie's dad paid us a hefty sum to keep her protected, despite his daughter falling in love with her protector.

"I save us money. Bex undercharges our legal fees." Khan shifts in his chair, his massive size causing the wood to creak.

"That would be helpful if you weren't the one who costs us the most in legal fees," Goblin says under his breath.

I glance over at Roch. I can tell he's fuming and wants to say something, but words don't come easily for him, so I take the load off. "Truly and her mom save our asses by stitching us up."

Roch gives me an appreciative nod that I return.

It's a good thing Coyote's not on the ranks because, as far as I can tell, Riley hasn't done shit for us other than work at the strip club.

"Whatever. The point is, we don't know anything about this Cal guy. He could be backed by some major players. Before we do anything, we need Sly to do a deep dive and find out exactly who he's connected to and how loyal they are. He's selling women to very wealthy and powerful men who would probably like to keep their shit quiet. If we take him out, they'll come knocking at our door wondering what we know and if we can expose them. We can't handle that kind of heat right now." Loki digs his pack of cigs out of his pocket and lights up. He's been trying to quit for almost a year now, but none of us say shit about it.

"I'll start looking today, but regardless of who might want to protect him, we need to keep him far away from the club," Sly says.

"And give full protection for Dove," I add.

Loki's brows raise. "You claiming her?"

"We both are." Sly gives an uncharacteristically sinister look, daring anyone to argue.

Khan slaps the table loudly. "I fuckin' knew it. You dirty dogs."

Sly's face breaks into a cocky smirk. "What can we say?"

"Does she know?" Goblin asks.

"She will," I say, earning jeers from my brothers. "Fuck off. She's been through a lot of shit. She's almost ready."

Everyone boos, and the room breaks out into chaos.

Slamming his gavel down, Loki shuts everyone up. "All right, all right. So, for now, Petra has our protection, and Sly is researching the fuck out of this Cal guy. No moves will be made until we figure shit out. Let's get back to business. Goblin, grab Coyote, would you?"

Goblin steps out for a second, returning with our newest member.

"Coyote, how's the club doing?" Loki asks.

"Better than expected. The rebranding and remodeling are bringing in record numbers. Roxy let go of all the girls who weren't up to our standards and hired a bunch who are. Thanks to everyone willing to pull shifts so I can get some time off."

"Good. Between the runs, the club, and the construction company, our books are sitting pretty. Everyone's getting a bonus this month," Sly says, earning hoots and hollers from the guys.

"Fuck yeah," Loki says. "Anyone else have anything to add?"

We go silent, all our business handled.

"Then get out there. Keep an eye on the schedule Moto has posted. Everyone's doing runs, everyone's taking shifts at the club, and everyone's working a job site. No exceptions." Loki's gavel slams down one more time, and we disperse.

"I guess things are official," I say to Sly as we walk down the hall.

"Went better than I thought."

"Are you going into your den of nerdiness?"

"Yeah. I want to know everything I can find out on this guy." He stops me in front of Dove's door. "You saw her with me, right?"

"Yeah. Before you came in, we had a similar exchange."

"Her memory returning is the best and worst thing to

happen." His features look tortured, like he's happy but also worried as fuck.

"Agreed." I reach out and place a hand on his arm that could appear friendly. "We'll figure this out and take this asshole down once and for all."

"I know. I just . . ." He pierces me with eyes that are navy blue today, thanks to his dark blue shirt.

"Yeah, I know. It's a lot of responsibility to ask your brothers to fight for you. But we've done it for them, over and over. It's our turn."

He leans in close to my ear. "Meet me in my room later."

"Okay. Let me know what you find out, yeah?" My hand drops, and he starts down the hall.

"Will do."

Chapter
TEN

Petra

"**Y**ou have to try this on," Roxy says, tossing me something that looks like a pile of dental floss.

Apparently, being under the club's protection means that I have to be with a club member at all times. If no one is around at the clubhouse, I get to go to Royal Treatment. This couldn't have worked out more in my favor.

"I wouldn't even know how to put it on." I hold it up, trying to figure out if it's tangled or supposed to look like this.

She yanks it out of my hands. "Take off your clothes."

My face has never turned red faster, and panic bubbles in my belly. "What?"

"Clothes. Off."

"I don't think that's a good idea."

"Girl, you've seen me buck ass naked. We don't have secrets back here." She pins me with a look.

The problem is, I don't look like her. I have so many insecurities I'd need both our hands and toes to count them all. Everything about me is small: my breasts, my ass, my height, everything.

That's not it, though. Fuckwad and Anthony did things to me, left permanent marks, and my upper thighs took the brunt. There's a roadmap there of everything I've been through.

"I can't," I choke out.

"Why the hell not?"

"I told you what happened to me."

She taps her toe and pops a hip. "Not seeing the problem."

"I have scars," I whisper.

"So? Everyone has scars, honey. Even if you can't see them on the outside, they're there, on the inside."

"But I don't like to show them."

She plops down on the wooden bench next to me. "Look. It's just me, and you know I don't care."

Swallowing my fear, I toe off my shoes before pushing down Sly's sweatpants. My cheeks flame red, and I have to close my eyes as I continue to remove my clothes, telling myself this is for emotional progress.

"Holy shit, babe."

"I know." I open my eyes and watch her perusal as she circles me.

There are white strips that wrap from my inner thighs outward from Fuckwad's knife—he liked to watch me bleed—and small red burns cover my inner thighs from Anthony's cigars. When he was angry, he used me as his ashtray.

All the bruises, bloody lips, and black eyes have healed, but when I look at myself in the mirror, I still see them permanently etched in my memory.

"That's not what I'm talking about," she says, and I open my eyes. "You're giving me a lady boner."

I wasn't expecting her to say that, and a hysterical fit of laughter bubbles out of me.

"I'm serious. I'd kill for tits that sit that high. And your ass is so tight. Those men out there would go crazy if you were on stage."

"I don't think so."

"Here, step into it like this, and pull it all the way up." She holds out the strappy number, and I put it on as instructed.

She adjusts the fabric, spacing out the thin strips that run along each butt cheek and spreading out the ones covering my nipples. When she's done, I stand in front of the mirror.

To my surprise, I love it. It's edgy and sexy, and the way it fits emphasizes my assets. I'm not focused on my scars at all. I look and feel sexy.

"Get out on that stage, Petra. Do it right fuckin' now." She points at the ceiling, waving her hand back and forth.

"I don't think I'm ready for that, but I agree; I like it."

"If the scars make you uncomfortable, I'll show you how to cover them with makeup."

"You can do that?"

"Yep. And while we're at it, we can do something with your hair."

We head over to the wall of vanities and take a seat. Roxy hands me a beauty blender and a bottle of foundation. "This will cover anything. Put a dot on each thigh and blend, then we'll set it with powder."

I follow her instructions and am shocked at how my scars disappear. You can still see the bumps and valleys of each, but only if you look closely.

"See? I told you." She glances at the clock. "Shit. I'm on stage in ten, and I haven't put my own makeup on."

I pay attention to the way she lines her eyes and applies her face makeup so I can give it a try when she leaves. Even though I think I was pretty good at it four years ago, trends have changed.

She fluffs up her hair, making it wild and sexy, then applies a thick coat of red lipstick.

"That's it. When I return, I want to see what you come up with," she says.

"Break a leg."

"Be right back."

I carefully apply the makeup exactly like Roxy did, using cotton swabs to fix my small mistakes. By the time Roxy returns, fisting a stack of cash with a sheen of perspiration on her body, I'm done and proud of how I look.

"How'd it go?" I ask.

"Fucking amazing. There's a good crowd out there." She sets the cash down and sorts it.

"You probably make pretty good money, huh?"

"The best. Especially after the club took over. They classed up the joint, and now all the weird losers who used to come in can't even get through the door. It's awesome."

"I'd like to make my own money," I admit. "I've been living off the club for too long."

"We joke about it but would you ever consider dancing?" she asks.

"I never have before. I spent my early years in school—high school, college, med school—then immediately went into my residency and started working in an ER. Other than waitressing on weekends, that's the only job I've had."

Her jaw drops. "You're a fucking doctor?"

"I was. I don't know what I am now."

"Can you dance?"

"I remember loving to dance, but I don't think I'm especially good at it."

"How late are you here?" She waggles her brows.

"Moto said they'd be done an hour after closing because they're doing the bank drop tonight."

"Perfect. Keep all this on and pick out a pair of shoes. We're going to have a dance lesson once we close up."

"I don't know."

"No one will see. It'll be just me and you." She stands to go lock her cash up. "And Petra, I'm not taking no for an answer."

I chew on the inside of my mouth, wondering if this is a good idea. I guess if no one is around, it'll be okay.

"Okay." I smile, realizing I might have an actual friend.

It's been so long since I had a female to talk to. It feels good to have someone to confide in. I love my guys, but there are things I don't feel comfortable talking to them about.

I put my sweats on over the sexy outfit and decide to help Riley. We serve dinner and restock products for the girls to use while they're here. Everything from tampons, travel-size hygiene products, and snacks are kept in bins for them to take.

I can't believe how well they're treated, but the only experience I have with strip clubs is what I've seen on TV and in the movies. Those aren't reliable sources. Or maybe the club just appreciates them more than others. I don't know.

Riley's someone else I hit it off with. She's sweet and caring in the way moms are.

We talk while we work, and she tells me how she had a one-night stand with Coyote and got pregnant. Then they reunited four years later but had some major drama with a different MC, the Sons of Erebus. I'm glad they made it through that. It's obvious she and Coyote are in love.

"So, are you *together* with Sly and Moto?" she asks.

I choke on my Dr. Pepper. "What?"

"I'm only asking because you're under the club's protection, and they don't do that unless a member claims the woman in question."

"Claims?"

"Oh boy." She rests a hip on the rectangular table the girls eat at and folds her arms across her chest. "How much do you know about club life?"

"Apparently, not very much."

Before my memory came back, I spent as little time in the main spaces as possible. I didn't want anything to do with the big, scary men who milled about out there. It's slowly changing, and I find myself eating meals with them and getting to know them, but as far as club rules? I'm clueless.

"The only people the club protects are members, their family, and their ol' ladies. You're not a member, you're not family, which means they claimed you."

"Both of them?" I ask.

"Don't you like both of them? You three are hardly ever apart."

I decide to change the topic slightly and get some answers of my own since Riley is blunt and seems to have no problem divulging information.

"Do Moto and Sly often get with the same women?"

"I've never seen them with anyone except you, but I've heard stories. Apparently, that's their thing. They like threesomes."

I sit down, spinning my can of soda, trying to make connections in my mind.

"I'm so confused."

"Are you attracted to both of them?" she asks.

"Well, yeah. They're the hottest men I've ever seen in real life, and I've connected with them both on a deeper level."

I think back to the last week where there have been these moments I thought for sure each of them would kiss me. And to my surprise, I wanted them to. After it passed with no kiss, I was ashamed to feel the same amount of desire for each.

The part that throws me off even more is the occasional affection they show each other. Sometimes it's just a look, but lately, it's more. I feel the sexual chemistry between them, and it makes sense. They're closer than any two people I've been around. They finish each other's sentences and check in with each other throughout the day. Something they don't do with any of the other brothers.

I've pushed it aside, thinking I'm making things up in my head, but now that Riley has spoken it out loud, it makes sense.

"Has anything happened between you three?"

"No. Separately, there have been times I thought it would, but they never pull the trigger. I was beginning to feel guilty for being attracted to both of them."

"I don't think you have to worry about that. I think you can have both cakes and eat them too." A sly smile breaks across her face.

"I've never even entertained anything like that."

"Maybe you haven't, but I guarantee they have. My guess is they don't think you're ready." Riley leaves me, getting back to work.

I cradle my head in my hands, resting my elbows on the table. My mind is reeling from this new information, and I don't know what to make of it.

I stay that way until the dressing room floods with women, signaling the end of the night. Outfits and makeup come off, comfy clothes are put on, and the security guards open the back door to escort them to their cars.

The insanity lasts five minutes before it's quiet, with only a few remaining.

Roxy finds me at the table and takes a seat next to me. "You ready for this?"

Needing a distraction, I nod and follow her to the front of the house. Like she said, no one is around—just me, her, and the intimidating-looking pole.

"Take off the sweats," she instructs.

It feels ten times scarier being in this open space, but I do it, folding the sweats and setting them off to the side. I feel naked and exposed, the air conditioning hitting places normally covered.

"Let's turn on some music." She runs in her high as hell heels to the DJ booth and turns on an upbeat, sexy song. Running back, she blows out a breath and says, "Okay. Show me what you got."

"What?" I laugh nervously.

"Show me your moves. I need to know what I'm working with."

"You want me to just dance?"

She rolls her eyes. "Get it, girl. Show me."

"I haven't danced since before." It's a lie. After Sly gave me that Alexa, I've been playing music nonstop, and as a byproduct, I started dancing again. I quickly remembered the freeing feeling of drowning out the world and moving my body. While I'd never consider myself a dancer, I love doing it.

"Show me," she insists.

And I do. I rock my hips, run my hands over my body, and move to the beat in a way that's much sexier than anything I've done before. Maybe it's the song or the lack of clothes and atmosphere, but whatever it is, it inspires me.

This moment is perfect. It makes me feel like my old self, before I saw the horrors of the world and things were much simpler.

"Yes!" Roxy claps. "That's what I'm talking about. You'll be easy to teach."

I beam over at her, feeling the glow inside me reigniting. It's been a long time since I've felt like this, and I don't ever want it to go away.

I'm too old to start a career as a stripper, regardless of what Roxy says, but it might be what I need to heal myself on the inside and accept myself on the outside.

Chapter ELEVEN

Sly

"**R**eady?" Moto asks.

I stand and collect the money bags. "Ready as a rocket. I haven't seen Dove in a while, have you?"

"No. I didn't have a chance to pop in on her. It was a crazy night."

"Roxy was with her. They're probably still playing dress-up."

We open the door to the dressing room to find it empty. None of the dancers are lingering.

"Where the hell is she?" Moto's panic is rising, I can feel it.

I slap a hand on his back. "Let's check the club. Come on."

Music is still playing, making the walls vibrate with the pounding bass. Usually, the DJ shuts it off before he leaves, so that gives me hope she's right where I think she is.

I open the door and follow Moto to the open room, nearly running into the back of him when he stops abruptly.

"What the hell?" I push him to the side, only to be stunned stupid.

There, up on the stage, is Dove. I'm sure Roxy is up there, too, but I don't notice her. All I see is our girl, wearing the skimpiest of outfits, dancing. And not just any dancing; her hands caress her body, her narrow hips thrust and gyrate, and her feet move so damn smoothly to the beat.

I nearly bite clean through my tongue. Holy shit.

"Goddamn," Moto curses, eyes big, mouth open.

"Goddamn, indeed."

The song ends, and Roxy tells her she's perfect for the stage, making her blush. When a new song starts, this one more sensual and moodier, she directs Dove to her knees, showing her how to move in a way that looks good from every seat in the house.

We watch, stupefied and unable to make our presence known because neither of us wants the moment to end.

Roxy rolls onto her back, and Dove follows suit, their legs rising to the ceiling. Dove's ass is fully exposed, the piece of floss she's wearing disappearing between her round cheeks. And though her cunt is covered, I can see the outline of it through the fabric.

"Jesus Christ." Moto takes a seat, and I chuckle. She's officially made him weak in the knees.

They do a routine, spreading their legs, closing them back up, and moving them side to side; all of it designed to show everyone watching what they can't have. And fuck me, I want what she's displaying so fuckin' bad. My cock is hard as steel and desperate for it.

After the song ends, it goes quiet, and they erupt into giggles, their legs falling to the ground.

"Gotta say, Dove. You look like perfection up there." I clap hard and loud, Moto joining. The laughter stops short, and they both sit up, Dove's hand flying to her chest.

"I didn't know we had an audience," Roxy says, standing and helping Dove up.

"We were just messing around." Dove attempts to cover herself, but her hands are small and don't hide shit.

"Don't get shy on me now. You look hot, baby." It's the first time I've called her that, and I decide I like it. It makes me feel like she belongs to me. To us.

Her cheeks pink up. "I should go change." She darts off to the back, and Roxy follows, flashing a conspiratorial grin. Apparently, she's on our side. Good.

Once Dove's back in her sweats, and I mean hers because I know we're not getting them back from her, we load up in the cage.

"I didn't know you were a dancer," I say, pulling out of the parking lot.

"I'm not." She finger combs her hair, bringing it around her face.

"Why are you embarrassed?" Moto leans forward from the backseat, popping his head between us.

She doesn't answer, and I can't stand the silence. "I couldn't take my eyes off you. Never seen anyone look so beautiful."

She looks toward me ever so slightly, just enough that I see her smile.

"Agreed." Moto leans back.

We pull into the clubhouse, and I immediately notice two bikes parked side by side out front, not in the carport where we normally park them.

"Who do those belong to?" I ask, getting out of the van. It's late, nearly four in the morning, so it doesn't make sense that anyone would be here.

The three of us walk over, and I notice they're brand-new Harley-Davidson Cruisers. Both are Street Glides, one in a custom matte army green, the other in midnight blue.

"You don't think these are for us?" Moto asks.

"Miguel did say he'd make it right." That's when I notice there's a tag on one. I pluck it off and read. "Hope this squares us up. I'll be in touch."

"Holy shit." Moto straddles the midnight blue one. "This one's mine."

"They're so pretty," Dove says.

"Hop on, let's try them out." I straddle mine and motion for her to get on, surprised when she does.

Moto's still in a sling and pouts like a child when he sees I'm going for a ride. I feel bad for him, but there's no way I'll be able to sleep without giving her a test ride.

"Sorry, bro," I call out.

"Fucker," he shouts, but he's smiling.

"What about helmets?" she asks.

"We'll just take her for a spin." I start it up, and the engine purrs to life. Goddamn. I'm almost glad Moto got shot.

I take us on a quick loop around the compound, speeding up when I hit the straightaway. Dove's arms tighten around me, and I feel her chest vibrating against my back. I think she's crying for a second, but when I quickly glance over my shoulder, I realize she's laughing.

I hit the gas again, sending us shooting forward, and she lets out a whoop of excitement. She's fuckin' perfect, and so is this bike.

All too soon, we're back at the compound entrance and parking.

"I can't wait to take her on a long ride," I say, holding a hand out to help Dove off.

"How'd she ride?" Moto asks.

"Like a dream." Dove beams. MC life suits her. "That was fun."

We walk inside, stopping at Dove's door.

"Guess this is goodnight." Something about this night has me feeling brave, so instead of the usual hug I'd give her, I tip her chin up and say, "Can I kiss you?"

Her eyes dart to Moto. "Right now?"

"Don't worry, Dove. He's planning on kissing you too."

There is no plan, of course, but I know I don't have to talk Moto into following suit.

"Both of you?" Her eyes go wide.

"Baby, I know you know who we are and what we like. That hasn't stopped you from getting close to both of us, which tells me you're okay with this. If I'm wrong, tell me. But if I'm right, then I'm gonna kiss the shit out of you right now."

She doesn't stop me. Instead, she licks her lips, and goddamnit, that's all the invitation I need.

I plant my lips on hers and moan when she responds, kissing me right back. As much as I want to make this kiss last all night, I know I need to pull away, but not before I part her lips and get a taste. Our tongues meet, slipping and sliding together, giving me all sorts of ideas. But again, that's not what this is about, so I end the kiss. Leaving her with one last peck.

"You taste like fuckin' heaven, Dove," I say, releasing her.

Moto steps up, drawing her to him. Her eyes are still closed, a euphoric look on her face. "My turn."

My cock's already hard but watching Moto claim her lips has my pulse beating in my pants, desperate for action. Something that can't happen. Not yet. She's been through too much, and sex comes with a lot of responsibility.

We gotta take it slow, give her a chance to acclimate and watch her cues to make sure nothing we do brings back bad memories for her.

"Good night, Dove," he says, squeezing her tight before releasing her.

"You good?" I check in with her.

"Yeah, I'm good." She gives me a dreamy smile before disappearing into her room. I was right. She's with us.

Moto takes my hand and drags me into his room. He barely gets the door shut before sinking to his knees and tugging at my belt. It's an impossible task with one hand, so I help him out, chuckling at his desperation.

"Did you see that?" He reaches into my boxers and pulls out my stiff length. "She wants us."

"I saw," I say, amused at how much this is turning him on, even though it did the same to me.

He sucks on the head of my cock, his eyes locked on mine, and shit, it's hot. I tug his hair free and fist it at the root, giving me control. Guiding him up and down, I relish the wet sounds he makes as he sucks me off.

"Soon, I'll have you both on your knees, and you can take turns. You'd like that, wouldn't you?" I grit out.

He nods, mouth full of cock.

"Take it deeper." I push him down, and he opens his throat. "Just like that."

I fuck his face and nearly lose it when he swallows around me. He releases his grip around my base to roll my balls in his hand. My head falls back, and I close my eyes, allowing myself to feel every sensation for just a minute before pulling free.

"I want your ass," I say.

"Then take it." He stands, and I help him undress.

I love his body. He's thicker than I am, but it's all solid muscle. His chest and abs are chiseled and so fuckin' smooth. He keeps himself hairless, and though I keep things tidy, I don't have the energy for that kind of dedication. Even if I love the way it looks on him.

He watches as I remove my own clothes, stroking his cock lazily. I grin over at him, proud that I can do that to a man as sexy as he is.

We can only do one position right now given he's still recovering, so I sit down on his bed, resting against his headboard.

"Grab the lube and sit on my cock."

After reaching into the nightstand and finding the tube of glide, he straddles my thighs, adjusting himself so his cock is resting on top of mine. He drizzles the lube down his length, and I take us both in hand, smothering our dicks in the slippery goo.

"We look so good together like this." I jerk us up and down.

I admire his dick for the thousandth time. He's girthier than I am and cut, while I'm longer and intact. We're perfect together, and if this is all I have for the rest of my life, it'll be more than enough. But having Dove here would make things that much better. "Come up higher so I can prepare you."

I release our dicks, and he moves up my body, lifting onto his knees so I can reach under. I circle his rear entrance with my lubed-up fingers before pushing one inside. He's always a tight fit and requires some stretching, something I'm happy to provide.

"You feel so good, love." The only time I can be free with him like this, calling him pet names and ordering him around, is in bed, so I make sure to do a lot of it to get it out of my system.

The rules are unspoken, but somehow, we're both on the same page. Whether the guys would freak out if I called him 'love' outside the bedroom or not, I don't know. But keeping this secret only serves to turn us on more, so we have no desire to test it out.

What we share is for us alone. We don't need to bring the club into this relationship. I don't know how bringing Dove into the mix will change things, but we'll figure it out.

I add another finger, scissoring his hole as I pump in and out. His cock drips precum onto my chest, and with my other hand, I scoop it up and suck it off my fingers.

"Fuck me," he curses, panting and needy.

Taking his cock in hand, I stroke him slowly, squeezing a bit harder when I reach his tip, milking even more precum from him.

"You ready?" I ask.

"So fuckin' ready." He repositions himself over my pelvis.

"Go slow. I want to feel every inch sink into your tight hole." I grip my dick at the base, and he lowers himself down at a snail's pace. "Yes. God, yes."

He pauses once he's fully seated, taking a moment to adjust.

Then he lifts up, clenching as he goes, squeezing my cock in the most delicious way. I fist his dick as he fucks mine, increasing his speed slowly, drawing out our pleasure.

He reaches back, placing a hand on my bent knee for leverage, but his quads will get a major workout since his other arm is useless.

"I'm going to come," he moans.

"I'm right there with you."

He slams down on me over and over. I can barely keep my wits about me enough to continue stroking him, but I manage to stay with it. He comes first, grunting as his hot seed shoots up my abdomen, chest, and chin.

The sight of it is all I need to let go. I thrust up as he comes down, driving even deeper into him as I coat his insides with my cum.

"Fuck!" I roar, way too loudly, but I don't give a shit because it's never felt this good. My orgasm lasts until I think I'm going to pass out before I finally crest and come back down.

"Pretty sure the whole house heard that." He chuckles, wincing as he dismounts, falling to my side.

"Did I hurt you?"

"Not in a bad way, but you shot off so deep, I think I can taste your cum in my throat."

"Idiot," I joke.

"Tonight was a good night." He stands, reaching for the pack of baby wipes we keep in the nightstand. We share a bathroom, but you have to leave the room to get to it, and neither of us wants to walk across the hall covered in jizz.

"I'm staying here tonight," I say. It's not something we usually do, but I want to stay close to him. If I'm honest, I always want to be close to him. Maybe it's time to make some adjustments to our rules.

"Good." He grins, and I know I made the right choice.

Chapter
TWELVE

Moto

I knock on Dove's open door, popping my head in. "Ready?"

"Yeah." She hops off the bed and pushes her feet into a pair of Birks.

"What are you wearing?" I ask, noticing her usual sweats have been replaced with a pair of jean shorts and a cropped tee.

She tugs on the hem of the shirt, looking shy. "You don't like it? I can change."

"No, not what I meant. I like it. I'm just surprised, is all."

She looks hot as hell, but after months of wearing pretty much the same thing every day—except for when we're at the club and Roxy dresses her up—it takes me by surprise to have her look so normal.

"I thought it was time to stop hiding." Her chin lifts with pride.

It's been a fuckin' honor watching her come back to herself. Each day, she lets more of herself shine through, and I don't think I've ever witnessed anything as beautiful as that.

"You're the prettiest goddamn woman on this planet." I cradle her head in my hands. "You know that, right?"

"I know that's what you think."

"Good enough for me." I kiss her long and hard, exploring her mouth and memorizing every inch.

It's been two weeks since our first kiss, and now Sly and I take every opportunity to taste her sweet lips. Though none of us have made a move for more. The buildup is torture but necessary.

I pull away and take her hand. "We better go."

Loki's brows raise when he sees my claim on her as we walk through the clubhouse and outside to the van, where I open the passenger side door for her. My arm is healing, and I can use it with minimal pain now, though the vibration and strain my bike puts on me is still too much.

I open the driver's seat, but before I can climb in, Sly takes my place.

"I'm driving," he deadpans.

"You don't have to drive every time."

"Yeah, I do."

"Asshole," I mutter and slam the door, climbing into the back.

It's another night at Royal Treatment, and since no one's home, Dove's coming with us. But even if someone was home to protect her, she'd still want to come.

She loves it there and has made friends with all the girls, though she and Roxy are inseparable. She even had Roxy over to the clubhouse for girl time. Whatever the fuck that is.

"What was your childhood like, Sly?" she asks out of the blue.

"Why?"

"Just wondering."

"Pretty fuckin' shitty. Parents were con artists but were really bad at it. One or both of them was always in jail for mail fraud, check forgery, shoplifting, you name it."

"How did you get into hacking?"

"Despite the shit genes my idiot parents passed down to me, I was smart. Like really fuckin' smart. Especially with electronics and computers." I flash her a smug grin. "So, I had parents whose only influence was lying and cheating, a computer, and a natural ability to figure shit out. It was the perfect storm. I think I was twelve when I sent out my first phishing email."

"What's phishing?" she asks.

"I created very real-looking emails from various banks and sent them out with a link to a website that appeared to be legit. People would log in, thinking the bank was sending them an important notification, and bam! I had their bank login and access to their funds."

"That's kind of mean."

"I know. I'm not proud of it."

"How did you get into the club?"

"Is this get to know Sly day?" he asks. He doesn't like talking about what he's done in his past.

"I want to know everything about you. About both of you," she says.

He blows out a breath, weaving through traffic because the jerk has no patience.

"I quickly discovered the dark web and met a guy who took me under his wing. He taught me all about black hat hacking, and I started taking jobs doing that."

"What does that mean?"

"Some companies or individuals will hire black hat hackers to break into their competitors' systems and implant malware to either take their system down or destroy files. I was good at it. Really fuckin' good."

"Until you weren't," I say.

"Shut up. I was always good, but I got cocky and took jobs that fucked with power companies, hospitals, and government agencies, which alerted the FBI. They only knew my pseudonym, but I could feel them getting closer to figuring out who

I really was. I didn't want to get locked up, and by that point, I was moving to a new city every five or six weeks to stay on the safe side. It was exhausting and lonely. When I landed in Reno, I liked it so much I decided it was time for a change and disappeared from the web altogether."

"What about the club?" she asks.

"I was at a bar, and a bunch of bikers walked in. I didn't have any friends or family—I wasn't talking to my parents at all—and seeing the dynamic the bikers had, I realized that was something I wanted. I approached the guy with President on his cut and asked if I could join. He laughed in my fucking face."

"Was that Loki?"

"No, it was his dad, Trucker. Beast of a man, very scary." He laughs, and I join in. "You'll meet him sometime, I'm sure. He still comes around, though not that often after his wife was killed."

"Oh, that's sad."

"Yeah. She was good people. Anyway, he let me start hanging around, which is the first step to prospecting. At the time, I was this skinny computer nerd. I didn't belong anywhere near the club life. But Loki invited me to work out with him, and I bulked up. After six or so months, Trucker agreed to let me prospect, and the rest is history."

"Wow."

We pull into the parking lot and get out. There are a few cars here already, which tells me it's going to be a crazy night.

"Are you heading to the dressing room?" I ask.

"Yep. I'll see you guys later." She wraps her hand around the handle, but before she can pull, I'm yanking her toward me for another searing kiss. Our lips have barely parted before Sly's dragging her over for one of his own.

"Stay out of trouble," Sly murmurs against her lips.

"Always." She slips into the dressing room, and we head to the security room.

"Learn anything new today?" I ask, knowing he's been on the hunt to learn more about Cal.

"Without his last name or even knowing if Cal is his real name, it didn't leave me many options. Then, I got the idea to find him using facial recognition."

"What did you find?"

"It took some time to hack into the DMV's system, but when I finally got in, I was able to take a screenshot from surveillance footage at the clubhouse and run it through. His name is Tyler Sorenson."

"He gave Dove his real name."

"Yeah, well, he didn't think she'd live this long, so there was no point in lying."

That thought sobers me up real quick. Who knows if she'd even be alive if we hadn't broken into Anthony's house that day. I doubt she would be. She was on the road to killing herself with alcohol and pills if Anthony didn't get to her before then.

"So, now what?" I ask.

"Now I'm going to learn everything I can about him and take it to Loki. Come up with a plan for taking him out."

"Good. I'll feel better when he's out in the desert getting picked apart by scavengers."

"Same."

For the next two hours, we handle minor security issues—mostly drunken idiots—and keep tabs on everything happening via the cameras covering every inch of this place.

"Here." I hand Sly a sandwich one of the girls brought over for us.

"Thanks." He's unwrapping it when the radio interrupts him.

"Sly, Moto, you guys might want to get out here," Kevin, one of our bouncers, says.

"What is it?" I ask in a terse tone.

"You need to see it with your own eyes."

Mine and Sly's eyes meet briefly, exchanging a "what now" look before jumping to our feet and heading into the club.

It's packed. There's not one open seat, which leaves some guys loitering around, waiting for something to open up. I scan the room, looking for the threat, but everything looks fine. No disruptions, no girls in distress. What the hell did Kevin want us to see?

My gaze lands on the main stage, and now I know. He wanted me to see Dove dancing, front and center, for everyone to see.

She has on a strapless, rainbow-colored bathing suit-looking thing, except it's made of fishnet, so you can see more skin than not. Her nipples are barely covered with pasties, and though there is a strip of fabric over her pussy, it's so tight that the outline of her lips is on full display.

"Are you seeing what I'm seeing?" Sly asks.

"Yep."

She moves to the music, and though I can tell she's nervous as hell from the look in her eyes, I don't think anyone else notices. Every eye in this place is glued to her magnetic appeal that's screaming sex. I can't believe this is the same girl we pulled from Anthony's house.

Stepping up to the pole on clear acrylic platform heels, she swings around, one leg out straight, the other wrapped around the pole. Her head is held high, and she makes eye contact with the crowd like a damn professional. I'm so fuckin' proud of her. She's so brave.

"Did you know Roxy was teaching her this?" I ask.

"Nope."

"Goddamn. Part of me wants to drag her off stage because she's showing these assholes more skin than she's shown me," I start.

"And the other part?"

"Is getting off on the fact that all these men are watching

our woman and lusting after her. It's a turn-on knowing they can't have her."

"It's not like we've had her yet," he huffs.

"No, but we will. And that's more than any of these assholes can say."

"True." I back up into his front, reaching behind me to feel that he's just as hard as I am. It's dark, and no one's paying us any attention, so I continue to rub up and down his length.

He leans forward so his lips are next to my ear and says, "Unless you want to get fucked right here in the middle of this club for everyone to see, I suggest you quit that."

I laugh and remove my hand because even though I take no issue with public fucking, a strip club isn't the right place for that.

We watch, fuckin' entranced by this woman who never fails to shock me. She falls to her knees, gets on all fours, and crawls across the stage to a group of young dudes with stacks of cash in front of them. Rolling to her back with her ass in their faces, she does the thing we saw her do a couple weeks back.

The guys lose their shit, hooting and hollering, tossing cash on the stage, and getting rowdy.

A little wave of nerves hits me, and I get out my radio. "Make sure they don't touch her."

"Got it, boss," Linc says back, and I see the very large man step out of the shadows and take position.

"Good call," Sly says.

Dove stands right when the music ends and is met with a round of applause, including from Sly and me. That shit was impressive, and I can't wait to tell her how much so when she gets off stage. Her smile is bright as she bows like this was a recital. It's cute as hell.

I turn and pat Sly's shoulder, signaling for him to follow me back so we can meet up with our girl, but he turns stock still, his proud smile fading. I flip back around and see Dove, frozen on stage, a look of true fear in her eyes.

"What is it?" I ask.

"I don't know. Something's wrong." He presses the button on the little radio that sits on his shoulder. "Who's she looking at?"

"Some guy up in the booths. I'll check it out." Linc pushes through the group of guys to check it out.

Sly and I make our way to the stage, hopping up and reaching her in seconds.

"What's wrong, baby?" Sly asks, crouching a little to meet her eyes.

"It's him," she says, her lips moving but the rest of her rigid.

I wrap my arm around her waist and follow the direction she was looking. Now that the dance is over, people are milling about, and the dancers walk around giving out lap dances. It's chaos, and I can't find what she sees.

"Tyler." Her voice is flat, like all emotion and feelings have been sucked out of her.

His name is all it takes for me to scoop her up and carry her backstage, where Roxy is waiting, her head tilted and her lips pursed.

"Can you watch her? Lock the dressing room door. Don't let her out of your sight. I'll send Linc in to guard you."

"Yeah, okay." She takes Dove by the elbow and guides her over to the benches.

I radio Linc, telling him to stand guard over the dressing room, and jump off the stage. I'm assuming Sly is already searching, and I'm correct when I find him walking the floor.

"You see him?" I ask.

"No, but there're two hundred dudes in here, and it's dark as fuck."

"Shit."

We split up, each of us going in different directions. I scour each face, searching, but he's nowhere to be found.

"You with the girls, Linc?" I radio.

"I got 'em, boss."

Relieved she's protected, I keep looking until I run back into Sly.

"Anything?"

"Not a fuckin' thing. What the hell?" He runs a hand through his dark hair, loosening the gelled curls.

"Maybe there was someone who looked like him. It's dark, especially with the spotlight shining on you."

"Maybe," he agrees.

"Let's go back and talk to her." I follow Sly, pausing so he can press his finger to the pad to unlock the door to the back of the house. I teased him for all his security measures, but now I'm fuckin' glad he has them in place.

In the dressing room, we find Dove—dressed in the clothes she came here in—sitting in front of the vanity while Roxy wipes away her makeup. Her eyes are watery, and her arms are wrapped around her middle, hiding as much of herself as she can. I'll put a bullet through Tyler's head for stealing her thunder.

Sly gets his phone out and types out a message.

"Who are you texting?" I ask.

"Coyote. Asked him to come down and take over for the rest of the night." His phone chimes, and he glances at the screen. "He'll be here in ten."

I crouch next to Dove, placing a hand on her knee. "Hey, Dove. You okay?"

"Did you find him?" she asks, her voice shaky.

"No. Are you sure it was him?"

Her gaze meets mine. "I'm sure. He traced his throat with his thumb. Who does that in real life?"

"I don't know, but he's gone now. Must've known we'd come looking."

"I'm scared." She falls forward into my arms, where I catch her.

"I know. But you're safe, Dove. I'll never let anything happen to you as long as I'm alive."

"Promise?" she asks.

"We both do." Sly rubs her back.

"Coyote will be here in"—I glance at my watch—"seven minutes. Finish taking off your makeup, and we'll take you home, okay?"

She sits up, wiping her nose with the back of her hand. "Okay."

I stand and nod to Roxy, who takes over, comforting Dove while she cleans her face.

"We gotta figure this out," I say to Sly. "Like right fuckin' now."

"I know. It's my fault for taking so long."

"You're doing the best you can. I know these things take time, but our time is up."

"Agreed."

Chapter
THIRTEEN

Petra

I stare out the window the whole way home, my mind a jumbled mess.

The whole time I was on stage, I kept thinking about how proud I was of myself. Being in front of a group of men nearly naked, dancing, and having a good time doing it. After all I've been through, this is something I never thought I'd do.

Then I saw him, and I was back to being that scared girl.

Tyler's not even the one who abused me all those years, but it was his face I thought of most while I was being raped and assaulted. He's the one who forced me into this situation. It was his fault, so while I was being tortured, humiliated, and abused, I mentally checked out and spent that time thinking of all the ways I'd kill him if I ever saw him again.

Yet both times it's happened, I froze. Now I'm pissed at myself for being so weak.

"Dove, we're home," Sly says, breaking me from my thoughts.

Roxy put my hair in a high ponytail, but I ruin it when I pull two front pieces free to curtain my face as Moto opens my door and helps me out. Right now, I need the security hiding my face gives me.

Tonight wasn't supposed to be like this. It was supposed to be about me showing the guys I'm ready for more than their kisses, that I'm ready to explore the next step. Now, look at me. No good for anyone or anything. Just a statistic, another girl, broken because of a man. How pathetic.

"Can you walk?" Sly asks, then waggles his brows, attempting to lighten the mood. "Or shall I carry you?"

"I can walk." I give him a tight smile. It's all I can muster, but even that is difficult.

Going straight to my room, I'm surprised when they both follow me in. I was hoping to avoid any discussion about tonight. All I want to do right now is change and go to bed, but that's not happening. I should've known they wouldn't let this go.

"Where are your sweats?" Sly asks, opening my dresser drawers.

"In the bottom one," I say.

He finds one of five pairs of sweatpants I've stolen from them and one of the six RBMC T-shirts I've swiped. I expect him to crack a joke about me being a thief, but it doesn't come. He simply sets them on the bed next to where Moto is sitting and says, "Arms up."

I look at him like he's gone mad.

Before my run-in with Tyler tonight, I was prepared for them to see me naked. I was even excited at the prospect. But my bravado is gone.

"Dove. I just saw your entire ass and most of your tits up on that stage. Don't get shy now."

He's right, and God, being up there made me feel powerful. Who would've thought I could feel that strong while mostly naked in a room full of men? Especially knowing how weak I used to feel in a room with only one man in it.

Enough of that power returns for me to lift my arms up in

the air. He tugs off my cropped tee, leaving me bare-chested for only a second before he pulls on the oversized shirt. His gaze never leaves mine as he unbuttons the shorts and pushes them down my legs, then promptly allows me to use his shoulders for balance as he pulls the sweatpants up.

His respect and kindness heal a little of my wounds from the evening.

From their outward appearance, you'd think it would be the opposite. The worn jeans, faded T-shirts, and leather cuts with skull patches don't instinctually instill trust. It was the rich, well-dressed men with manicured nails who took what they wanted from me, while the unkempt, rough-around-the-edges bikers were the ones who treated me like a queen.

"Climb in bed," he instructs, and I obey, rolling onto my side.

Sly gets in facing me, and Moto follows, spooning me from behind.

"Thank you for taking care of me," I whisper.

"Always." Moto slides the hair tie from my ponytail and releases my hair, finger combing it into submission.

"Ignoring the fact that the night went south pretty damn quickly, I'm proud of you for getting on that stage," Sly says.

"It was the single hottest thing I've ever seen in my life," Moto adds.

"I wasn't going for hot," I admit.

Sly grins. "What were you going for?"

Being tucked protectively between them, I feel safe again. Some of my bravery reappears, giving me the strength to go with honesty for this conversation.

"Jealousy."

"Jealousy. Why?" Moto's arm falls around my middle.

"It's been two weeks since you guys kissed me for the first time. I know you're going slow because you think I can't handle it, and I appreciate that. But I thought if I got on stage, you'd be so jealous about all the other men seeing my body that you'd take me right then and there."

Sly gasps dramatically. "In front of everyone? How exhibitionist of you."

"No." I let out a small snort. "I thought you'd bring me home first." I bury my face in Sly's chest. "Would it have worked if Tyler hadn't shown up?"

"It did work, but not in the way you think," Moto says.

"What do you mean?"

"There're still some things you don't know about us."

I peek over my shoulder, uncomfortable with the conversation but dying to know what he's talking about. "Like what?"

The guys share a look before Sly blurts out, "We're freaky."

I lift my head up fully and shift my gaze between the two men. "How do you mean?"

"Things like public sex, or in this case, seeing you up on the stage nearly naked in front of all those people, didn't make us jealous. It turned us on," Sly says.

"Really?" I knew they had certain proclivities. After all, most men in relationships don't seek a woman to join their dynamic. But I didn't know it extended beyond that.

Moto's lips brush the back of my neck, sending chills racing up my spine. "Really."

"What else are you into?" I can't stop the curiosity from growing.

I know all about the illegal and unethical dark side of kink, the side that has men buying women, forcing themselves on them, and then getting off on their pain and suffering. But I know that's not what they're about.

Still, the idea of what they could be into frightens me some.

"Let's leave it at that for tonight." Sly smooths my hair back comfortingly.

"Why?"

"Because that's all you need to know right now." He palms

my cheek and pecks my lips, making me forget my protest. With his lips on mine and the soothing way Moto runs a hand up and down my back, I forget about how wrong the night went and remember why I got on that stage. I want them. He pulls away, leaving me breathless, and says, "Tonight can go one of two ways, Dove. You can go to sleep and carry on like tonight never happened. Or, we pretend that things went exactly as planned and show you what it's like to be worshipped by two men who want to bring you more pleasure than you ever imagined. Either way, we're staying here with you tonight."

If he'd asked me that a half-hour ago, I would've gone with option one. But somehow, they turned things back around with how they took care of me. It would be easy to lump all men into the same category, the one that Fuckwad and Anthony are in, but how can I when they've spent months proving how different they really are and how much they care about me?

"Option two," I murmur, tilting my head up and inviting him in for another kiss, but he stops me.

"I need to say one thing first." He rests a hand on top of Moto's that's resting protectively on my hip. "If you feel uncomfortable or want us to stop for any reason, you need to promise you'll speak up."

I stare into eyes that are gray in the dim glow of the lamp sitting on the nightstand. Could I be brave? Five years ago, I was a fighter. I didn't let anyone walk all over me. But I lost that along the way and eventually let things happen to me without so much as a no.

But this is different. So very different. Sly and Moto aren't here to hurt me or bring me down. They want to bring me back to life. And they have been. Day by day, hour by hour, I'm returning to who I once was.

I had a setback tonight, but that doesn't mean I have to start all over. I can regain my power and prove to myself and them that I'm healing. It's why I stepped onto that stage in the first place and why I'll give myself to them tonight. And if it's too much, too soon, I can be open about that and know with every fiber of my being that they'll stop and not punish me or be angry with me for it.

"He means it, Dove. I could be balls deep inside you, and if that's not what you want, we need to know you'll say something. And you need to know that if you do, everything will stop, and no one will be mad or disappointed. You feel me?"

My chest warms, and I feel my eyes water.

Goddamn it. Not now.

"Are you okay?" Sly asks.

"I'm perfect," I say. "And yes, I promise to let you know."

Sly flashes me a wolfish grin. "Good girl. Now lie on your back."

I roll over, and Moto devours my lips like I'm his life source. We don't come up for air. Who needs to breathe when you have a man like him kissing you?

Sly snakes a hand under my shirt to stroke the skin on my abdomen. He inches lower and lower, and my pussy responds to his close proximity. Wetness coats my panties, and my clit throbs. It's a sensation I never thought I'd have again, and the excitement at knowing I'm not broken only turns me on more.

My eyes are closed, but I feel Sly's heated gaze on us. Knowing he's watching me kiss his boyfriend is arousing, and I'm beginning to think I know nothing about what turns me on anymore. Or maybe that part of me has changed along with everything else.

Prior to the last four years, which I don't think even count as experience since I wasn't a participating party, I was quite vanilla. My previous relationships were with college boys who would take me home after a date, turn the lights off, deliver an adequate orgasm after some clumsy foreplay, then go home while I lay in bed wondering what all the fuss was about.

Things like threesomes weren't even in my vocabulary. Even

in my wildest fantasies, it wasn't where my mind went. Maybe I allowed myself to dream up something like oral sex or multiple orgasms. But never a threesome.

Thankfully neither Fuckwad nor Anthony wanted to share me. That's where their decency ended, though. They got off on my fear and pain until I never wanted to be with another man again.

Until now, and it strikes me that all that fear is gone.

Sly and Moto are dominant men, but their dominance is quiet and controlled. They make demands and tell me what to do but give me ultimate power over what happens between us. It's exactly what I need to confidently explore this new world.

"Sit up. Let me take this shirt off," Sly says.

I do as he says, not surprised that he's the one taking the lead between the two of them. Moto has no problem stepping up to the plate and doing what needs to be done without direction, but I see how he defers to Sly, looking for his approval. Apparently, that extends to what they do in the bedroom too.

He lifts my shirt up and over my head while Moto takes it from him and tosses it to the side. It's as though they're performing a synchronized dance. Even though I know it's because they've perfected their method by sleeping with an unknown number of women, I don't care. I'm the one benefitting from all their previous experience.

"Goddamn, these tits." Sly pushes me back, and I'm bombarded with sensation as they each take a nipple into their mouths. Moto sucks and licks while Sly nips and bites. My core clenches tight, and my clit pulses with need. I could come from this stimulation alone, but I fight it. There's so much more coming my way. I can feel it.

I moan wantonly, and the sound doubles their efforts, hands roaming up and down my body as they give my breasts more attention than they've ever had before.

Moto releases my nipple with a wet *pop* and says, "Now the pants. I need to bury my face between your legs."

"Oh God," I whisper, loving his dirty words.

They both stand and strip to their boxers while I wiggle my sweatpants and panties down. When I look up, I'm struck dumb.

Two naked bikers.

Both with raging erections barely contained behind fabric.

And they're staring expectantly at me.

A wave of intimidation washes over me at the sight.

What did I get myself into?

I don't have time to think about it when Moto positions himself between my legs—pushing my knees wide open—and Sly settles back at my side, reclaiming my breast with his mouth. A warm tongue licks up my center while another swirls around my nipple. My whole body shudders.

"So responsive. I see a lot of orgasms in your future, Dove," Sly says before kissing up my chest and neck, stopping at my lips.

Moto hums as he rubs up and down my slit, spreading the moisture already seeping from me, then parting my folds. His warm, wet tongue finds my clit and flicks it over and over before changing things up and flattening his tongue, licking up my seam. When he goes in for the kill and latches onto my clit, I explode in a mind-bending orgasm that comes on so fast there's no time to prepare.

Sly swallows my cries with his kiss while he pinches my nipple and gives it a tug. I lose control and ride the wave, my heels digging into the mattress, goosebumps spread over all of me. My vision becomes spotty until I eventually come down. I've never come this hard in my life, and that one orgasm did nothing to satiate my desire for these two men.

"My turn," Sly says. "Suck Moto's cock while I eat you out and finger fuck your pussy."

Um, yes, please. I want that too, so I nod, giving him the permission he's asking for.

Moto moves to my side, lifting onto his knees and pushing down his boxers while Sly settles between my shaky legs. A finger probes my entrance, stroking up and down a few times before slipping inside, filling me up.

"You're so tight, Dove. It'll take us weeks before we can both fit in this pussy," Sly says, his voice husky and full of lust.

Wait, what? Both of them? At the same time? There's no way. I push that thought aside, saving it for future consideration, and focus on the cock leaking pre-cum bobbing near my mouth.

I take Moto in hand, stroking down from his swollen, spongy head. Opening my mouth wide, I wrap my lips around him and suck, moaning when his pre-cum bursts on my tastebuds.

"Fuck me, Dove. You have no idea how sexy you look with Sly's face between your legs and your mouth full of my cock." He tenderly strokes a hand down my cheek.

His words are filthy, but his actions are sweet. A combination I didn't know I was missing from my life, but here we are.

"Mm, she tastes so good. Doesn't she, Moto?" Sly asks.

"So fucking good. Like a juicy pineapple."

Sly presses two fingers into me, curling them to reach the place inside that has my eyes rolling back while I bob up and down on Moto's dick. I can't take him all the way, so I use my saliva as lube to jack him while I suck. He weaves a hand into my hair, not to force me down further or control the movement, but to keep me here with him.

"She gives amazing head," Moto groans.

It's hard smiling with your mouth full, but I feel the corners of my lips turn up anyway. I like them talking about me like this. It's empowering and only encourages me to keep going, even when my jaw starts aching because the man is thick. Everywhere.

Sly's fingers move faster in and out of my pussy, and his tongue flutters like hummingbird wings against my clit. I lose my breath as another orgasm unexpectedly crashes over me. I've never felt anything this good, this intense.

My hips thrust up, and I hold Sly to my core, keeping him where I need him to ride this out. I try to focus on Moto's engorged cock, but the sensations are overwhelming, and I have to release him to squeeze my eyes shut and cry out my screaming release.

Sly works me back down, slowing his movements until I collapse back to the bed, my energy waning.

I didn't expect it to be like this. I anticipated them being as much about each other as they are with me, but that's not what's happening. I'm getting a hundred percent of their attention. It's heady and intense in the best way possible.

"We're losing her," Sly says, noticing my lax body.

"Guess it's time to fuck her and really show her what we can do."

Chapter
FOURTEEN

Sly

I was right. Dove is the one. There's no question about it. I feel complete, and judging by the blissed-out look on Moto's face, he's feeling the same.

"Get on all fours, Dove. It's my turn to feel your mouth while Moto gets the first dip into your tight cunt," I say.

Moto moves to get behind her but stops midway to give me a kiss. Her flavor is on both our tastebuds, and fuck me if it doesn't make my cock harder. I don't spend much time questioning why certain things get me off because there's no point. We like what we like, and fuck anyone who judges us for it.

He pulls away and continues behind her, his heavy cock glistening with saliva and pre-cum, making my mouth water. There are so many things I want to do with them, but Dove's fading fast. She doesn't have our stamina yet, but we'll work on that.

I pull down my boxers and kneel on the mattress. Her head tips back, and she meets my gaze. She's fuckin' beautiful like this with lips that are red and swollen but still hungry for more cock.

I don't give it to her, though, not yet. I'm too invested in watching as Moto grips his dick at the base and drags it up and down her slit. His chest is heaving with anticipation, but he's taking his time, making sure to get this right. He's a patient man who takes his time with everything he does in order to do things perfectly on the first go-round.

He's the opposite of me. I dive in and make a million mistakes, learning as I go. It's why I trust him to be the first to fuck Dove. I know he'll pay attention to every cue she gives off, every breath she takes, every change in the atmosphere, making sure we'll never be the reason for this woman to experience any more trauma.

He works in slowly, giving her time to adjust to his girth. Each time he pulls out, his cock comes out more and more slick with her juices, a sure sign she's enjoying this as much as he is— as much as I am, for that matter. When he finally pushes all the way in, his eyes close, his mouth drops open, and his head falls back on his neck.

"Tell me how it feels," I say.

"Shit, bro. She fits like a glove." He grips her by the hips, holding her in place while he enjoys the moment.

My focus is interrupted when Dove wraps a hand around my cock, bringing it to her mouth and placing a kiss on the tip.

"Greedy girl," I murmur, pinching her chin.

"I want it to be all three of us, together." Her words are soft and shy.

"Then that's what you'll get. Open for me."

Her lips part, and I guide my length into her mouth while Moto begins to move. She drops her hold on me and places her hand back on the mattress for balance, which also means I'll be in control of this blow job. That's dangerous.

"Tell me if I get too rough. It'll be hard for me to control myself." I grip myself at the base and press deeper into her throat, feeling the tight constriction as she swallows.

She nods slightly, mouth stuffed with cock, and it's the

sexiest thing I've ever seen. I'm tempted to ask her a string of yes and no questions just to watch her answer.

Moto grinds into her, finding a rhythm that I follow. He thrusts forward at the same I do, spearing her from both ends. She makes muffled sounds of pleasure, and I know from Moto's appreciative hum that she's clenching her cunt down on him while her throat tightens around me.

"Look at you, taking us both like the good girl you are." I gather her hair into a ponytail and wrap it around my fist. If she were anyone else, I'd fuck her face roughly. It'll take some time to figure out how far is too far, so it's best to go easier until we learn more about her likes and dislikes.

Moto kneads the flesh of her ass, parting her cheeks to get a view of her puckered hole. I know what he's thinking. He can't wait until he can take her there while I fuck her pussy. From that position, we'll be able to feel each other through the thin membrane separating her holes, something that makes us both lose our minds.

In time, brother.

"Fuck, I'm going to come if I keep this up. You need to feel this cunt. It's the best I've ever had," he says, pulling out.

It strikes me that there was no discussion about condoms. Something else we haven't done with anyone else except each other. We get tested every three months like clockwork and know that the doctor who looked at Dove after coming to the clubhouse tested her. She confided in us how relieved she was that the tests didn't show any STIs.

That only leaves pregnancy. The thought would've terrified me before Dove. I don't want to knock her up, not before we've bound her to us for time and all eternity, but it's not the worst thing that could happen.

Coyote has a kid, and she's cool as hell. I'll bet our kid would be even cooler.

It's irresponsible not to sheath myself before swapping

places with Moto but still, I don't. I want to feel every inch of her without any barriers between us, like when Moto and I are together.

Moto lies down beneath Dove, making it easier for her to suck him off while I take position behind her and take in the sexy as hell view. Her pussy lips are puffy, swollen, and dripping with her arousal.

"Such a pretty cunt." I stroke myself while I rub a thumb against her clit, which is swollen and ready for yet another orgasm.

Bringing some moisture up to her ass, I circle the hole with my thumb while working over her tiny bundle of nerves, testing the waters. She might not be okay with anal, and it's even more reason we need her to open up to us about her sexual history. Maybe after this, she'll trust us enough to confide all those details. Not just from the last few years but before that too.

Her breath hitches, and she pushes into the pressure, forcing my thumb inside, just past the first ring of muscle.

Oh yeah. She's into it.

Sloppy sucking sounds fill the air, and I see Moto relaxing back like a king, hands behind his head as Dove sucks him off.

My balls tighten with need.

That's enough playing around. I need to fuck.

Knowing she's been primed for me, I grip her hips and pull her back while pushing inside in one fluid motion. A guttural moan leaves me as I force everything from my mind and just feel.

Tight grip, warm comfort, insane pleasure.

"Good, right?" Moto asks, a cocky grin on his face.

"So fuckin' good. Best we've ever had."

She pops off his cock to peer over her shoulder at me with a beaming smile on her lust-drunk face.

I smack her ass, leaving a handprint. "Our girl likes compliments. We'll have to remember that."

She sticks her tongue out at me in a rare show of playfulness.

Goddamn, I don't know what this feeling is brewing around in my chest, but it sure feels like love. Different than what I feel for Moto. My love for him is bone-deep and vital, grounding me to the earth. But what I feel for Dove lifts me up, fills me with air and light.

I need them both in equal measure.

"Fuck, Dove. Pull off now if you don't want me coming down your throat." Moto caresses the back of her head.

My brows raise when she stays put, moving up and down with even more vigor. He bites his lip, eyes glued on her. His upper body is taught, all his muscles engaging, making him appear chiseled from stone. A stark contrast to the curve of Dove's hips and round ass up in the air.

My body is a coil of tight heat, and my spine tingles. I know what's next.

"Rub your clit, baby. I want you to come with us," I say.

She balances on one hand, reaching between her legs. I hold my orgasm in, giving her more time, but it's too late for Moto. He curses, holding her down on his cock as he blows down her throat.

It spurs her on, and her walls tighten around me, spasming and drenching me even more.

"Shiiiiit," I draw out the curse as I release deep inside her, coating her walls with my seed.

I nearly black out with pleasure. When I come to, the room stills, the only sound is our heavy breaths and pounding hearts. Or maybe it's only mine I hear. I don't know.

"Get over here," Moto says, breaking the silence and pulling Dove up onto his chest and off my dripping cock. "You too."

I crawl up the bed, taking my place on her other side. It won't always be like this, Moto and I focusing our attention on her. But it felt important for our first time to be centered around her. She needs to know we're here for her in all things.

Despite being sweaty and sticky, Moto and I hold her tight

for a long time, basking in the afterglow. I tickle my fingers up and down her bare spine, eliciting goosebumps across her skin while she caresses Moto's torso.

"I need a shower," she says.

Moto kisses her forehead. "Let's do it."

"All of us?" she asks.

"Yeah. We can fit."

I climb off first and help Dove to her feet before hoisting Moto to his. Dove has one of the few rooms with an attached bath, and thank fuck for that.

The bedroom was so dim that when I flip on the light in the bathroom, it brings a whole new reality to what we just did. Dove positions herself so she's facing the wall, but I brush it off as bashfulness and wait while Moto adjusts the water temp. Once steam is billowing from the stall, we step inside.

Dove is quiet, too quiet, and it has me wondering if she's regretting things. I fuckin' hope not because that was the single best moment of my life.

"Let me take care of you," I say, and squirt some of her girly-smelling body wash into my palm and rub my hands together. Crouching down, I rub her calves, working her overused muscles. I make my way up to her thighs and freeze. "What the hell?" I ask.

Dove tries to turn away from my view, but I grip her hips, keeping her in place.

"I know. They're ugly."

I'm speechless as I take in the scars marring her upper and inner thighs. Some are red and angry looking, fresher, while others are white and completely healed. How did I miss this? Even with the room only lit up by a lamp in the corner, I can't believe I didn't see this before.

"What are these?" I ask. The first thought that comes to mind is that she's been doing this to herself, right under our noses.

"It's not what you think." She presses her thighs together, trying to stop my inspection. "They were punishments."

"From them?" I tip my head up to look at her and what I see punches me in the gut. She looks mortified. Why the hell would she be embarrassed about something she had no control of?

"Yes."

"Fuck me." I trace the scars while she squirms. I'm making her uncomfortable, but I need to burn every single scar into my memory so when I finally get my hands on Tyler, I can do the same to him. Then after I'm done squashing the life out of him, I can find Fuckwad and repeat the process. Anyone who has wronged this woman is going to pay.

"Let me see." Moto takes my place.

"I'm gonna kill everyone who has ever hurt you," I say.

"Since Anthony's already dead, you're partway there." Dove laughs humorlessly.

I turn her to face me, cupping her cheeks. "I mean it. They're dead men walking."

"I know." Her eyes flutter closed, like she can't bear to look at me.

"Eyes open, Dove."

Reluctantly, they do. "I'm sorry. I'm sure you're used to perfection. I've seen the women who hang around the club. They're all so beautiful."

"Fuck perfection. We want you, scars and all."

Moto sighs, then stands and tightly wraps his arms around her waist from behind.

"Then you can have me," she says.

We take our time washing and worshipping every inch of her skin before quickly cleaning ourselves.

"Here." Moto steps out and holds a towel open for her.

We dry off, and while Moto and I only put our boxers on, she climbs into the bed completely naked. I guess now that we've seen all of her, she doesn't feel the need to hide.

I fuckin' love that.

"What now?" she asks once we're snuggled up under her white comforter.

"What do you mean?" I ask.

"What does this mean for us?"

"Tonight didn't change anything," Moto says, not realizing how she'd take it.

She deflates and grows quiet. She thinks he wants everything to return to the way it was. But that's not it at all.

"What he means is, you were ours before tonight. Having sex doesn't make it more real. It's just a bonus." I kiss her forehead. "Giving us your body doesn't make us love you any more or less."

I want her to understand that. Sex was the difference between survival and punishment before, and she needs to understand that's not how it is with us.

"Love?" she asks.

That came out of my mouth so easily, without any thought. That must mean it's true.

"Love," Moto affirms, and I'm glad he's on the same page. "If you haven't guessed, we're pretty crazy about you."

Her head pops up from my chest as she glances between us. "I love you both too. Much more than I ever thought I could love any one person, let alone two people."

"Thank fuck for that." I reach over and stroke Moto's cheek. He's just as pleased as I am.

We're finally complete.

Chapter
FIFTEEN

Moto

Sly walks in—still stripped down to his boxers—carrying a tray with coffee for him and me, tea for Dove, and a plate full of eggs, bacon, sausage, and pancakes for us to share, thanks to Tabs and Sissy, who make sure we eat like kings.

"I'm starving." Dove skips over the tea and snags a piece of bacon before the tray even hits the mattress.

I like watching her eat. After months of coaxing her to eat a slice of toast every morning, I'll never get over how happy it makes me to see that her appetite has returned.

"Same." I reach for a pancake and sausage, rolling them up together and taking a massive bite.

We settle in, Sly and I only in boxers, Dove in my T-shirt. We slept that way after the most incredible night I've ever had, and that's saying some shit. I spent my first eighteen years under my parents' thumb, depriving myself of most earthly pleasures. They were deeply religious, and almost everything that made a person feel good was a sin.

Once I got to college, I went hog wild. My parents thought they were instilling values, but that's not how it went. They made everything taboo, and my rebellious side craved everything they had been hell-bent on saving me from.

"How are you feeling?" Sly asks Dove after the food frenzy slows.

"Good." She grins shyly, her chin tucking to her chest and casting her eyes down. "Really good, actually."

"I'm glad because that was just the beginning. We'll be repeating that every night until the end of fuckin' time." Sly tosses the remainder of his pancake on the plate and lies back.

"I'm okay with that," she says.

"Before we get to that, we should probably talk about a few things." I gulp down the last of my coffee and move the tray to the ground.

"Do we have to, Daddy? Can't we just let things happen?" Sly jokes and pulls Dove down next to him, but I know he's thinking the same. His goofy-ass just doesn't want to be the one to lead this conversation.

"Sorry, kids. It's a must," I say, stretching my sore arm. This is the most I've exerted myself since getting shot. I'm still a little achy, but nothing that won't work itself out. "First thing's first. Are you on birth control, Dove?"

Her smile flattens as the real world comes crashing through her happy bubble. "I was given an IUD after I was taken, which is good up to ten years."

"Good," I say, even though the reason for it pisses me the hell off.

"Is it?" Sly asks. "Wouldn't it be fun to have a little boy running around with my good looks and Dove's book smarts?"

I slap a hand to my forehead. Sometimes it's like wrangling a troop of monkeys with him. "I think we can all agree that isn't a good idea. Not yet."

"Wait, what?" Dove's eyes widen.

"You don't want kids?" I ask.

Sly and I have had conversations about someday finding

the perfect woman and having a family, but it was all talk. We've only just stepped into relationship status with Dove. There are a million steps that need to happen before we can even entertain the idea.

"I don't know. I used to think I did, but I never thought I'd get the chance. And now"—she pauses, staring blankly at the wall for a long moment before sighing—"I don't know. It would kill me if my daughter ever had to go through what I went through."

All playfulness leaves Sly in the blink of an eye. "That would never fuckin' happen. I wouldn't let it."

"You can't control that. Okay, maybe until the child is eighteen, but they'll live their own life after that, and bad things happen in this world."

"Not to my kid, it won't." Sly's fierce determination does wonders to ease Dove's fears, but they don't disappear completely.

"We'll come back to this conversation in the far, far future, but I'm happy it won't be an issue until then," I say. "Next thing we need to discuss is something we should've talked about long before we ever had sex."

"It was amazing sex," Sly groans. "Like, mind-blowing. Am I right, Dove?"

She giggles. "It was."

I shake my head, wondering why I put up with this guy. Oh, right. The amazing sex. "I also agree, but to do it again, we need to know more about your history."

"History?" Dove's brows raise.

"Your sexual history," I say carefully.

"Like what? How many guys I've been with?"

"To start."

"Five, I think, including . . . you know."

"Okay, good." I rub a hand across the back of my neck. This conversation isn't uncomfortable for me, but I know it might be for her, and I want to make it as easy as I can. "Can you talk about the time you were away? You usually avoid saying anything about it, but now that we're sleeping together, it would be good for Sly and me to avoid any potential triggers."

"What do you want to know?" She folds her arms across her chest, and Sly is right there, pulling her closer to him for support.

"We want to know anything you'll tell us," he says.

"I'll tell you all of it, or at least what I remember. I have nothing to hide."

For the next two hours, she talks while I actively work not to show just how pissed the fuck off I am. It's so much worse than I thought, and by the end of her story, I'm left wondering how this woman is still standing, how she's managed to enjoy life again. I don't think I could.

Sly holds her the whole time. Thankfully, she can't see his face because what's written there is pure, unadulterated rage. If he could find a reason to leave the room right now that wouldn't make Dove doubt or fear what she's told us, he'd go straight to working around the clock to take Tyler's entire operation down.

She's been chained, hit, punched, raped, starved, debased, and had a hundred other horrible things done to her. The least of which was the drugs and alcohol Anthony got her addicted to, though the effects will last a lifetime.

My breakfast was threatening to come back up as I listened to it, and I'm angry at myself for not talking to her about this long before now. We could've set her healing back years if we had done one thing wrong last night.

Though Sly and I had a visceral reaction to her words, she held her composure, speaking of her experiences as though they're historical facts, not horrific situations she lived through.

"How do you feel now that you've told us everything?" I ask.

"Not so good, actually."

Sly releases Dove and sits up. "Why?"

"Because now you're both looking at me like that." She points between us.

"Like what?" I ask.

"Like I'm a broken piece of machinery you want to fix, but even after you do, you'll never trust it to not break down on you again."

"That's not how we feel," Sly says.

"He's right. That's not it at all."

"Okay, so the next time we have sex, you aren't going to picture everything I've been through, wondering if you get rough with me or get into any of the kinky stuff you won't tell me about that I'll freak and crawl into the corner crying?"

Sly and I share a look because that's exactly what we were thinking.

"See?" She jumps up from the bed. "It was a mistake to tell you."

"No, Dove, wait," I say, but it's too late. She's already dashing out the door.

"Fuck me," Sly curses.

"Goddamn it." I jog out the door after her but have no idea where she went. I check my room and Sly's room, but she's not in either. Sly catches up and slaps a stack of clothes on my chest. Only now do I realize I'm roaming through the clubhouse in my boxers.

"What about out back?" He motions for me to follow, and I pull on the pants and T-shirt on the way.

We find her in the middle of the massive backyard, a pack of Roch's pit bulls surrounding her. There's a reason his road name came from the patron saint of dogs. All it takes is him hearing about a pit in need of rescue for there to be another one running around here the next day.

Not that we care. They're a good security system and have built such a strong loyalty to all the brothers that there's no doubt they'd rip anyone to shreds who dared sneak onto the property.

But currently, they're licking Dove's face with their tails wagging furiously, or at least the ones who didn't have their tails removed when they had shitty owners. Those ones are shaking their asses happily.

"All right, get out of here." I wave them away, trying not to crack a smile when they turn their affection on me. I love the bastards, but I need to talk to my girl.

Roch hears the commotion and helps me out by whistling and shaking a bag of treats. They take off running, leaving room for Sly and me to sit next to Dove.

"Clearly, we don't understand what you want from us. Everything you told us today broke our fuckin' hearts and made us want to burn the world down looking for those responsible. What are we missing?" I ask.

"Before I told you all that, you looked at me like a woman. A woman you wanted to fuck." It's strange hearing the curse word glide off her lips, but I like it.

"Trust me, we still want to fuck you." Sly grins, bumping his shoulder against hers.

"Maybe, but now you think I'm broken and you need to wear kid gloves with me."

"We don't think that, but we know some of the experiences you've been through possibly turned you off certain things we might unknowingly subject you to," I say. "All we want is to know what those things are so we can avoid them."

Her cheeks turn splotchy, and her eyes redden. Oh, fuck. She's gonna cry. I can't take it when she cries.

"What if there is, and you decide I'm not worth avoiding things you like?" Her lower lip trembles, breaking my fuckin' heart. I'll give her whatever she wants at this point. Anything.

"Stop that bullshit," Sly says, and I want to punch him out. What the hell? She's taken aback, too, because her lip trembles even more. "I only mean, if there's a guy or guys out there who you're not enough for because of things you don't want to do, they're not fuckin' worthy of you." His chin lifts with confidence. "However, you hit the jackpot because these two guys? They don't care about shit like that. There are thousands of ways we can make you come, Dove. Thousands. You don't like one of them, we'll cross it off the list and move on to the next one."

He turned that one around real quick, thank God. I thought for sure I was going to have to kick his ass.

"He's right. We love you, Dove. That doesn't stop because there's something you don't want to do in bed. We both have things too, but we talked about it, and now we know to stay away from them."

"You do?"

"Yeah. Sly doesn't like to have his ass eaten, so I don't eat his ass." I chuckle when her jaw drops, but it's true.

"Not my cup of tea because it tickles, but I like doing it to others." He waggles his brows at her.

She chokes on her own spit. "I am not prepared for this conversation."

"You need to be," I say in all seriousness. "We gotta know because you went through some heavy shit, babe."

"Yeah, I know." She sighs.

We take her back inside, but we go to my room this time.

"So, hit us with everything you think could possibly trigger you." Sly throws his arms open wide.

"If I tell you what my hard limits are, you have to tell me what your kinks are." She's bargaining. I like it.

"Deal," I say.

"Okay, I don't want to be hit or kicked or punched." She thinks for a second. "Except when you slapped my butt, I liked that."

"You're setting the bar pretty low, Dove," I say.

She ignores me. "Your turn. Tell me one of your kinks."

"You already know we like it when other people see you and want you, but we also like a little exhibitionism." Sly grins.

"Really? Like public sex."

"Oh yeah, but even just some PDA is good. And of course, we only do it when the time and audience are appropriate."

"I didn't think I'd be into that either, but I kind of liked having all those people watch me up on stage."

"See? It's hot." Sly shoves her playfully. "And so is public sex."

"Maybe," she says, but I see the interest. "Okay, my turn. I don't want to be peed on. Any degradation, really."

I know it's a common kink, but it pisses me off that she was forced to be a slave, and the assholes took a piss on her just to drive the point home further. Fuckin' animals. Dead animals. Fuckin' roadkill after I get ahold of them.

"Not our thing either. See? We're lining up more than you think." Sly grabs her hand and places it in his lap. "What's another of our kinks? Hmm, we both really like edging."

"What's that?"

"Bringing each other to the brink of orgasm and then pulling away. Then starting all over again," I explain.

"I think that sounds interesting." Her posture straightens. "I'm not against anal sex. I thought I was, but I liked it when you were playing with me. I just need to make sure you use lube and take your time."

Once again, I see red. The things I'm going to put Fuckwad through will be so painful. It'll be a whole different kind of edging. I'll take him to the brink of death and bring him back, just to do it over and over again.

"Anything we do will be safe. That includes using lube and making sure you enjoy it," I say.

"Good. Now it's your turn."

"We should probably make it clear that we want to be with each other as much as we want to be with you." Sly takes my hand and places it in his lap.

"I figured that out already. I've honestly never thought about being in a relationship with two men. Before I met you two, I probably wouldn't have given it a chance. But it makes me happy to see the relationship you two have, and I'd never get in the way of that or how you express it."

"There could be moments of jealousy," I say.

"If there are, I could talk to you about it. Right?"

She's more than perfect.

We go back and forth like that for another hour. Dove tells us she's nervous about being tied down but is willing to leave it open to try, along with things like clamps and toys. Her hard limits were things that we wouldn't do to her anyway, like locking her up or gagging her.

We tell her more about what turns us on, which lines up with things she's willing to try. She doesn't have a lot of positive experiences with sex, and Sly and I vow to change all of that for her. She hit the lottery when we came into her life, even if she doesn't know it yet.

Chapter
SIXTEEN

Petra

I slowly lower into a hot, lavender-scented bath. After our talk, the guys insisted I relax alone to process everything that's happened in the last twenty-four hours.

I protested, not wanting to be away from them for a second, but they said they had club business to tend to and wanted me to unwind before going to Royal Treatment later.

The second I'm submerged, I'm grateful for their insistence. It feels so good, and they were right about needing some time to think. Things have drastically changed for me, and while it's exciting and thrilling, it's a lot to take in.

I can't believe I had sex with two men last night. And I loved every second of it.

I cover my giggle, thinking about the three orgasms they gave me. Because of our chemistry and the trust I have in them, I knew it would be good. But I had no idea it would be three orgasms good. I think they enjoyed it just as much. I mentally pat myself on the back, proud I kept up and pushed away all my fears about sex enough to enjoy it.

Wait until I tell Roxy about this. She is going to flip.

She was the one who encouraged me to get up on stage and gave me the confidence to do so. She'll never know how much of an impact she's made on my life. Just as much as Mia did. She was my ride or die and the only one of my friends who understood the demands of my job and didn't take it out on me when I turned down invitations.

Oh, God. Mia.

My mood turns somber. She was the best friend I ever had, and I have no idea where she is or what she's doing. There's a good chance she's either dead or still being trafficked.

Sly will find her. I know he will. Even if something tragic happened, he won't stop until we know the truth. But things are moving too slowly. I need answers and vengeance. It's the only way I'll be able to move on with my life.

Not knowing is the biggest reason I refuse to go home and see my family. I feel so much guilt about being alive and free. I could never look Mia's family in the eyes and tell them I'm the reason we got separated. That it's my fault we couldn't stay together and keep each other safe. And while I'm out here living my life, she's God knows where, doing God knows what, being abused by God knows what kind of men.

It's not fair.

The muscles that were relaxed only minutes ago tighten painfully. I don't deserve to rest until she's found and away from her abusers.

Standing up, I wrap a towel around my body and step out of the bath. I had picked out a cute outfit for the club tonight, but with my soured mood, I toss them aside and reach for my comfortable sweatpants and tee.

A knock sounds on my door the second I'm dressed, and I open it to find Sly, arms above his head, hanging onto the top of the door frame, his thickly veined arms on display. My mouth goes dry.

He's wearing worn, dark wash jeans and is shirtless, showing off the sexy tattoos covering his torso and arms. He's a tall man with broad shoulders and narrow hips. There's a small patch of coarse hair in the center of his chest and a happy trail he keeps trimmed, and he has a perpetual five o'clock shadow of dense facial hair. His lips are pouty, and his hooded eyes are set deep, creating a shadow over his eyes that makes him look dark and dangerous, all of which is true. But he's also goofy, caring, and loyal.

There's no question I've absolutely fallen for this man.

Moto appears behind him, hooking his arm around his waist. They look nothing alike but are equally as good-looking in their own ways. Moto's long black hair is damp, telling me he's just stepped out of a shower. He's also shirtless but has on casual-style leather pants, not the super shiny, rock star version.

He's built more like a brick house, his whole body big, boxy, and powerful. The kind of man people fear at one glance. Unlike Sly, he's hairless and smooth as a baby's bottom. I love running my hands all over his torso.

There's no question I've absolutely fallen for this man too.

"Is it time to go?" I ask, toweling off my hair. I don't ever do much to it. It's stick straight and doesn't hold curls for longer than an hour, so they're a waste of time.

"Soon. Just wanted to check on you." Sly steps inside the room, stopping to place a kiss on my lips. Moto follows, doing the same. Butterflies swarm, and my cheeks heat. I could get used to this new version of us.

"I'm fine." I close my door and sit down on the corner of my mattress. "I'm glad you're here, though. I wanted to ask how the hunt for Mia is going."

Sly shares a look with Moto before saying, "It's going. Still no closer to finding her, but I did find who Tyler works for this afternoon. I want to show you his picture to see if it's someone you recognize."

He pulls out his phone and shows me a man with a thick

head of salt and pepper hair and a bushy mustache and eyebrows. He's stalky, and the slight smirk on his face is sinister and creepy.

"No. I don't think I've ever seen him before. Who is he?"

"Franco Corsetti." Sly pinches the bridge of his nose like a headache is brewing.

"Corsetti?" My chest tightens. My late piece of shit ex-husband's last name was Corsetti.

"Yeah. Anthony's dad and Max's grandfather." Sly sits down next to me, rubbing circles on my back.

"Explain," I say, leaning forward to rest my forearms on my thighs and dig my hands into my hair. What are the odds? Maybe greater than I think, but I don't make the connection.

"Franco Corsetti runs a sex trafficking ring out of New York. His oldest son, Dom, was supposed to run the West Coast operations here in Reno. But he sucked at it, so Franco yanked it away and hired outside of the family. The person he hired was Tyler."

"On top of killing Anthony and Max, the club also killed Dom," Moto says.

I turn my head, still cradled in my hands, to face him. "I know why you took out my ex-husband and his shitty kid, but why Dom?"

"Dom was the one responsible for taking Birdie."

I learned all about how Loki and Birdie met during my long conversations with the guys. Back when I was too scared to talk to anyone, they sat on the opposite side of my room and talked for hours about anything they could think to say, trying to prove they had no intention of doing the things Anthony and Fuckwad did to me.

Birdie experienced a lot of the same things I went through, though only for a couple of days, while my torture lasted years. It doesn't make it any less terrifying.

"This is crazy. What are the odds that all of this is connected?"

"The dark and seedy world the club lives in isn't all that big. There's probably a maximum of six degrees of separation between us and the cartels, sex trafficking rings, or any other criminal organization out there," Sly says, his hand now massaging my shoulder.

"This is fucked up." I don't know how I got to this place where conversations about organized crime are commonplace. I grew up in Henderson, Nevada. I went to private schools. I'm a doctor, for God's sake. My only mistake was going to a dance club, something millions of women from all over the world do every weekend.

"It is but actually, it's good news because Franco isn't all that connected. His idiot sons burned a lot of bridges, and no one really trusts the Corsetti name anymore. Franco obviously hates us for killing Dom and Anthony, but he's never come after us because he knows he couldn't win. That means we can go after Tyler and not expect a massive retaliation." Sly's tone is reassuring.

"And even if he does, we'll be prepared," Moto says.

"Okay. So, you can find Tyler?"

"Yes, but Dove? He won't be leaving here with his life. Not after what he did to you."

I gulp but not because I don't think he deserves to die. He does. It's still hard for me to grasp that this is the world I live in now.

"When will it happen?" I ask.

"We need to take it to church first. Probably tomorrow. Still need to clue Loki in." Sly stands. "It's getting late. We should go."

"Are you ready?" Moto stands and offers his hand to help me up.

"Yeah." I look down at my oversized clothes. "I think I'll take it easy tonight."

"You do whatever you want. You know we don't care about what you wear." Sly runs a hand down the back of my head and brings me into his hard body. He smells masculine and intoxicating. Like clean musk.

"The question is, are you two ready?" I laugh, motioning to the bare chests.

"Guess we need shirts." Moto rubs a hand over his bare chest.

It's then I wonder if they showered together. A slight pang of jealousy hits me, though it's not logical. They were a couple before I got involved, and I can't expect them to stop what they have together and include me in every interaction. Yet, it's still there.

I wonder if I'll be able to handle a three-way relationship where we have separate dynamics and a group dynamic. I should talk to them about it, but it's embarrassing. Neither of them seems to have any jealousy. Matter of fact, whenever I spend time with one of them, and the other finds us together, they look almost pleased about the situation.

That's not what I'm feeling at all.

"Dove?" Moto breaks through my internal debate.

"Yeah?"

"I said, we're grabbing shirts, and then we can go."

"Yeah, okay. I'll wait in the dining room."

We arrive at the club before all the men getting off a work shift, meeting up for a bachelor party, or just plain lonely show up. Every other time I've walked through the doors of this place, I felt a rush of excitement and possibility. There are such negative connotations with a strip club, but I see it differently.

These women have talents most don't possess. They're

basically makeup artists, costume designers, dancers, pole experts, and actresses, all in the span of a shift. The lights, the music, the anticipation, I love it all. It's why I let Roxy convince me to get up on stage.

But all of that is gone. Tyler ruined it for me. That memory has tainted this place.

"You heading into the dressing room?" Sly asks.

"No. I think I'll stay with you guys tonight."

"Why?" Moto's brows furrow.

I shrug, not wanting to get into it. "No reason."

"Dove." Moto stops in my path and grips me by the shoulders. "He can't get in. I made every security guard study his picture and posted it at the entrance in case they forget. Bullet is standing at the back exit, and Ford"—he waves over my shoulder—"is going to be the perfect gentleman and be your personal bodyguard. Right, Ford?"

The look he gives the newbie member sends a shiver down my spine, but Ford takes it in stride.

"Absolutely. Let's go get dolled up." He slings an arm over my shoulder that Moto pushes away.

"No touching."

He holds his hands in the air, taking a step back. "Hands off. Got it."

I roll my eyes but lift onto my toes, fisting the front of Moto's cut. "Thank you for making me feel safe." Touching my lips to his, I prove my appreciation. He predicted my unease before I even knew it would happen, which means the world to me.

"You're welcome."

"Hey, I helped," Sly protests.

I release Moto and cup Sly's cheeks, dragging him down to my level before giving him a kiss with the same level of heat. "Thank you."

"Always, baby."

They continue down the hall while Ford and I step into the dressing room.

"Petra!" The ladies call out, already busy getting ready.

"Everyone, this is Ford. Ford, this is everyone," I introduce.

Catcalls echo against the tile floors. Clearly, they approve, and I don't blame them. He's a good-looking guy with long, flowy hair and tattoos. He reminds me of an old-school '80s rocker but not in a slimy way. In the rock god kind of way.

He waves and follows me to my honorary locker. Technically, I don't work here, so I can't be given one permanently. But Riley didn't see a problem with me storing outfits I've acquired to wear after the club closes, and Roxy stays late to teach me tricks.

"Hey, Petra, can we talk?" Riley pops her head around the row of lockers.

"Sure." I follow her, Ford following closely behind. "You can stay here."

"Sorry, babe. I have orders not to let you out of my sight. No matter what."

"Fine." I find Riley in the kitchen area, setting up a spread. "I thought you weren't coming in tonight?"

"I'm not here. You didn't see me. But I hate it when Coyote makes me take a night off, and there's no dinner for the girls."

"Where does Coyote think you are?" I flash her a conspiratorial smile.

"The store, which wasn't a lie because I had to stop there to get stuff for sandwiches. It's not fancy, but it'll do."

"I know they appreciate it."

"I hope so." She places her hands on her hips, a small baby bump showing. "You were a hit last night. There have been a lot of requests for a repeat performance."

Pride fills me from head to toe. I know it's not saving a life or finding a cure for cancer, but it was the first thing I've done in the outside world since before my nightmare began, and to know people enjoyed it thrills me. Almost enough to overpower how it ended.

"That's exciting," I say.

"I'm glad to hear you say that because Coyote and I think you should do it on a more permanent basis."

"You want to give me a job?"

"Yeah. Part-time for now because we already have a full roster, but we want to offer you two sets a week, Friday and Saturday night. So prime time."

The thought of making my own money and providing for myself is so tempting. Moto and Sly can tell me I'm not a burden all they want, but the money they spend on me is money they don't have in their pocket.

"Can I get back to you?" I ask.

"Of course. Think about it. Let me know, and in the meantime, you are more than welcome to take the nine-fifteen slot tonight."

I wasn't prepared to do it again so soon. My mood has been all over the place today, and in order to perform, you can't be down. The customers sense it and don't have a good time, which means their wallets will stay shut. But all the praise I've received has me feeling much better. And knowing Tyler can't get in has me not wanting to hide anymore.

"Okay. I'll do it."

"Great! I'll mark you down."

Chapter
SEVENTEEN

Sly

Moto and I keep ourselves busy by plotting out how to find Tyler while we watch the cameras. It shouldn't be hard. He wants to get close to Dove, so reason tells us all we need to do is dangle her around, and he'll come out of the woodwork. Using Dove as bait isn't ideal, but if we plan it right, she'll never be in any real danger.

"Are we going to let Khan do the interrogation?" he asks.

He's typically who we rely on for these kinds of things. The fucker gets a sick thrill out of torture, and he's the most intimidating of all of us. I may be as tall as he is, but Khan has at least fifty pounds of muscle on me.

"No. This is personal. It needs to be us."

"And when we have our answers?"

"Then we kill him."

Moto's eyes darken. "Good. We're on the same page."

Our gaze returns to the security feed, and a wave of long, black hair catches my eye. I installed the cameras and made sure the image quality was the best on the market, so when I zoom in on the main stage, I can see every detail of Dove's striptease.

She has on a long black trench coat that's open to reveal a see-through, sparkly gold bodysuit. I smack Moto's arm and point to the feed. Strutting out in the tallest platform heels I've ever seen, she takes a seat on a wooden chair that's been placed in front of the pole.

I know Roxy works with her on the pole every night we're here, but Dove's mentioned she isn't comfortable using it quite yet, so it has me grinning to see she's found a different implement.

"Do we go out there?" Moto asks.

"Hell yeah. Let's go."

We all but jog into the club, forgetting our responsibilities. The second I see her on stage, my mind blanks out. This place could catch fire, and I wouldn't move from this spot. Her beauty is mesmerizing.

She sheds her trench coat, leaving her in just the bodysuit. The gold is classy, but metal chains dangle over her hips, giving the whole outfit an edge. When the beat drops, her thighs part, and she gyrates her hips. Her hair is down and wild, and her make-up is gold and black. Even her lips are painted in gold sparkles.

"She looks like a million bucks," I mutter, almost too stunned to speak.

She lowers her body back over the side of the chair, upper body hanging down, and her hair dusting the floor while her legs shoot straight in the air, giving the audience a look at the G-string tucked between the cheeks of her ass. I glance around the room, seeing men and women alike practically drooling over our girl.

I reach down and adjust myself. I don't know what turns me on more. Seeing how badly everyone in this room wishes they could take her home or knowing we're the men who will be taking her home. It's a toss-up I have no interest in figuring out the answer to. All I know is I'm horny as fuck now.

Her thighs jiggle side to side, which shows everyone in here what they would see if they were fucking her from behind. An image I know well since I'm the lucky bastard she chose to give that reality to.

She sits up, and her hand reaches to the back of her neck. She unclasps the bodysuit, and the top part falls, revealing the tiny sequined pasties covering her nipples. The rest of her small but full breasts are exposed, and she shimmies her shoulders, making them sway back and forth.

"Fuck me," Moto grinds out, reaching down to adjust himself.

I wish like hell I could fuck him while we watched her. No one would notice; everyone's attention is glued to the beautiful woman on stage. Even the bartenders and servers have stopped what they're doing to watch.

But I better not risk it. Loki would be pissed if someone reported us for lewd conduct.

Dove stands and pushes the rest of the bodysuit to the floor, revealing the tiniest thong I've ever seen. Her pussy lips are barely covered. I fight the urge to pull her off stage, not because I don't want her showing her goods—I don't give a shit about that—but because I need to fuck her. It's beyond a want at this point.

She uses the chair to dance, straddling it backward and forwards, grinding on it, and laying across it. I've never been more jealous of a fuckin' piece of wood in my life, but I'd kill to be the one getting all that attention.

Turning her back on the crowd, she hooks her thumbs into the small strings of her thong on her hip and bends forward, pulling it down right as the lights go off. A round of applause mixed with boos at not getting a glimpse between her legs erupts in the club.

Seconds later, the lights come back on, and Dove's gone. The club slowly goes back to business, but as we walk around, we listen to all the conversations about how incredible that last dancer was. I light up with pride and arousal, knowing they'll all be picturing our girl when they return home to their boring wives or lonely beds while Moto and I will be fucking the sexiest woman alive.

Arms wrap around me from behind, but Dove's voice shouts over the music before I have a chance to react. "What did you think?"

I turn around, placing a possessive hand around her waist. "You were fuckin' amazing."

Her little nose scrunches. "Really?"

"Really."

I release her, and she takes two steps to the side for Moto to place a claiming hand around her. She's got that gold bodysuit on again, and now that I'm getting an up-close view, I notice how sheer it really is. Damn, she's sexy.

Moto kisses the top of her head. "Proud of you, Dove. I can't believe the woman up there is the same one we rescued all those months ago."

"Thank you. Who would've guessed stripping was what I needed to bring me back?"

I lean over and nuzzle into her neck. "Is it time to go home yet?"

She giggles, pushing me away. "Not yet."

"How much for a lap dance?" An older man, probably in his late forties, interrupts. He's in an expensive-looking suit, which isn't a surprise. We cater to higher-end clientele than the other clubs in Reno. The atmosphere we've created, our drink prices, and the caliber of our women ensure the people who walk through our doors are executive class.

"I'm sorry. I only dance on occasion."

I get in her ear and whisper, "Do it. I want to watch."

Her eyes widen, and her thighs push together. She likes

that idea too. But she holds a hand up to her cheek to block the man's view and mouths, "I don't know how."

Again, I whisper, "Just pretend he's the chair."

Her hand falls away, and she smiles big. "Okay, let's do it."

He takes her hand and leads her over to his booth, where his buddies are waiting. Moto and I follow, standing guard in case they don't use their manners. They give us a side-eye but lean back and outstretch their legs, ready for the show.

A sensual song comes on, and if Dove's nervous, you'd never know. Her hips sway, and her hands move up and down her body, stopping to cup her breasts. The men grin, throwing out hoots and hollers.

She sidles up to the first man and straddles his lap. He keeps his arms extended along the back of the bench like a good boy. It turns me on to watch her dance in front of other people, but no one's allowed to touch her except me and Moto. If he breaks that rule, I'll break his hand.

She weaves her fingers together at the back of his head and grinds down on him, pressing his face into her cleavage. When she stands, his stiff dick is visible through his trousers. He'll be beating off to this memory for months to come while I'll be the one balls deep inside her whenever I want.

The more she moves, the hungrier the man's eyes become. He's envisioning taking her home and sinking balls deep into her sweet cunt. I'm tempted to tell him how delicious and responsive she is. How her thighs tremble when she comes. I'll bet that would drive him even wilder.

She finishes the dance by going down the row of men, giving each of them a little attention and leaving them all with a hard-on. The song ends, and wads of cash are pushed in her direction. She thanks them, collecting the money with a beautiful smile and her skin glistening with perspiration.

She looks fuck hot.

"I'm done sharing," I say to Moto, and he nods, agreeing.

He takes her by the hand and leads her back to the dressing room.

"Do you think they liked it?" she asks, truly not understanding what she does to every person she meets. Women and men alike, they all want her.

"They'll have blue balls all night," I say, then dip down to kiss her gold lips. The glitter is rough, and I know the lipstick will transfer to me, but I don't give a fuck.

She pulls away and slaps my chest. "You're ridiculous."

Moto steals her away, grabbing her hands and tugging her to his chest. His hands go to her ass, and he kisses her roughly. I watch his tongue thrust into her mouth and see how her body melts against his.

How are we going to make it four more hours without fucking her?

"Don't you two have a job to do?" she asks, laughing at our fierceness.

"Yeah, we should probably get back to it," I say.

"Are you performing any more tonight?" Moto gives her ass one last squeeze before releasing her.

"No. I'm done. But I promised Roxy I'd help her get ready for her Bat Woman set."

"Sounds interesting. We'll be in the security room if you need us." Moto gives her one last peck.

It's then I notice Ford standing in the shadows. He managed to keep an eye on her this whole time without me seeing him.

"Good man," I say, waving at him.

"It's a tough job." He shrugs, but there's humor in his eyes.

He holds open the dressing room door, and she walks through, hips swaying and ass jiggling.

"Fucking hell," I curse.

The second we get through the clubhouse doors, I throw her over my shoulder and storm to her room, Moto following behind.

"I can walk, caveman," she protests but is laughing, so I know she doesn't mind.

I toss her on the bed while Moto closes the door. Wordlessly, Moto and I strip down to our boxers as Dove watches. Her makeup is gone, and she's back into sweatpants and a tee, but she's no less beautiful than she was on that stage.

I catch sight of Moto—the muscles of his nearly naked body taut with excitement and a gleam in his brown eyes—and wonder how the hell I got this lucky.

Deciding to start with him, I stalk over and grip him by the base of his throat. He gives me a challenging glare, but it's gone in seconds when I tip his chin up slightly since I'm three inches taller and kiss him, my tongue plunging into his mouth. He tastes good, like the wintergreen gum he was chewing.

Knowing Dove is watching us only spurs me on more, and I dip my hand past the waistband of his boxers so I can grip his steel length. His cock is velvety and smooth, yet hard as a rock and dripping with pre-cum. I stroke him as I devour his mouth, moaning at the pleasure.

I pull my hand free, my fingers gleaming from the clear liquid seeping from his tip. Walking over to the bed, I hold them to Dove's lips, wondering how she'll react. She leans forward and sucks them clean, her warm, wet mouth a precursor to how it'll feel when I'm buried in her cunt later.

Moto climbs behind Dove, spreading his legs wide to make room for her. He lifts up her shirt, and I'm surprised to find she's not wearing a bra. Her brown nipples pucker from the cold air, and I cup one, strumming my thumb over the stiff peak.

Standing over them, I feel like a king, even though they are the ones in charge. I might be the director, but my naughty fantasies would never come true without their consent.

"Look at you both. So fuckin' sexy. Pull down your pants and spread your legs wide. I want to watch Moto play with the pretty pussy everyone in that club wishes they could have," I say.

She shimmies them and her panties down her legs that, despite her short height, seem to go on forever. Once they're tossed into a pile on the floor, she opens for me. I bite my lip, seeing that she's already soaking wet. Moto pushes her hair over one shoulder so he can bite and suck on her neck while he plays with her pussy.

"Fuck me, you're so wet for us," Moto murmurs, latching onto her collarbone.

"I'm not used to men who like to share. I didn't think it was something I wanted. But seeing the way you watched me give that lap dance turned me on. I liked it." Her words come out breathy, a sound that goes straight to my dick.

Pushing my pants down, I kneel in front of her. "You're perfect for us. You know that, right? We might like other people to desire you, but we'd never really share. We want to be the only ones who ever get to experience *this* with you."

She licks her lips, eyes on the bobbing cock in front of her. "I know."

"Good. Now suck me, Dove. I've been dreaming of your mouth on me all night."

I grip myself at the base and feed her my length, inch by inch. She whimpers sweetly, and I'm not sure if it's from Moto's fingers in her tight heat or my pre-cum landing on her tongue.

"Play with your tits, baby," I say. Her hands knead her flesh before pinching her nipples and giving them a little tug. "What a good fuckin' girl."

It's a feast for my eyes, with Moto planting open-mouthed kisses along her neck, his fingers working her over while she sucks my cock and plays with her perky breasts. This is better than a fuckin' porno.

Feeling a little guilty that Moto isn't receiving the kind of pleasure Dove and I are, I reluctantly pull out of her mouth. "I want to fuck Moto while he eats you out."

"Oh my God, please. I want that too," Dove says.

Moto jumps to his feet and drops his boxers, his hard cock springing free. Dove scoots back on the bed, practically panting for what's coming next. After last night, I took it upon myself to stock Dove's nightstand with supplies. Thank fuck for that because the last thing I want to do right now is walk across the hall sporting the hard-on of the century.

I lube myself up while Moto gets on all fours, diving into Dove's pussy. He hooks his arms under her thighs and spreads her outer lips, exposing her tiny bundle of nerves.

"Look at how ready she is, brother," he says before flicking her clit with the point of his tongue.

"I'm jealous. Tell me how she tastes."

"Sweet and juicy." He licks up her slit while I position myself behind him.

I've fucked his ass more times than I can count, but it never gets old. I'll never tire of how it feels for such a masculine, strong man to open his body to me like this. Never.

I drizzle some lube down his crack and press a finger inside. He makes a pleasured sound that vibrates through Dove's pussy, causing her to make a similar noise. Increasing to two fingers, I hook them inside to press against his prostate while running a hand down his spine. His skin feels so good against my calloused fingers.

Once I feel he's ready, I grip my dick and slowly press inside, groaning as my fat head passes the first ring of muscle. I don't prefer his ass over Dove's pussy. They are equal in my eyes, both making me feel like I'm experiencing a bit of paradise.

Little by little, I press more of my length inside until I'm buried to the hilt. Moto pauses what he's doing, the pleasure too much for him to concentrate. "Oh my God. Feels so good."

"Are you ready for me to move?" I ask.

"Yes. Do it."

I pull out completely and then push back in, loving how that first ring of muscle squeezes my head. I'm so lost in what I'm doing that I completely forget this is the first time Dove's seeing two men fuck. But that's not the only first happening right now.

Moto and I have never fucked while with a woman. It was something special between us that we never wanted to share with anyone. Until Dove.

We're keeping this woman. Forever, if she'll let us.

When I glance over Moto's shoulder, I see she's propped pillows under her head for a better view of what I'm doing. Her lips are parted, and her nipples are hard. And I don't think it's just from Moto's mouth. It turns her on to see us like this.

For the hundredth time, the words "she's perfect" cross my mind.

Chapter
EIGHTEEN

Moto

Sly fucks my ass without mercy, increasing his speed until the sound of his hips slapping against my ass fills the room. It's hard to concentrate, but I focus on pleasing Dove, pushing two fingers into her channel while I suck on her clit.

I wasn't lying when I said she tastes like a peach. Her pussy is mouthwatering, and I could stay here all day feasting on her. But if I know Sly, he'll make us switch positions any minute now. Even if he's enjoying what he's doing, he likes controlling what we're doing even more.

I don't care. He always makes it good for me.

Sly smacks my ass. "Switch positions with Dove. I want your cock down her throat while I fuck her pussy and stretch her ass with my fingers."

We asked Dove how she felt about eventually taking us both, and she's on board. It'll require time and effort, but I could come just from the thought of both of us fucking her at the same time. I'm glad Sly is starting that process now.

He slams into me one last time with a grunt, bumping against my prostate. I squeeze my eyes shut and swallow, pushing away the orgasm wanting to burst free. I feel empty when he pulls out but knowing my dick will soon be in Dove's pretty mouth stops the protest sitting on my lips.

Sly cleans up while I swap spots with Dove, but before she can get on all fours, I pull her to me and suck a nipple into my mouth. The bud puckers at my attention, and I flick it with my tongue while palming her ass. She's so petite and fragile that I constantly remind myself she's breakable.

When Sly and I are alone, we're like wolves, feral and wild. We're aggressive with each other in a way that we walk away bruised and sore after a good fucking. With Dove here, we have to tone it down.

I don't care. I love her soft and sweet just as much.

She pulls my hair free and runs her hands through it. "Your hair is beautiful."

I release her breast. "So is yours."

She kisses me soft and gentle. Knowing she's tasting herself and not caring turns me on. Watching her lick my pre-cum off Sly's fingers turned me on. Everything this woman does is one big fuckin' turn-on.

Taking my cock in her soft hand, she pulls away, bending over and sticking her round ass in the air. Sly steps up behind her, eyes glued to the spot between her legs. I'd be jealous if her lips weren't wrapping around my cock and her warm, wet mouth wasn't sucking me down.

Sly pushes into her in one solid thrust, hand gripping her ass roughly, turning her pale skin red. Violence was a hard limit for her, but to her surprise, she loved it when Sly slapped her ass. I won't lie that I get a little nervous when he does something for the first time. My worst nightmare would be for one of us to unintentionally do something that makes her not want us anymore.

It makes me go easier on her, but Sly's not like that. He's

full steam ahead, all the time. I have to hope he keeps his wits about himself enough to not go too far.

Dove's slurping and suction noises bring me back to the moment. She cups my balls, rolling them in her palm as she sucks me off. It feels so fuckin' good, but I can't see shit because her hair is a thick curtain around her head. I gather it up in a ponytail and hold it there.

"Give me your eyes," I say, and her gaze shoots up to me. Her brown irises sparkle as she moves up and down, her lips stretched wide to accommodate my girth. "Fuckin' beautiful."

A cap opening gains my attention. Sly drops a stream of lube down her crack and then works his thumb inside her back hole. Dove moans, and the vibration feels phenomenal.

I watch as his thumb disappears between her cheeks. We're one step closer to taking her at the same time. I can't fuckin' wait.

"You're ours, Dove. You know that, right?" he asks, a manic look of possession in his eyes. I know what he's thinking. He's thinking about all the horrid stories Dove told us about her time being trafficked.

As much as we try to not think about it, it's impossible. Even during sex. Especially when we're close enough to see the scarred skin between her legs and on the back of her thighs, the way he can now. She covers them in makeup when she's at the club, but she doesn't hide anything from us.

She releases my dick, a string of saliva still connecting us, and her breaths coming fast and hard. "I know."

"We're going to worship this body every chance we get, the way it always should've been."

"Yes. Oh my God. I'm going to come."

He picks up his pace, twisting and turning his thumb inside her as he fucks her hard. She pushes back against him, tilting her hips to hit in the right place. I scoot forward, and she drapes her upper body over my shoulders. I reach between her legs and rub her swollen clit drenched in her juices.

Her warm breath skirts over my neck, and she cries out in pleasure, her body tightening and her thighs shaking. She's so fuckin' beautiful when she comes, and it turns me right the hell on to be part of it. It has me feeling like a bomb, ready to detonate.

"I think Dove should swallow both our cum," Sly says, and that sounds like the best idea I've ever heard.

"Do you have enough strength to get on your knees?" I ask. She nods, and I pinch her chin before bringing her mouth to mine. I can't get enough of her kisses. "Good girl."

She slinks off the bed and lowers to her knees, sitting up tall. Sly and I jerk our cocks, eyes trained on the naked woman in front of us. She takes over for Sly first, stroking him and sucking on his tip. It's a fuckin' sexy sight, and it doesn't take long for an orgasm to build back up.

This time I don't fight it.

"Fucking hell. I'm going to come," I groan.

She releases Sly and moves to me, stroking my cock with a firm grip, her lips wrapped tight around my tip. I lose it when her tongue cradles the underside of my head and slides side to side against it.

"Shit," I curse, every inch of my body tingling as fire shoots through me and my load releases into the softest mouth it's ever been in. She doesn't stop until she's milked every single drop from me. "Show me." She releases her hold and sticks out her tongue. "Now swallow."

She gulps it down, looking like it's the best thing she's eaten all day, when I know that can't be true. Even so, I appreciate her gesture. She moves over to Sly and gets back to work, making him feel as good as she made me.

I run a hand up his chest, feeling the definition of his muscles and running my fingers through his small patch of hair. Then I kiss him, giving him a taste of Dove.

When he pulls away, his breaths increase, and I know he's

coming. I want to watch it happen. His hands weave in her hair and fist it, giving him something to hold onto while the pleasure moves through him in waves.

She greedily takes everything he's got, but it's too much and spills out the corner of her mouth. I collect it with my finger and suck it off, not wanting a drop to go wasted. Sly's gaze burns into me.

After all these years of knowing each other, it still makes me feel so fuckin' good when he looks at me like that. Like I'm the most important man in the world. Like I'm not just the man he fucks or his club brother; I'm a fundamental part of who he is as a person.

We help Dove to her feet and get her in bed. Before climbing in myself, I close the curtains to block out the sunlight cresting over the mountains. We'll be sleeping in.

"Hello?" Sly's sleepy voice wakes me, and I turn over to see him on his phone.

Whatever the person on the other end of the call says has him flipping the comforter off and jumping out of bed. Something's wrong, and I'm instantly on edge.

"Not fuckin' happening. She's ours." He tugs on his messy bedhead.

Dove stirs, her eyes fluttering open. She looks innocent and young when she firsts wakes up. I place a finger to my lips and then point at Sly.

"I'll kill you before I let that happen, you know that, right?"

Fuck. This isn't good. It must be Tyler on the other end. It's the only thing that makes sense.

Dove's eyes widen, and she sits up, exposing her bare tits. The second the cold air hits her skin, she pulls up the sheets.

It's too bad because my blood pressure lowered substantially the second I saw them.

"Try me, asshole. I dare you." Sly ends the call and tosses the phone on the nightstand.

"Tyler?" I already know the answer, but he's not saying anything.

"Yeah." Pacing back and forth, he digs the heels of his hands into his eyes.

"What did he want?" Dove asks.

"He wants you. He said he doesn't leave loose ends."

"And I'm the loose end?" There's no panic, just resignation in her tone.

I bring her to me, cocooning her in my arms. "He'll never touch you again, Dove. Not ever."

Sly places his hands on his hips and looks down at me. "I'm sick of this shit. Get up and get dressed. We need to find Loki."

An hour later, Loki calls church, and all my brothers are sitting around the enormous wooden table with our logo hand-carved into the center.

"Let's put Dove on the billboard above the club to advertise her performances," Sly suggests.

My brothers are straight-faced and not happy about being pulled into yet another war against the Corsettis, even if the chance of retribution from Franco is small.

"What's that going to do?" Loki asks.

Sly pulls the pen he's been chewing on out of his mouth. "We need to get him back at the club. When he shows up, we can grab him and go from there."

"What if he doesn't show? He knows you saw him. It would be stupid for him to return," Khan says.

"Then we'll find another way. But I think it'll work. He's arrogant as fuck and obviously thinks he's protected. Otherwise, he wouldn't have shown up at the club in the first place."

"Or called you this morning, warning you," I add.

"I don't have any problems with that. Our *marketing* lady"—Loki rolls his eyes—"got some good pictures of her last night for the website. I'm sure we can use one for the billboard. I'll send her a message."

Before buying the strip club, we didn't bother with things like marketing for our legal businesses since we didn't care how successful they actually were. On paper, they look incredibly successful since all our gun-running cash gets cleaned through them.

Things changed when we bought the club and saw how much money pussy brought in. It had us taking that shit seriously real quick. We hired a marketing team and put money into advertising and fuckin' promotions. And, we don't have to worry about shipments being stolen or jail time.

It feels a little like selling out, but we're in this for money and freedom, not time served.

"Cool, thanks," Sly says.

"Anyone have anything else they need to discuss?" Loki asks, twisting his skull ring around and around. The fucker is finally taking quitting smoking seriously, and it's made him pricklier than a pissed-off porcupine.

Goblin makes an amused sound and lifts a finger. "I get that things are going real well for the three of you, but I damn near stormed into Petra's room early this morning thinking someone was being murdered."

Sly messes up his hair. "Aw, did we interrupt your beauty sleep, old man?"

Goblin bats his hands away, cursing. "I'm not fuckin' old."

Sly pokes him in the side. "You should listen in next time. Might learn a thing or two about makin' a bitch scream."

The guys bust up laughing at Goblin's expense, and even I'm grinning despite the internal panic seizing my gut. All they know is me and Sly sleep with the same chicks. They don't know about the relationship me and Sly have on our own. Or maybe they do. I don't fuckin' know.

Sometimes I want to blurt it out and get it over with so I don't think about it so much. But if they took it badly, I don't know what would happen. This club and my brothers are everything to me.

Goblin pushes back from the table, irritated as all hell. "Are we done here?"

"Yeah, we're done." Loki slams the gavel down.

Chapter
NINETEEN

Petra

"**T**here's a billboard. Of my ass." I gesture to the gigantic electronic sign a couple hundred feet away from where we're standing in front of Royal Treatment. It's facing the freeway and was included in the purchase agreement when the Royal Bastards bought the place.

Sly slings an arm over my shoulder. "There's no ass. I think there are laws against that."

He's technically right. The picture is of me from my performance a couple weeks ago. I'm lying on top of a chair, my legs crossed and straight up in the air. In the original picture, you could see my entire ass, but on the billboard, they've strategically placed a red box with wording over the area that says "classy" in a pretty script font. Except the letters A-S-S are big and bold.

Ignoring that part, I do look amazing. My long hair is flowing to the ground, and I'm making eye contact with the camera. My lips are shiny and red, my makeup is smoky and sexy, and I'm chewing on the end of my nail sexily.

I cock my head to the side. "Do I really look like that, or is it altered to make me look better?"

"We hardly had to touch up a thing. There was some scarring on the back of your legs that was showing, so we airbrushed that out. But other than that, it's all you," Marissa, the marketing lady, says.

Moto growls menacingly, and Marissa takes two steps away from him. My protective men, always sheltering me.

I give his hand a squeeze. "I can't believe that's me."

"Thanks, Marissa." Loki shakes her hand.

"I'll be in touch." She all but jogs to her car and peels out of the parking lot.

I turn to Moto. "Was that necessary?"

"Yes," Moto and Sly reply at the same time.

I roll my eyes, but I'm smiling. My moms were fierce like that, and I didn't realize how much I missed having people in my corner. A pang stabs through my heart, and I rub at the spot. I haven't given myself the space to think about my old life, but as I settle into my new one, the memories come through more and more.

I miss them.

"I think you look hot as hell, P," Roxy says.

"Yeah, P." Ford sidles up next to her, folding his tattooed arms across his chest.

My bodyguard is getting awfully friendly with my new bestie, and I don't think it's one-sided. I make a mental note to ask her about it later. Though I don't know when, since Ford is my literal shadow when I'm at the club. Maybe I should ask her to come over one night when there's a party at the clubhouse.

"Thank you," I say. "Think this plan will work?"

I was a little weary when Moto and Sly came to me with this plan. I'm not scared of Tyler; I'm terrified of him. But I can't live in peace until he's no longer a threat, and I trust my guys to keep me safe.

"I think so." Sly turns to Coyote. "Did you tell all the bouncers about the plan?"

"Yeah. They know they can let him in and notify us when he shows."

"I guess now we just wait?" I shade my eyes with a hand, taking the billboard in one more time.

"Yep," Sly says.

"What are these parties like?" Roxy asks as she overlines her lips with a blood-red liner.

We're in my bathroom getting ready for the party, to which Roxy very enthusiastically accepted my invitation. I asked her opinion about Ford, and she gushed for ten minutes about how amazing he is and told me he's basically been living at her place for a week.

It would be nice to have a friend who's dating a club member. I'm friendly with the ol' ladies, but I don't click with them the way I click with Roxy.

"I don't know. A lot of dudes and a lot of booze." I take the liner out of her hand and apply it to my own lips.

She snickers. "So, like a normal Friday night for me?"

I hand her back the liner. "Exactly."

"Is that what you're wearing or . . ." She motions down my body. "Because if that's the look we're going for, I'm wildly overdressed."

Roxy went all-out biker chick with her look and is wearing a faux leather jacket, a little black dress, and chunky boots. I'm still in my usual borrowed—stolen—sweats. I look ridiculous considering Roxy curled my hair, and I put on an insane amount of makeup.

"I'll change. I just wanted to be comfy until the last moment."

The music is already blaring, and I know the guys started

drinking well before the sun went down. There's growing chatter outside my room, so I know people have already begun to show up.

Roxy places a hand on her hip. "Might wanna get that done, babe. Sounds like we're missing the fun already."

"Fine." I open my closet, seeing all the many things Sly and Moto have bought for me. I didn't ask for any of it, but sometimes I borrow Sly's laptop to look at things I might want. Since he's nosy, he goes through his browser history, and if I've added something to my cart to save for the future, he buys it.

Even after fighting with him over this, he still does it, and I've now acquired quite the selection of clothing that hardly ever gets worn. I only get out of my sweats for club parties and when I'm working. Neither of which are frequent events.

Tired of watching me stand there and stare, Roxy pushes me out of the way. "I'll decide."

It takes her all of five seconds to pull out a scandalous number with a cream-colored, sheer corset top and a floral print, flowy skirt. I take it from her and hold it up to my body. I've never worn this one, but it's beautiful, and I know my boys would love it.

She kneels down and scours through my shoe collection that's smaller than my dress collection. I'm not into shoes, so I only have staples.

"These will have to do." She hands me a pair of cream sandals with ties that wrap up my ankle and calf.

There's nothing on each other's bodies that we haven't already seen, so I strip down and put the dress on.

"Can you do up the back?" I ask, pulling my hair to the side.

"Of course." She does up the hook and eye closures running up my spine.

Once she's done, I turn and hold out my arms. "What do you think?"

"You look fine as hell."

"But you can see my nipples through the fabric." I look down. The boning of the corset travels up the center of each of my breasts, but the sheer fabric shows my areolas clear as day.

"Remember how you told me that Moto and Sly like it when you get attention?" She quirks a brow.

"Good point." Wetness seeps into my panties, and I wonder if I should even wear them. Knowing that I'll be turning them on with every glance from another man turns me on. I'm suddenly excited to get out there.

Sitting on the corner of my bed, I lace up my heels as fast as I can. The sudden urge to see my guys is strong.

Once we're finished primping, we make our way out into the main area of the club. It's packed with bikers, hang arounds, and women. The pungent scent of alcohol hits my nose, and for a second, I think tonight is the night I see if I can handle drinking now that I'm in a better place in my life.

Then Marcia's voice from all those weeks ago plays in my head, warning me about how dangerous that thought is. I hate that I can't be like everyone else and have a drink. Being the only sober one in a room full of happy drunk people sucks. It's not fair.

But if there's one thing I've learned, it's that life isn't fair. Four years ago, I was a year away from having my dream career. My life was full of friends and family. I had everything going for me. Nothing about my life has been fair, but it happened, and I need to live in the here and now.

"This is wild," Roxy says, looping her arm with mine.

"Wait until you see outside. Are you hungry? Khan is some kind of barbecue mastermind, and he always cooks an insane spread for these things."

"I could eat."

We weave our way through the crowd, gaining plenty of attention. The men wolf whistle, and the patch pussy—a term I hate—glare daggers in our direction. After a quick stop to get Roxy a beer, we walk out the back sliding doors and are hit with a different, yet just as enticing, scent.

Meat.

"Do you see Moto and Sly?" I ask, wondering where they are. I might've missed them inside, but they usually keep an eye out for me, knowing parties make me uncomfortable.

"Not yet."

"Let's go grab a plate then." I lead her over to the picnic tables, and we each load up on the classic barbecue spread, then find empty seats at one of the tables inside.

I take a small bite of potato salad, desperately trying not to get lipstick on my upper chin—a problem us women with plump lower lips face—when I feel lips dance along my neck. I know who it is without looking. My core heats, and a shiver races up my spine before the motor oil and leather scent hits my nostrils.

I cup his cheek and lean into the touch. "Where have you been?"

His lips nestle themselves into the shell of my ear. "Watching you."

"Should've known."

He sits down next to me, and Sly dips in for a quick kiss—not giving a damn about the lipstick—before flipping a chair around and straddling it. "Hey, baby."

"Hey. Did you guys eat?"

Sly smirks. "Saving my appetite."

"You three are gross." Roxy stands. "I'm leaving to find my own fun."

"By yourself?" I instinctually ask, but it's a dumb

question. I would never mingle in a crowd of strangers, but Roxy absolutely would. She's not afraid of anything.

"I think I found someone to show me around."

I follow her gaze and see Ford leaning against the porch post, his eyes on her, looking every bit the bad boy his image leads him to be.

"What about your food?" I ask, but she's already gone.

"I'll eat it." Sly hops up and takes her place on my other side.

"Do you have a drink?" Moto asks.

"No."

"Can I get you something?"

"Sure. Thanks." I don't give him any guidance as to what I want. The little voice inside tells me if he brings me alcohol, it's a sign I should drink it. Hope blooms inside me, despite the humiliation it makes me feel.

I should've known he'd never compromise my sobriety like that because he returns with three water bottles a minute later. I deflate a little, even though it's for the best.

"Just because I can't drink doesn't mean you two can't," I say.

"We're staying sober tonight." Sly winks. "We want to have our wits about us."

Moto runs a hand up my dress before settling on my bare thigh.

"Oh." My mouth goes dry, and suddenly I'm not hungry for food.

Since our first night together, I can't get enough of them. It's like my body is making up for all the years I didn't feel an ounce of desire. Now, all it takes is being in the same room as them, and I'm squirming in my seat, counting down the minutes until we can be alone.

"Spread your legs for me," Moto says in a conversational tone.

"Right now?"

"Spread them," he demands, and my legs automatically part, like he's the one controlling my body, not me. His hand moves to the apex of my thighs, cupping me over my damp panties. "What has you this wet already?"

My lips part but nothing other than a strangled moan comes out when his finger reaches my clit.

Sly scoots closer, resting his elbow on the table and propping his head up with his hand. "I think I know, but I want to hear it from you."

Moto's hand returns to my thigh, making me scowl. "Tell me what, and I'll make that pretty cunt sing."

Do I want that? There are hundreds of people walking around, and all it would take is one look at my face to know what's going on. My cheeks heat, and my panties grow wetter because that thought turns me on more.

"My top is see-through, and I knew it would turn you guys on to know everyone will be staring at my breasts all night," I admit in a hushed tone.

"Let me see," Sly says.

I've been hunched forward over my food, but now I lean back, giving them full view. Sly traces the boning, starting at the top of my breast, down my very erect nipples, and stopping when he reaches my lower belly.

"Goddamn, you're sexy." Moto's hand returns to cup me, his thumb stroking back and forth on my clit.

"How did it feel walking through the crowd, knowing every man in here was getting hard?" Sly asks, tracing his way back up my body, stopping to circle my nipple.

My eyes roam the crowd, but no one's paying us any attention. "I liked it."

"Like? Your pussy is telling a different story. She's telling me you loved it."

He's right. I loved it so much that it won't take me long to orgasm.

"Take your panties off," Moto demands.

My eyes pop wide. "Right here?"

He nods. "Do it."

My gaze shifts side to side, and I nonchalantly reach under my dress and slowly tug them down my thighs. Once I need to lift my ass up, I push the chair back and pretend to pick something up off the ground when really, I'm pulling my thong down my legs the rest of the way. It's not a lot of fabric, so I can hide it in my hand before returning to my seat.

"Give them to me," Sly says. When I hand them over, he brings them to his nose, making a show of breathing in before tucking them in his pocket. "Good girl."

"What now?" I ask.

"You're going to sit on my lap." Moto pushes back a little, making just enough room for me between him and the table.

"You're joking." They told me they were into public sex, but I thought that meant a quickie in the bathroom or hiding around a dark corner.

"Not joking." He unbuckles his belt, then pops the button of his jeans before unzipping them.

"Everyone will know," I protest.

"Kind of the point, baby," Sly says, his eyes going half-lidded and full of lust. "But I don't think anyone's paying attention. They're all involved in what they're doing."

Looking around, I know he's right. Groups of men are gathered around, laughing and talking, women doing much of the same, but no one even glances our way.

"Oh my God," I say and shift from my seat to his lap, giving him enough cover to pull his dick free. I lift my ass up a little and lower onto him, gasping at how thoroughly he fills me.

Sly moves over to my chair and scoots as close as

possible, resuming his position with one elbow on the table, propping his head up on his palm while his other hand slips under my dress and finds my clit. I'm so turned on I wouldn't have to move to get off, but that's not what Moto wants. He places his hands on my hips and guides me back and forth in an almost imperceptible motion, just enough to create friction.

"You feel so good. Fuck me. Your pussy is the best I've ever had," Moto says.

"You're so wet, baby. It's dripping down to Moto's balls already." His fingers leave my clit and travel lower. Though I can't feel it, I know he's rubbing my arousal over Moto's sack.

I moan as quietly as I can muster, desperately not wanting to draw attention but wound so tight that I have to let it out. This is the single most arousing moment of my life, and that's saying a lot because these men do things to me that turn my world upside down.

"I'm going to pump you so full of my cum, it'll be dripping down your thighs. Every man here will know this pussy has been claimed. But I need you to come first. Can you do that for me?" Moto murmurs.

I nod, and Sly's fingers return to my clit, rubbing fast circles. I close my eyes, knowing I'll never get there if my mind is caught up in making sure no one's looking. A whimper begs to come out, and I bite down on my lower lip to keep it at bay. God, he feels so good.

Moto encourages me to move back and forth a little faster, and his cock swells even more.

"Come, baby. Come now. I want to watch you fall apart on Moto's fat dick," Sly says.

His dirty words spur me on as my pussy spasms and pleasure overtakes me. To stop from screaming, I bite into my lip so hard I draw blood, the metallic tang bursting on my tongue. Then I feel a gush of warmth deep inside, and I know Moto followed right behind.

"Fuck me. I love seeing my man and my woman come together."

I open my eyes and smile, feeling satisfied and scandalous. It doesn't last when I realize the precarious situation I'm now in. I have no panties to pull on, I'm full of cum, and I'm surrounded by people.

"Now what?" I ask.

"Now I'm going to clean you up." Sly ducks under the table.

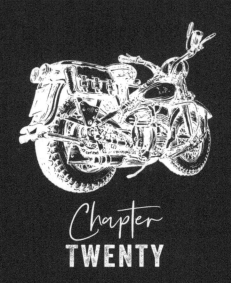

Chapter
TWENTY

Sly

I crouch under the table. It's uncomfortable as shit, not just because I'm a big man trying to hide under a table but also because my dick is hard as stone after the show Dove and Moto put on. I wasn't sure how she'd react to doing something like this with so many people around, but damn, did she go with it.

"Move over to your chair." Moto slaps her outer thigh.

"But I'm—"

"Dove, do it."

She lifts off his softened cock and takes her seat. I'll get to her in a second. Moto jolts when I suck his sensitive dick into my mouth, cleaning it off before tucking him back into his pants. He takes over, buckling up as I move over to Dove's cum-filled pussy.

I spread her thighs wide and pull her to the edge of the chair. Lifting her skirt up, I dive in. The taste of Moto's cum mixing with hers covers my tastebuds. It's the most erotic flavor I've ever tasted, and I'm immediately addicted.

I lick her clean until the only thing left is her own arousal that's flowing again. The muscles in her thighs quiver, and she gently rocks against my face. I wasn't sure she'd relax enough to allow me to get her off again, but our girl surprises me with every turn.

Thrusting my tongue in and out of her hole the way I would if it were my cock, I strum her clit with my thumb. While I can't make out his exact words, I hear Moto's low murmuring, no doubt sweet-talking her and getting her even more worked up.

I wasn't lying when I said how much it turned me on to watch them fuck out in the open. My only regret is this painful hard-on I'll be sporting until after the party when I get a turn. It'll be worth it, though. Tonight's the night we will fill both her holes at the same time.

We've made good use of the last couple of weeks while we wait for Tyler to show his face. If we're not on a run or working at the club, we're fucking. Moto and I have been inside Dove's ass and pussy more times than we can count, preparing her, and we all agree it's finally time.

Knowing that will get me through the blue balls I'll have the second we get back to the party.

I change things up, pushing two fingers in her cunt and flicking her clit with my tongue. She moans, probably too loudly, but I fuckin' love hearing it. I hope everyone hears her. Matter of fact, I hope she loses her mind and screams my name. It's unlikely, but a man can hope.

Her inner walls clamp down on my fingers, and her thighs squeeze around my head. She's coming. I suck hard on her clit while I finger fuck her through her release. Her cum is so sweet and juicy that I could use it as a mixer to cut my tequila, and it would be the best tasting drink in the world.

Fuckin' love every part of this woman.

Once she relaxes back into the chair, I kiss her pussy, lower her dress, and then unfold myself from under the table. My neck is kinked, and my back aches, but I couldn't care less. My man and my woman are satisfied. What more could I ask for?

Dove blushes furiously and adjusts her dress when I climb up to my seat. I pick up a fork and dive into the plate of food in front of me, distracting myself from my still hard dick.

"I won't survive you two," she says, hearts in her eyes as she looks from Moto to me.

"Death by orgasm. Not a bad way to go." I shove a hunk of steak in my mouth.

"I don't know. You look more alive now than you ever have." Moto drapes an arm over the back of her chair.

"I feel more alive than ever, to be honest. I thought my life before was perfect. I was happy and doing something I loved. After I was taken, I had a lot of time to think, and I realized that I wasn't happy; I was busy. I spent my entire adult life at school or work. I rarely took time to have fun or travel. If I hadn't been taken, I would've died without doing or seeing anything. I wouldn't have found love." She stares out at the backyard, unseeing, but we stay silent, knowing she has more to say. Eventually, she smiles, and fuck me, it's a gorgeous smile. "I can't regret those four years of hell because they brought me here, to my guys, and I'm truly happy now."

Moto cups her cheeks and rests his forehead against hers. "This is going to sound cheesy as hell, but I'm saying it anyway. You fuckin' complete us, Dove."

I grin as they kiss, proud of Moto for saying it because he's right on both ends. It needed to be said, and it sounded corny as fuck.

"Love you, baby," I say when they part, and she leans over to kiss my cheek.

A commotion steals our attention, and I narrow my eyes on the crowd forming.

"Oh my God. I have to see this," Ford yells, grabbing Roxy's hand and tugging her into the yard.

We follow where he's pointing and see Khan, Duncan, and

Miles sitting at a table, each with a plate of brown powder in front of them. Fuckin' idiots.

"What are they doing?" Dove asks, standing.

"Cinnamon challenge," Moto groans.

"What?" She steps around the table to get closer.

"They eat a tablespoon of cinnamon and try to swallow it without water." Moto walks to her side.

"It went so well last time. I'm glad they're trying again," I say sarcastically and reluctantly walk away from my food. "Might as well go watch the train wreck."

Birdie stands in front of them with a checkered flag, explaining the rules like this is a race, not some idiots playing an impossible game.

"Ready, set"—Birdie raises the flag—"go!"

The flag lowers, and my brothers spoon the powder into their mouths. Duncan and Miles instantly recoil, brown puffs of air leaving their mouths and even coming out their noses. But Khan, the giant bastard, swallows and flips the table as he stands, his mouth dropping open and his head turning side to side to show the crowd inside. His tongue is brown, but he did swallow it without water.

He roars and flexes his muscles, making a show of his win as the other two cough and sputter. Duncan doubles over and stumbles toward the keg. Grabbing the spout, he sprays beer into his open mouth, showering everyone within a three-foot perimeter, causing them to block their faces with their hands and run.

It's chaos. Me, Moto, and Dove snicker as we watch the scene unfold. It's fuckin' hilarious.

Khan grabs Bexley around the waist and tries to kiss her, cinnamon mouth and all, but she slaps him and storms off. He laughs as he watches her leave.

"I don't understand those two," Dove says. "She seems to hate him more than she loves him."

"Just watch." I brush her hair over one shoulder and kiss her neck.

A minute later, Khan sidles up to Bexley and whispers something in her ear. Her sour expression slowly morphs into one of desire. She grabs his hand and tugs him inside, no doubt so they can go fuck in his room.

Loki, Roch, and Khan have houses in Tahoe next to each other, but they keep rooms here in case of a lockdown or if they need a place to crash after drinking too much at one of our parties.

I wonder if that's our next step. The clubhouse has been home for so long that I never pictured myself living anywhere else. Matter of fact, I planned on dying here—hopefully from old age. In my head, this was mine and Moto's retirement home.

But chicks don't want that. They want a place of their own, and someday we'll get Dove's IUD taken out and fill her with both of our cum every night until we knock her up. To me, our clubhouse is the perfect place for kids to grow up. It's safe, there's lots of room to run and play, and it's where we spend most of our time. I doubt Dove would want that, though.

"I guess they're off to . . .?" Dove asks, letting me fill in the blanks.

"Oh yeah. They'll fuck." I chuckle.

"Truly's here. I'm going to go say hi," Dove says.

Moto and I settle back at the table, watching our woman talk to Roch's very pregnant ol' lady. Dove crouches down and places her ear on Truly's belly. I can't hear what she's saying but judging by the serene expression on her face, she's cooing something sweet.

"Does one of us need to marry her before we knock her up, or can we skip right to planting a baby in her?" Moto asks.

"You read my mind." I shovel some macaroni salad in my mouth. "We should probably wait a while to talk to her about that."

"I know, but I can see the future so clearly, and it's fuckin' beautiful, man. Can't help but want to jump ahead."

I place a hand on his muscled thigh and squeeze, trying to tell him how much I love what he's laying down but not having the words. I want to lean over and kiss the shit out of him but it would expose our relationship, something I don't think I give a shit about anymore. But he's not there yet, so I keep my lips to myself.

"How long are we gonna hide what we mean to each other?" I ask.

"What do you mean? I think everyone knows we're with Dove."

"I don't mean with Dove." I turn to face him. "I mean you and me. We're a forever kind of something. Even if Dove didn't exist."

"I know."

"When?" I ask again.

"Does it matter?"

It hits me that it's never mattered to me. I went along with it because I knew it would bother him. But I don't want to hide anything from my brothers. And if they can't accept us for who we are, they're not the men I thought they were, and this isn't the family I want to belong to.

"It matters to me. There shouldn't be secrets between us."

His jaw ticks, and the veins in his neck pop out. I'm pushing buttons I've never pushed, but shit, it's got to come out sometime. Minutes pass, and the more he thinks about it, the more pissed off he gets. His nostrils flare, the knuckles on his hands that are fisted together on the table grow white with tension, and his leg bounces furiously.

I'm ready to tell him to forget about it and deal with it later when he jumps to his feet. He's going to run away and leave me here feeling like shit. I can kiss the night we had planned goodbye.

"Moto, wait," I say, reaching for him, but he's too fast.

My gut sinks, and I'm pissed at myself for pushing so hard. I knew he wasn't ready. Banging the same chick with your club brother is celebrated around here, something they'll pound you on the back for and say, "you dirty dog." But admitting you also like to fuck or get fucked by your club brother is something different. At least in his eyes.

The thing is, that mentality isn't putting trust in your brothers. The same brothers you trust with your life on the daily.

A commotion breaks out where the keg is, and I walk over to check it out. The crowd is gathered in a tight circle, stopping me from seeing what's going on. I weave through them and find Moto at the center.

"Shut the fuck up and listen. I got something to say." His arms are folded across his chest, and he has the same irritated look on his face. "Dove is mine and Sly's ol' lady."

"No shit, Sherlock," someone shouts, and I huff because they're not wrong. We've never hidden our relationship with her.

"Did I not tell you to shut the fuck up and listen?" Moto growls. "What you don't know is Sly and I have been together for a long time. Years now. And if anyone has a fuckin' problem with it, you can take it up with me."

It's silent for a few seconds before Loki shouts, "That's what you had to say?"

Moto nods, probably cracking a molar with how hard he's clenching.

"Bro, we already fuckin' knew that." Loki waves him off and walks away like it's nothing. I could kiss Prez right now because even if everyone didn't know that, he set the tone. No one's brave enough to go against his opinion on something like this.

The crowd walks away—slapping us both on the back as they pass—leaving me, him, and now Dove standing there. She must've heard the commotion at some point and joined in.

My fuckin' chest feels like it's going to explode with the

pride I feel for him, and I wonder if it's asking too much to kiss him right now. He makes the decision for me, charging toward me and planting a bittersweet kiss on my lips.

"Happy?" he asks, pulling away.

I grin wickedly. "So fuckin' happy."

"I'm so proud of you," Dove gushes, stealing him away and kissing him long and hard.

His anger melts away, and I'm grateful for it. Moto and I don't have the ability to soften for each other; it's full throttle, all the time. That's why we need Dove. She files away at all our hard edges and comforts us in a way we can't do for each other. She's our missing piece.

Have I mentioned how fuckin' perfect she is?

Chapter
TWENTY-ONE

Moto

I didn't want to do it, but now that it's done, I feel lighter. I didn't realize how heavy not being open with my brothers weighed on my chest. No one said shit about it, but I'll never know if it's because of Loki's easy acceptance or if everyone already had suspicions.

Not that it matters. It's out now.

As the party goes on, the vibe changes from energetic and chaotic to slow and sexual. Everywhere I look, there's hedonism.

Two women lie naked on the bar while Duncan and Miles drizzle their nipples with lime juice, then sprinkle them with salt. My brothers rest a shot glass of tequila between each lady's tits, then take their time licking off all the salt on their chosen woman. Once their nipples are licked clean, they bury their faces between the women's breasts to latch onto the shot glass, not using their hands at all. Through a chorus of cheers, they tip their heads back to drink down the liquor before diving back into bare tits for the lime juice.

In every corner of the house, club whores are on their knees, sucking the cocks of hang arounds. I'm sure they'd rather be servicing a patched-in member, but there are only a handful left without ol' ladies, and those have already chosen a partner for the night. The hang arounds are the next best option.

If I'm not mistaken, Roxy is one of the women on her knees, servicing Ford.

Guess they hit it off.

Sly, Dove, and I watch it all from where we sit on the leather sofa. Dove is between us, squirming as we caress and kiss her shoulders and neck. Her nipples are hardened points and visible through her corset top. She's so fuckin' hot, and we're minutes from taking her back to her room.

As for our other brothers, Khan and Bexley haven't resurfaced from his room. Loki and Birdie are still around, but they'll disappear soon, judging by their proximity to each other. Roch and Truly took off hours ago because the pregnancy makes her tired. And Coyote and Riley left not long after that because they have a kid at home and one on the way.

"Can we go back to the room now, please?" she begs, squirming and rubbing her thighs together.

"I think that's a great idea," I say.

We choose Sly's room, stumbling through the door and slamming it shut in our haste. The next few minutes are a frenzy of clothes being ripped off, and I mean that literally because Dove's damn top seems to be sewn to her body. I try to undo all the little hooks running down her back, but impatience has me tearing it apart at the seam instead.

"Hey, I liked this top," she whines, her plump lower lip pouting, but the complaint is short-lived as I cup her breast and pinch her nipple. "Oh, God."

"That's what I thought," I say, but it lacks heat because Sly has a hand around my cock and his tongue in my ear. "Fuuuuck."

Sly leaves me to sit on the chair situated in the corner of his room. He spreads his legs wide, his hard dick pointing straight up and resting on his chiseled abs, looking like a goddamn king on his throne. "Get over here, Dove."

She scrambles to do his bidding while I stay put, stroking myself as I watch him turn her around to face me before lowering her onto his cock. She moans as he runs his hands up and down her body from behind, stopping to tug on each of her nipples.

"Gotta open up those legs so Moto can eat you out while I fuck you," he murmurs loud enough for me to hear.

He grips the back of her thighs, bringing her legs up and out so her feet are now resting on his thighs. I almost nut on the spot seeing her tight cunt full of Sly's long dick, her arousal dripping down onto his balls.

"I want this image tattooed into my brain," I say, walking over slowly, taking my time to admire this scene before sinking to my knees.

I lick a path from his heavy sack up the side of where they're joined, stopping when I reach her swollen and needy clit. I flick that little bud over and over with the tip of my tongue, loving the pleasure-filled sounds coming from her.

Sly tilts his hips, his movements small and slow, but coupled with my oral attention, are enough to drive her to the brink of orgasm. Her hands weave into my hair, fisting it as she pulls me closer to her center. I love the way she smells, like a mix of sex and soap. It's a heady combination that I inhale deeply.

I cup Sly's balls, rolling them in my palm as I lick her, while my other hand snakes up her body to knead and massage her tits. Sly curses, and her moans intensify. I don't know how Sly is holding onto his control. I'm not sure I could if I were in his position.

"I'm coming," she mewls, her toes curling and her head falling back to rest on Sly's shoulder, making her back arch as she shoves her gorgeous tits in the air.

I flutter my tongue against her clit faster, and Sly speeds

up his movements. He can't give her the long strokes she's used to, but he makes up for it with short, fast ones.

"I can feel your pussy spasming around me, baby. Fuck, it's so good," Sly says.

My cock throbs, knowing what it feels like to be in his position. Her cunt is straight up heaven.

We carry her through her release until she collapses, boneless, legs falling down the side of Sly's, as I pull away. She's fuckin' stunning like this, her creamy skin flushed red, little strands of her black hair plastered to her dewy brow, and a satiated smile on her beautiful red lips.

Sly nuzzles her ear. "Ready for more?"

She nods eagerly and lifts off him, causing Sly's cock to slap against his stomach when they disconnect. It's nearly purple from all the blood flow that's rushed south, proving how much restraint he used to not blow inside her.

"You gonna last, old man?" I kid before taking him into my mouth, sucking all of Dove's juices off him.

"I'm only four years older than you," he says, his voice deep and throaty.

I release him with a pop. "A lot can happen in four years."

He jokingly pushes me away with a hand to my forehead. "Get on the bed."

I lie down, waiting to see what his next instructions are, and knowing that whatever he's conjured up in his filthy head will be good for all three of us.

My trust in him goes deeper than our mutual pleasure. It's woven into me right along with my DNA. That man could lead me straight to hell, and I wouldn't question it.

"You next, Dove." He slaps her ass, making her jump and let out a squeal. "I want to see you sit on his fat cock."

She stands straddled over me, giving me a brief view of her puffy, wet pussy lips. My tongue craves more even though her essence is still on my tastebuds.

Lowering to her knees, she grips me at the base and sinks down, sheathing me in her tight heat.

"Fucking hell, your pussy is so tight," I groan, trying to think of anything other than how good she feels. Now that I've ribbed Sly about almost becoming a two-pump chump, I can't come before him. We're both competitive by nature, which doesn't go away during sex. Sometimes our fucking will last for hours with us trying to outlast the other.

Sly kneels on the bed behind her, settling between my legs. He places a hand between her shoulders and eases her forward so her breasts are pressed against my chest, and we're eye-to-eye. Those brown eyes that were dull for so many months, now sparkle bright.

"Kiss me," I breathe out, and she leans in, her soft lips moving against mine, our slick tongues sliding together. I love the harsh, teeth-clattering, forceful kisses I share with Sly just as much as I love Dove's sweet and smooth ones.

Now that she's in position, I see Sly's vision. All foreplay is over, and we're heading into the main event. Thank fuck because my balls are near bursting.

The lube cap pops open, and Dove pulls away slightly, her warm breath dusting across my cheek. She lets out a sigh of pleasure at what I can only imagine is Sly rimming her back entrance.

"This ass can handle my fingers with Moto's cock buried in your pussy," Sly says. "Now let's find out if it can handle my cock."

Her brows furrow, her lips purse, and her eyes squeeze shut. I don't have to see what's going on to know Sly's working himself into her tight hole.

"Open your eyes and look at me," I demand.

They flutter open, but her face is still scrunched in discomfort. This will never work if she doesn't relax.

"I'm so fuckin' proud of you right now, Dove. But you gotta relax so he doesn't hurt you. Can you do that for me?" I tuck her hair behind her ears and stroke her cheek with the back of my hand. My touch calms her, and the muscles in her face go slack. "There's my good girl."

I can't see shit but holy hell, do I feel it through the thin tissue separating us. Sly's mushroom head pushes in, pressing along the side of my length. My eyes roll back into my head as Dove becomes impossibly tighter, packed full of our cocks.

My first job in this is to check in with Dove and make sure she's okay, but I give myself this one selfish moment to just feel. And fuck me, I'm feeling a lot. My dick begs to speed things up, fuck the shit out of this woman and get myself off. If it were a club whore, that's what we'd do. It makes me an asshole, but it's what they sign up for. They know they'll be ridden hard and get off on that.

But Dove is no club whore; she's our everything. I blink my eyes back into focus. Dove's gaze is on me, her lips parted and her chest heaving.

"You okay?" I ask.

"Better than okay." She grins, biting her bottom lip. Fuck, that's sexy. "Ready for more."

"Thank God." Sly's voice is pained, and I know he's feeling every bit as good as I am.

He moves, setting a slow and dizzying pace that I try and mimic. When he pulls out, I push in, making sure to put the least amount of strain on her body. Sly's balls brush against mine with every thrust, and goddamn, does it turn me on.

"You're so fuckin' amazing, taking us both like this," Sly murmurs, picking up the pace.

"Yes. Oh my God, yes," Dove breathes out.

"You want more, baby?" he asks.

"Yes. Give it to me. I want everything you have."

I hear a slap, and Dove moans in a feral tone I've never heard from her before. I run a hand up her side, over her shoulder, and fist the hair at the back of her nape while the other hand grips her hip tight. Using her for purchase, I thrust into her fast and hard. I fall out of sync with Sly, but she seems to enjoy the building frenzy.

Dove's hard nipples brush back and forth against my chest with every thrust, and the added sensation only fuels my need to fuck her without abandon. Tugging on her hair, I tilt her head back and latch onto her neck, biting and sucking her sweet flesh.

Her pleasured moans grow louder until she screams non-sensically, completely blissed out. My name, Sly's name, Jesus himself; it all flies out of her mouth. Goblin will definitely have something to say about this tomorrow.

"We're going to fill your ass and pussy so full of cum, baby. Do you want that? Do you want our cum?" Sly grunts out.

I watch Dove's response to his dirty words, relishing in the way her pupils blow wide, her brows furrow, and then she calls out, "Yes! Oh, God. I'm coming!"

She clamps down on my cock, her body becoming rigid and her nails digging into the back of my neck. Ah, fuck. It's too good, too tight, too much. I lose myself to the sensations and come right along with her. My balls draw up, and I blow inside her, exploding with overwhelming pleasure like I've never felt before. Like I never thought possible.

"Shit," Sly curses, low and throaty. He's coming too.

It's a trifecta of pleasure. All three of us chase our release and find it in each other for one solid minute of mind-blowing gratification.

The fever slowly cools, and the room becomes quiet. The only sounds are our panting breaths. Dove's body falls heavy on mine, and I wrap my arms around her waist, holding her tight to me.

"You good?" I ask.

"So good," she says sleepily.

"Get over here, Moto. Let's watch the cum drip from this gorgeous pussy and ass."

Dove rolls her eyes. "Really?"

"Hell yeah." I release her, wincing as I pull out of her tight heat.

Despite her sass, she cooperates and keeps her ass high up in the air, holding herself there while I slide from under her. Sly's pearly cum drips from her ass, mixing with mine from her pussy before dripping down to the bedding. It'll have to be changed before we can sleep, but I don't give a fuck because this is the sexiest thing I've ever seen.

I drag a finger from her back hole down to her messy cunt, swirling it around before pushing it back in. How much can an IUD really work? Good enough to withstand two men filling her with our cum every day, sometimes multiple times a day?

"That won't work, you dirty fuck," Sly says, giving my ass a squeeze.

"It might."

Chapter
TWENTY-TWO

Petra

I stare at my reflection, still dazed from last night.

That was the best sex of my life, which says a lot because lately, we've had some pretty intense fucking. But none of it even compared to this. I'm pretty sure I blacked out at one point. If women knew how good sex could be with two men, monogamy would be a thing of the past.

I've never felt more cherished, more worshipped in all my life. My chest warms with all the love I feel for my men. Lucky doesn't even begin to explain how I feel.

"Petra, you're up next, and you're not even dressed." Roxy breaks my trance. I shake my head and blink rapidly.

"Sorry." I shake out my curls and jump to my feet.

Roxy follows me to my locker and sits on the bench as I strip out of my sweats.

"What did those bikers do to you to put that look on your face?" she asks, and I grin. "Ooh, spill all the dirty secrets."

"I don't have time now, but I'll tell you all about it after I get off stage." I pull on the brand new one-piece I purchased last week. It's a neon yellow sheer bodysuit with a cutout that stretches from just under my breasts to right above my pussy, exposing my abdomen. It has two ties, one at my neck and one at the middle of my back. The back cuts into a thong, but there's a belt of holographic fringe that hangs over my butt cheeks. "What do you think?"

Roxy stands and turns me in a circle. "Where did you get this? It's gorgeous."

"It's handmade off some crafter's website I found." I push into my sky-high clear heels.

"This fringe will catch the lights and sparkle beautifully. I love it."

"Thanks," I say, darting off to the backstage area.

"Wait. You forgot makeup."

I pause, running through the last twenty minutes. I know I applied eyeshadow, eyeliner, and lipstick and put on my foundation, blush, and contour. What did I miss?

Roxy catches up to me, makeup compact in hand. "Your thighs."

I look down and see my scars on full display. "Shit. I don't have time."

"So leave them. I doubt anyone will see, and even if they do, so what? They're part of you."

The only people I've let see those scars are her, Moto, and Sly. Covering them up is usually the first step when I get ready. I can't believe I forgot.

"I guess I don't have a choice." I shrug, surprised not to feel my usual anxiety about hiding them. I guess this is what happens when you're with someone—or someones, in my case—who makes you feel like you're the most perfect woman to walk this earth.

Not giving myself time to doubt my decision and hearing my name announced on the speaker, I take a deep breath and stride on stage the second I hear the first note of my song.

I've been working on a pole routine and tonight is the first time I'm performing it. Don't get me wrong, it's not as difficult as what Roxy and the other girls perform, but I'm proud of how far I've come. I know I look good doing the basic moves.

There's a huge crowd tonight. I heard one of the girls mention the National Paper Association has some big convention downtown. Apparently, they decided to spice up their lives by coming here tonight.

I flow through the dance, the music moving through me. The cheers and applause from the crowd spur me on, encouraging me to put on a show. My ass pops out a little higher, my breasts shake a little more, and I make eye contact with each of the men and the one woman sitting in the chairs directly below the stage.

I know my men are out there watching, getting off on the fact that all these people are staring at me with desire in their eyes. My clit throbs knowing what this is doing to them, knowing what they'll do to me later. At thirty-one years old, I'm having a sexual reawakening.

I'm nearly to the end—the part where I crawl across the stage and shove each of my assets in the faces of those lucky enough to get the prime seats—when my stomach sinks and goosebumps spread across my skin.

Not the same ones that Moto and Sly give me when they're worshipping my pussy, the kind that tells me something is off.

I fall on my hands and knees like I'm supposed to, but my eyes search further into the crowd. He's here. I can't see him, but I know he's here.

When I find Moto and Sly, my intuition is confirmed. Their mouths are set in a firm line, jaws clenched tight, and arms folded across their chests. Instead of their gazes on me, they're staring out toward the back of the room.

I follow their line of sight until I see him. My stomach sinks, and for a second, I think I might throw up. I get the urge to run but fight it off. Sly ran through this scenario over and over with me. I know what I'm supposed to do.

"Don't let him know you see him. Keep dancing, and let us handle the rest."

But talking about it and living it are two separate things.

I take a breath and continue my routine, managing to crawl around the stage, letting the customers slip bills into the belt of fringe. Their fingers graze my ass, lingering for as long as it takes for me to pass by. It's a cheap thrill that drives them crazy and has them digging into their pockets to pull out more money for the chance to do it again.

Usually, this is my favorite part—my guys getting off on watching how much I turn other people on. And I do too. But tonight feels perfunctory and robotic. Moto and Sly are focused elsewhere, and I'm not in this for the money.

The second the music stops, I jump to my feet and dash offstage as fast as my heels allow. Ford is waiting for me, holding open my robe and helping me in it.

"He's here," I say.

"I know, but it's okay. We got you." He passes me off to Roxy.

"I'm here, girl." She wraps an arm around my shaking body.

I don't keep secrets from her. She's the one person I've divulged every painful detail to, other than Moto and Sly. She walks me over to my locker and sits me down on the bench.

"What do we do?" I fold forward, placing my head in my hands. We've been over this, but my mind is blank, my heart is racing, and I might puke.

Ford sits down next to me. "Deep breaths. We've got this place covered. There's no escaping, and tonight, you'll get your answers."

Roxy claims the spot on the other side of me and rubs a hand up and down my back. "It worked, babe. He came, and now your guys will get him."

"No, there's something wrong. It doesn't feel right." I can't explain it. This doesn't feel like the end.

"That's your nerves talking. You'll see. By the end of the night, this will all be over," Roxy says.

Except she's wrong because the power to the building shuts off, and we're suddenly plunged into darkness. The other dancers squeal, and I hear shouts coming from the club. I sit upright, clamping a hand down on Roxy's thigh and Ford's knee, tethering them to me.

"It's fine. The generators will kick on in a minute. This doesn't mean anything," Ford says. But they're wrong again because gunshots sound from inside the club.

There shouldn't be gunshots. That wasn't part of the plan. They were supposed to take him, load him in the van, and get him to the clubhouse. That was the plan.

"What if . . .?" I can't finish my question. Giving a voice to my fears will make them real, but it doesn't stop the question from flashing through my mind.

What if one of my guys got hit? What if one of them is lying on the floor bleeding out?

"You have to go," I say to Ford.

"No. I was given clear instructions. Stay with you and protect you with my life. That's what I'm going to do."

"Please," I beg. "They need you."

"No. Sly called Khan, Loki, and Goblin in the second he saw Tyler. Way before you went on stage. That's why Moto and Sly were waiting to act. The second the others showed up, they were taking him down. Plus, we have our security team out there."

The room lights up in a red glow, confusing me.

"What's going on?" I ask.

"The generators. They aren't meant to power the place, just light things up enough to get everyone out safely," Ford says.

More gunshots sound, and screams come from the club. Oh, God. My teeth chatter, and my entire body shakes. The emergency lights do little to settle my nerves. Instead, the ominous red glow unnerves me and reminds me of a horror flick.

"I can go," Roxy suggests.

"No," Ford and I say in unison.

"Why not? Tyler doesn't know me. I'm just another dancer."

"It's too dangerous. I need to know you're safe." Ford's gaze on her is fierce, and it hits me just how close he and Roxy are now.

"I'll be right back." She stands and darts for the door. Ford takes off after her, but despite her heels, she's quick and through the door before he can stop her. He glances back at me, his expression showing the war going on in his mind. It's either the club or his girl. Which will he choose?

In the end, he lets her leave, knowing he's a dead man walking if anything happens to me. He's patched in, a full member, but Moto and Sly hold a position of power, and to defy direct orders is a death sentence. A Royal Bastard's loyalty always falls to the club first.

"Motherfucker," he shouts, kicking the door closed with his heavy boot. I jump at the outburst, and tears spring free.

"I'm sorry," I cry.

He runs a hand over his head, muttering something under his breath before setting back on the bench. "Not your fault."

There's a loud commotion going on out there, people shouting and trying to escape the mayhem. All while we sit here in utter silence. The other girls have crowded against the far side of the room, awaiting instruction, knowing this is the safest place. They have no idea what's going on out there, and I feel terrible for being the reason they'll have nightmares about this night for a long time.

I didn't consider any of this when we made this plan. I didn't think people would get hurt or worse.

Ford's phone buzzes, and he holds it up to his ear. "Yeah." Pause. "She's good." Pause. "What?" Pause. "Shit."

My anxiety grows with each second, and I wish I could hear what's being said on the other end. Whatever it is isn't good.

"Fucking come and get her. I need to go." Ford's icy tone sends painful shivers through my body. He hangs up and tucks his phone away.

"What happened?" I ask.

"He got away." He stands. "And he took Roxy."

"No!" I wail.

"Goblin's coming to take you to the clubhouse. I need to go find her." He storms toward the door. "He's gone. You're safe. Just wait here, okay?"

"Ford," I call out, not feeling safe at all but knowing if anyone will get her back, it's him. "Bring her home."

"I will." It's more than a promise; it's an oath. I know it as much as I know the sky is blue. Royal Bastards don't say anything they don't mean.

I kick off my ridiculous heels and draw my knees to my chest, making myself as small as possible. I know what it means when Tyler takes you, and just the thought of Roxy suffering the way I did makes my skin crawl. This is all my fault. I should've left it alone. I was free. My friends were safe. I had my guys.

Now none of that is true, and it's all because I wanted revenge. What a fool I am.

"Darlin'?" Goblin approaches, startling me.

I didn't even hear the door open, too lost in my downward spiral.

"We gotta go, okay?" He sets a hand on my shoulder.

"No. I want to go help."

"That's not safe."

I stand, wiping my nose with the back of my arm. "If he's in the wind, we need everyone looking for him."

He shakes his head. "Can't do that. Moto and Sly need to know you're safe so they can focus. Only way they can do that is if you're somewhere Tyler can't touch you."

Even knowing he's right, I don't want to agree. My friend's out there, and every second counts.

"I abandoned a friend to Tyler years ago, and now she's God knows where. I can't do it again."

"I get that, darlin'. I really do. But you didn't have us out there looking for either of you back then."

"Goblin, please," I beg, knowing I don't stand a chance if I can't get him to agree.

"Do you trust Moto and Sly?" he asks.

"Of course." That's a stupid question because they're some of the few people in this world I trust implicitly.

"Then let me take you home."

Chapter
TWENTY-THREE

Sly

"**M**otherfucker!" I curse as I chase the black Audi R8 out of town, Moto, Loki, and Khan hot on my heels. How the fuck did this happen? We thought of everything. Each exit had security detail with orders to not let him escape, and our new hires weren't your average bouncers. We hired trained men, either ex-military or ex-law enforcement. He shouldn't have escaped.

Moto and I had almost reached him toward the back of the club when the power shut off. But that shouldn't have mattered. We knew he wouldn't come alone since he showed up at the clubhouse with security. But again, it shouldn't have fucking mattered.

Unless there was a rat. My fists tighten around my grips. I researched every person we hired, but everyone has a price, and I'll bet my left nut one of the outsiders was a cheap date.

"Where is he going?" Loki asks in my ear.

"No fuckin' clue." I mentally scan through all the information I collected on this guy, trying to pinpoint where he could be headed. He has property out in Washoe Valley. He could be taking us there. If he is, this is likely a setup, and we're driving straight into a trap.

When he takes the Eastlake Boulevard exit, my suspicions are confirmed, and now I need to decide how much I want this fucker. We all carry, but we're not prepared to take on whatever army Tyler has waiting for us.

"It's a setup," I say warily. Loki will no doubt call an end to this chase, and I'll be forced to tell Dove that Roxy is gone. "He's taking us to his property."

"We're getting out of here," Loki says, and his headlights get smaller in my side-view mirror, telling me he's slowing down. "I mean it, Sly. We're not doing this until we have a plan."

I'm glad he's not shutting me down completely, but I still don't want to see the look in Dove's eyes when I tell her we had to leave Roxy with Tyler for now. She'll be devastated and likely angry. Moto and I reassured her repeatedly that we had this handled and there was nothing to worry about.

We were wrong.

"Turn the fuck around, Sly. I mean it." Loki rarely pulls rank, only putting us in our place when it endangers the club.

I slow, noting Moto right behind me, waiting to see what I'll do, and I'm almost pissed to know he'd choose me over Prez. It's a stupid decision, one that would get him killed. Our brothers would die for us, but they'd also put a bullet in the back of our heads if we betrayed the club. It's not shocking; I'd do the same thing. We're nothing without our loyalty.

I make a U-turn and pull onto the shoulder where Loki and Khan are already parked. A van pulls up, and a crazed Ford pops his head out of the window.

"What are we doing?" he asks.

"Going back to the clubhouse. This was an ambush, and we're not prepared. We need a plan," I say, knowing he won't take this well.

"Fuck that. He has Roxy."

"If we follow him to his property, we're all dead. Including Roxy," Loki says.

"She's innocent," he snarls, and I recognize that look. It's the same one Loki had when Birdie was taken and again when Truly was taken from Roch. Our brother has staked a claim on that girl whether or not she knows it.

"We'll get her back. We just need a plan," I reason. Now that the adrenaline of the chase is fading, reason is setting in. Loki was right.

Ford's fist slams against the steering wheel. "Fuck!"

"We'll get her back, brother," Khan grumbles. "But we need to be smart."

Knowing we'll follow, Loki takes off in the direction we just came from without another word. And like the good soldiers we are, we follow.

"No!" Dove cries, slamming into my chest and pounding a fist on my shoulder. "No, no, no."

I rub her back and whisper reassurances while Moto stands close by, hands tucked in his pockets. He was raised to not express emotion, and while he's worked on that through the years, strong feelings still make him uncomfortable.

"She's not gone forever, I swear it," I say.

"You don't know that." She hiccups from crying, her tears soaking through my T-shirt. "If he sees value in her, he'll sell her. I know he will."

I glance at Moto, who gives me a nod, telling me I need to be honest with her.

"I do know that." I wince before revealing the thing she hasn't thought about yet. "She's his only leverage."

Her head lifts up, and those brown eyes that have been so

bright lately are dimmed. I'll kill that motherfucker with my bare hands for turning her back into the fragile girl she was when we first found her. "What do you mean?"

"He wants you, not her, and the only way to get you is to have something you want. He called me on the way back here and offered a trade."

Even I wasn't expecting this turn of events. I didn't know how far Tyler would take this. Sure, I knew he was mildly worried about her going to the authorities, but she's been free for months and hasn't reported her abuse. A fact I thought would clue him in that she had no intention of ever doing so.

Once Dove was clear-minded, her mind went straight to revenge and finding Mia. She never once considered reporting what happened.

It makes sense because you quickly realize how useless law enforcement is once you're exposed to the dark and seedy part of life. It's not the cops who saved her. It was an outlaw biker gang and us she turned to when she wanted answers and retribution.

"What?" Her voice cracks.

Moto takes a small step closer. "He's willing to trade you for Roxy."

"How does he even know Roxy means anything to us?"

"We didn't realize the lengths he'd go to," I say, lowering my head in shame. "He had to be watching you this whole time."

"Then let's do it." She wipes the sadness from her face with the sleeves of my RBMC hoodie she has on.

"Not a fuckin' chance," Moto growls, beating me to the punch.

"You don't understand. I can't lose another friend. I can't be responsible for someone else going through what I went through."

"This isn't on you, Dove. None of it is. Tyler's the only one accountable," I say.

"This is my choice, my life. Call him back and make the trade."

A rock forms in my gut, and I know I'm treading in dangerous waters. We can't take away her control and force her to do things our way. If we do, we'll lose her forever. That being said, we will never hand her over to that asshole. Not ever. No matter what she says.

"Listen to me," I say, bending at the waist to meet her stormy eyes. "We will get Roxy back. Tyler has no clue who the fuck he's messing with."

She shakes her head. "No. I can't risk it. Call him. Make the trade."

"He's not an honorable man, Dove. He won't follow through, and then both of you will suffer," Moto says.

"It's the safest option."

"No, it's not. The safest option is to keep you here and let us handle it," I plead, though it's all for show. The decision has been made, and a plan has been formed.

Granted, there isn't much to it. Gather our weapons and storm his property, killing on sight until we find where Tyler is hiding.

His hired guns risk their lives for an easy paycheck, leaving them with a whole lotta self-preservation still intact. We risk our lives for honor, brotherhood, and loyalty, meaning we fight to the death and do it with pride. They're no match for the Royal Bastards.

I can't tell her this, though. It's a conclusion she has to come to on her own. I don't want to think about what will happen if she doesn't go along with our plan because we're willing to stop at nothing to keep her safe. We just don't want to suffer the consequences of that. She'd hate us, and I don't think we'd ever get her back.

Dove paces the room, her hand clamped on her forehead as she thinks. I don't know what else to say to get her to understand. We're nothing without her, so if we have to take this guy down to keep her safe, that's what we'll do. And there's no doubt in my mind that we'll do it.

Moto steps into her path and cups her cheeks, tilting her face up to look at him. "Do you trust us?"

"You know I do."

"Then there shouldn't be a choice. Let us handle this."

"Okay. But if it comes down to it, promise me you'll let me do this."

No. Not a chance. Never.

"I promise."

It's the first lie he's told her, and I know it crushes him to do it. Before we sought her out waiting in her room, Loki called church, and we talked through everything. None of the scenarios we ran through ever put Dove back in Tyler's path, and they never would.

Moto kisses her, showing her how happy she's made him by backing down while I watch. My dick hardens when I see his tongue slip inside her mouth and how receptive she is when she lets out a small moan. Sometimes watching can be more of a turn-on than doing for me.

When I'm the one pleasuring her, I can't see the different ways her body responds; I can only feel them. So, I grab the back of her vanity chair and spin it around, taking a seat.

"Moto," she says in protest, her mind still reeling from everything that happened tonight.

"Nothing can be done tonight," he says with his lips pressed to her neck. "So let me make you forget. For just a little while, then I promise I'll stay up all night worrying with you."

"I don't know if I can. I'm so upset."

He backs her up to the bed until she has no choice but to sit. "Lie back and let me try."

She chews on the inside of her mouth, unsure. Until Moto strips his shirt off, and she scoots back, resting her head on the pillow. I don't fuckin' blame her. Moto's body is perfection. Thick, hard, tanned, and powerful.

Her head lifts, and she seeks me out. "What about you?"

"I'm happy where I'm at," I say.

"You're just going to watch?" Her scandalized look makes me laugh. How she's so innocent after everything we've done is beyond me, but it makes me hard as granite to see.

"I am. Better put on a good show."

She rolls her eyes, but then Moto drops his pants, stealing both our attention. He climbs in and straddles her, completely unashamed of his nudity. Pulling her to sitting, he lifts the hoodie up and over her head. Her dark nipples are puckered, and Moto wastes no time sucking one into his mouth.

I pop the button of my jeans and push them and my boxers down past my ass, setting my cock free. Taking myself in hand, I stroke up and down slowly, content to watch as Moto's hand slips under the waistband of Dove's sweats. Her back arches the second he makes contact with her clit.

"Always so wet for us," he murmurs, but it's muffled by the tip of her nipple pinched between his teeth.

"Please. I need you." Her hand skims down his back and settles on his ass.

He moves between her legs and kisses across her chest, between her breasts, and down her stomach, all while palming her perky breasts. He continues on, pulling her sweats down as he goes but doesn't go right to her pussy. Instead, he goes left, kissing down her leg.

Once the sweats are off, he playfully tosses them in my direction. They land at my feet, and I bend over to snag her panties. They're pink and made of silk and lace, perfect for what I want. I wrap them around my cock and jerk myself, loving the feel of the fabric on my sensitive skin.

I hope she's not attached to this thong because I'm about to destroy it.

He kisses up her inner thigh, heading right for her scars. Ever since she showed them to us, we pay extra attention there, trying our damndest to kiss away all the hurt.

She loosens the hair tie holding his ponytail in place until his long mane spills free. It's something both of us do every chance we get. His long hair is sexy as fuck. She weaves her hands into it, holding onto the sides of his head as he makes his way to where she wants him most.

I don't have a good vantage point from here, so I stand and move the chair to the side of the bed. Dove glances over but is too lost in the magic Moto is performing between her legs to be shy.

"Tell me how it feels," I demand.

"Warm and silky, and when he pinches my clit, a spike of pleasure shoots through me." Her voice is breathy and low.

Moto slips a finger inside, and she gasps, her hips grinding against his face. This clearly aroused him because the sound of his heavy inhales and exhales fills the room. It's the soundtrack of pure sex.

"Come for me, baby. I want to watch you lose yourself," I say, and she does.

"Oh, God. Moto," she cries out.

Her face scrunches, and her eyes close. Her head tips back, digging into the mattress and exposing her swanlike neck covered in red spots from Moto sucking and biting her there. She's so goddamn sexy.

Eventually, her body relaxes, and she lets out a content sigh, a smile crossing her lips. Moto sits up, his lips and chin glistening with her arousal. Unable to stop myself, I stand and grip him by the back of the neck. Planting open mouth kisses along his jaw and up his chin, I suck her juices off him, savoring her taste. I dip my tongue into his mouth, taking all that I can.

After getting my fill, I return to my seat and wait to see what he'll do next.

"Is it wrong that I get so turned on when I see you together?" she asks, a little sheepish.

"Fuck no. Unless you think it's wrong that I get hard sitting back and watching you and him." I take myself in hand and stroke, squeezing when I get to the tip, producing a pearl of pre-cum.

"Are those my panties?"

"Yup."

She giggles, but it's cut short when Moto drives into her in one forceful thrust. Her mouth drops open, and her attention returns to him. Her pelvis tilts up, ensuring each thrust in will hit her G-spot. She's gotten much more daring since the first time we fucked, trying new things and taking control of her own pleasure. It's an incredible turn-on.

"Look at this pretty pussy taking my fat cock." Moto spreads her outer lips, exposing her clit and the spot where they're joined. His thumb strums the swollen bud, driving her wild.

The base of my spine tingles, and I know I'm going to blow . . . and fuckin' soon.

Moto snakes his arms under her lower back, lifting her and spinning around so she's on top. She doesn't miss a beat, getting situated on her knees.

"I want to watch these tits bounce," he says, pinching a nipple.

She likes being on top but can only get off if she grinds. I know firsthand how good it feels for her to move back and forth, rubbing her clit along my length as she does. Just the memory of that has my balls tightening, bringing me one step closer to orgasm.

"Oh God. Feels so good." With her hands on Moto's stomach for purchase, she works herself back up, quickly bringing herself to another orgasm. She throws her head back, her long hair brushing her ass, and fuck me if it isn't the most magnificent thing I've ever seen.

My hand works fast and furious. The silky thong rubbing my length so good. I stand and move to Moto, who greedily opens his mouth. My cum shoots out, landing on his tongue and chin. His eyes go wild with lust. Watching us both get off has brought him to the brink.

He lifts up on Dove's hips, holding her in place so he can fuck her from below. His abdominal muscles ripple from the exertion, and his face screws up tight in concentration. I reach over and fondle Dove's breasts while we watch with rapt attention. The sound of him slapping his flesh against Dove's fills the silence, nearly getting me hard all over again.

"Gonna put my cum so deep inside you," he grits out, thrusting up one last time and holding himself there for long minutes. "Fuck me, that was good."

Chapter
TWENTY-FOUR

Moto

"Please be careful," Dove says, arms around my neck and lifting on her toes to give me a kiss. No better send-off than this woman in my arms and knowing I'm going into this with the man I love.

"I will."

She steps to my side where Sly stands, giving him the same. "You too, and take care of each other."

"We will, baby," he promises.

"I don't like this. I want to go with you."

"Not happening," I say. "Stay here with the women, and we'll be back before you know it."

"That's the most sexist thing you've ever said to me."

"Sometimes it's like that. Can't change it."

She sighs but kisses me again. "Please come back to me in one piece."

"Even if I don't, I know a doctor who can fix me up." I grab a handful of her ass.

"Not funny."

"Let's ride," Loki calls out.

"Time to go. Give me one last kiss," Sly says, but because he's Sly, he grabs her by the back of the thighs and lifts her up, her legs wrapping around him. "Love you."

"Love you too." They kiss, and just the sight has me wanting to delay this outing and go back to bed. But we arranged this trade with Tyler for an hour from now, and it'll take that long to get out to the middle of fuckin' nowhere and prepare.

Sly drops her to her feet, and we slap our domes on before mounting our bikes. I take one last glance back. I remember when Sissy and Tabs were the only ones standing outside to send us off. Now there's a line of women. Birdie, Bexley, Riley, and now Dove stand shoulder to shoulder with Truly and Roch off to the side. Since Truly's about to pop any minute, we all thought it best Roch stayed behind. He wasn't happy about it, but his ol' lady was giving him shit, too, so he eventually agreed.

Loki leads the way, and we follow, Ford driving the van behind us. In it are all our weapons. Long guns, grenades, basically everything we could get our hands on. We're prepared for everything, and during church, we talked through every scenario we could think of, including not doing anything at all.

Ford wasn't hearing any of it. He and Roxy formed a quick bond over the last couple of weeks while he was assigned protective duty over Dove. I can't say shit about it because things were pretty fast with Dove. I'm not sure if what they're feeling is the forever kind of thing like it is with Sly and Dove, but time will tell.

Besides that, the world will be a better place without Tyler, and Dove will sleep better knowing he's been sent to Hades. With any luck, we'll get a nice, long conversation with him first because we have questions that need answering. There's another asshole out there that deserves to die right along with him. Without Tyler's help, we'll never know his identity.

Then there's Mia. I have a sinking suspicion she's not on this earth anymore, but in order for Dove to move on, we need to know, and Tyler's the only one who can give us that information.

Before I know it and before my thoughts have time to settle, we're nearing the coordinates Tyler sent us. He thinks we're bringing Dove for a trade. We showed all our cards by protecting her the way we did. If we'd been smart about it, we would've continued making him think she was just a club whore. He might've even let her stay with us. But from the very first time he laid eyes on her, we made it clear she was ours. And that made her a threat.

We park at the entrance to the long dirt road that'll lead us to Tyler. We need a minute to scout things out and prepare. Northern Nevada is high desert, meaning there're plenty of cacti and lots of dirt but also mountains, hills, and trees. It's a unique terrain, but it's better than what they have near Vegas, where it's flat, and there's nowhere to hide.

"The coordinates are ten miles that way." Loki points in the direction of the road. "Sly, I want you and Coyote to ride as close as you can, then park and find good vantage points to set up. Ford, you know what to do."

Ford nods. He's in charge of grabbing Roxy and making sure she stays safe. Hopefully the second the shots start ringing, she'll be the least of their worries. Sly and Coyote are near-perfect shots, so it makes sense to have them hike in and take aim from whatever hill or tree they can find.

"Goblin, Moto, and Miles will ride in the back of the van. The second those doors open, it's open season. Me, Khan, and Duncan will be on the front line, doing what we can to get Tyler. Our main goal is to take him alive, but if it's a choice between any of us or him, you know what to do."

It would suck to go through all this and still not get answers, but sending him to Hades isn't the worst outcome, so we'll take it.

"I want all of you whole after this, you hear me?" Loki makes the demand as though getting shot is a choice, but we all nod anyway. "Okay, load up."

Sly and Coyote grab sniper rifles and head out, but not before Sly grabs the back of my neck and plants a firm kiss on my lips. I'm still not comfortable showing affection in front of my brothers but knowing there's a very real chance it could be our last has me putting every ounce of emotion into that quick press of his lips.

"See you soon," he says, and I nod.

The rest of us take turns selecting our weapons of choice. I grab a long gun and a grenade. If they get the upper hand, it's the easiest way to take out a group of them in one toss. Throwing extra ammo in my pocket, I step aside and let the others take what they want.

"All right, it's go time," Loki calls out.

I leave my new bike parked and climb into the van, hoping like hell it's not the last time I get to ride it. I was attached to my last girl, but she was giving me more problems than she solved, so those backward hillbillies really did me a favor. My new girl is sleek and modern, and the only time I have to work on her is when I want to upgrade parts or change her oil.

Goblin and Miles get in after me, and Ford gets behind the wheel. He leads this time since the van will give the other guys cover if they need it, and at the very least, it'll protect their bikes.

Those ten miles are the longest of my life, anticipation and adrenaline coursing through my body. It's the same feeling you get when you're on a rollercoaster climbing up and up. Each second feels like an hour, and the longer it takes to reach that peak, the more your stomach bottoms out, and you feel like you might throw up.

But the second the van comes to a stop, my mind clears, and I focus on the job at hand. I'm doing this for Dove, so she can move on with a clear conscience and a peaceful mind. She deserves that more than anyone in this world, and I'll fight like hell to give it to her.

I hear some talking, but we stay low so Tyler's men can't see us. For all he knows, Dove is sitting in here, ready to be handed over. Still not sure what his plan for her is. Maybe he'll sell her again, or maybe he'll put a bullet in her head the second he sees her. Either way, it doesn't matter. She's back at the club being protected by Roch, his pack of dogs, and three hang arounds looking to prospect.

"Hand her over, and we'll do the same of Petra," Loki says.

Petra. The name everyone calls her, but I never will. It's what *they* called her. I'll never know how she hears it every day and doesn't think about how she came to it. Maybe she'll want to go by Cameron again once this is over. The name suits her, but to me and Sly, she'll always be our Dove. A bird that symbolizes hope, strength, and renewed purpose.

I can't hear Tyler's reply, but Loki doesn't like it.

"Nah, man. It's not gonna work like that. I don't know you, and therefore, I don't trust you," Loki says in a cool tone that gives nothing away. "We'll let you see her, but you're not touching her until Roxy is handed over."

This is it.

The doors haven't even slid open all the way before I hear shots ring out. I jump out of the van, my long gun already in position to fire. The first asshole I see in black gets a bullet to his face. It explodes into a gory mess, his body frozen upright by muscle memory for a long second before collapsing to the ground.

My eyes home in on Tyler, who isn't all that surprised by what's happening but scared all the same. He darts toward one of the trucks he rode in on, somehow avoiding all the shots flying his way. Loki and Khan use the van as a shield and are distracted by men perched on the hill, firing at them, so I know this is up to me.

I run behind the back of the van, peering out to make sure the coast is clear before taking off after Tyler. I push the long gun back and reach for my Glock. A bullet whizzes past my head, and I see a man in black with his gun aimed at me. Before I can return fire, his head jerks to the side, and he crumples to the ground.

I shoot a quick glance to my left and can barely make out the top of Sly's head and the black barrel of his sniper rifle. He's for sure getting head tonight for that one.

From what I can tell, we're all still whole and seem to be wiping this place clean of all Tyler's men. It's too bad it had to happen like this. I'm sure they're here for the paycheck and would gladly turncoat if we could have a conversation with them. But they picked protecting a fuckin' monster, and for that, they'll pay.

Before I can reach the truck, I spot Ford running up the driver's side. He's not supposed to be here. He had one job, and that was to protect Roxy. If she gets hurt in all this, it's on him for not listening to orders.

He yanks open the door, gun aimed right at Tyler. But Tyler's prepared, and what I see next will haunt me until the day I die.

"We got you now, asshole." Ford yanks on Tyler's arm, pulling him out of the truck, his hands raised in the air. "Get on the ground, face down."

Ford digs a pair of zip ties out of his pocket and gets down on one knee. This was too easy. There's no way Tyler would facilitate all of this and just give himself up. It doesn't make sense.

Then I see it, the black handle of a knife sheathed underneath Tyler's shirt. My mouth opens to warn Ford, but Tyler has the knife in his hand before any words come out. He rolls to his side and pushes up on one hand, the other stabbing the knife forward into Ford's gut. Then, he twists, a wild snarl on his face.

Ford's eyes go wide, and his mouth drops open, shock

written all over his features. *No. No. Fuck no.* I sprint toward him despite feeling like I just got punched in the gut. I already know there's nothing I can do, but I'm sure as shit going to try.

Tyler isn't expecting me or the boot to the face I gave him, breaking his nose and knocking him out cold. I quickly roll him over and slip the cuffs on him before kneeling next to Ford, who's still confused about what happened.

Blood, so much fuckin' blood, is pouring down the front of him.

"Lie down, bro." I help him to the ground. Shots are still being fired all around us, but they're slowing down. A quick glance around tells me we're the ones left standing, which isn't a shocker.

"Fuck," Ford says. Blood trickles from the corner of his mouth now, and the last shred of hope I had is gone.

"Khan. Loki," I shout, gaining their attention. The second they see us, they come running.

"What the fuck happened?" Loki asks.

"Tyler got him," I say.

"Motherfucker!" Loki yanks the beanie from his head and throws it with the force of a man riddled in pain.

I place my hand on his wound, trying to hold the blood in, but it's no use. "Do we pull it out?"

"No. Keep it there. Let's get him in the van." Loki positions himself at Ford's feet, and I hook my hands under his arms. The second we get him off the ground, he screams. We panic and lower him back down.

"Don't bother," Ford chokes out.

"What do you need, brother?" Khan asks.

"Roxy."

"On it." Khan takes off at a pace a man his size shouldn't be able to reach. Thirty seconds later, Roxy is falling at his side.

"Ford. Babe. It's okay. It's going to be okay. Petra's a doctor, right? She'll fix you up," she says, tears running down her bruised face. Tyler clearly didn't keep his hands to himself. Yet another nail in his coffin.

Ford swallows. "I'm sorry."

"Sorry for what? You have nothing to be sorry for. We're going to get you out of here." Roxy's eyes dart to each of us. "Let's go. We're wasting time."

I look anywhere but at her, not wanting to be the one to tell her the truth.

"My time's up," Ford croaks.

"No." She takes his hand, kissing his bloody knuckles. "We just met."

"Thank you"—Ford coughs, red spittle flying from his mouth—"for making me happy."

She bends over, kissing him despite his gruesome appearance. This is their moment, but I can't look away. Their lips move, and maybe it's not love, but something close to it passes through them. Then Ford's lips go lax, and the rise and fall of his chest stops.

Roxy lets out a sob that I feel to the bottom of my black soul. The sound is something wild and feral and so drenched in pain, I hope I never have to hear it again.

"Come on, darlin'," Loki says, placing a hand on her back.

"Get your fuckin' hands off me," she spits out, jerking away from him.

She lies down next to him, snaking a hand under his head and turning his face to her. She cups his cheek and rests her forehead against his, whispering words meant only for him.

It's then I notice all shots have ceased, and my brothers are standing in a circle around the painful scene. Sly takes my hand, giving it a squeeze. We're not hand holders, but, in this moment, I'm grateful he's here.

This isn't how everything was supposed to go.

Chapter

TWENTY-FIVE

Petra

I read the text over and over, looking for a hidden meaning or clue as to how things went.

Sly: On our way back.

Four words. That's all I have, and not one of them comforts the anxiety coursing through my body. I try to focus on the fact that he texted me at all. That means he's alive. I wish I had confirmation that Moto is alive too.

"Here, sugar. Have some tea." Tabitha hands me a steaming mug that smells of lavender and chamomile.

"Thank you." I hold it to my lips, blowing on the hot liquid before taking a sip. It's my favorite blend, sweetened with the perfect amount of honey.

I don't wonder why she knows how I take my tea. During the first months I was here, she and Sissy helped nurse me back to health. They're the club's caretakers, and even though the thought of either of my guys getting pleasure from these women long before I met them makes my skin crawl, I try not to focus on it.

"This baby is trying to punch their way out of my uterus." Truly stands, looking uncomfortable.

Roch jumps up, placing one hand on her hip and the other on her belly, spanning his fingers wide. "'kay?"

Of all the bikers, Roch intrigues me the most. According to my guys, he experienced something bad while in the Army, and it took away his speech. The most I ever hear him say is one word, and that one word is usually shortened in some way. But Truly always knows what he's saying, most of the time with just a look.

"I'm fine," she winces. "Just Braxton Hicks."

I took a rotation in OB, and I can't tell you how many women came in, positive they were in labor, only to be sent home an hour later after being told it was false labor. While I enjoyed bringing life into this world, it wasn't for me. Too many bodily fluids spewing all over the place. Blood doesn't bother me but vomit and amniotic fluid do.

"Doctor," he says.

She glares up at him. "We talked about this. I want to have this baby at home where all my stuff is and where my dogs are."

He gives her a look that even I understand.

"It's completely safe. We have a midwife who spends more time delivering babies than most doctors do," she says. "Besides, you don't get a vote. You're not the one pushing something the size of a watermelon out a hole the size of a lemon."

He cringes, then kisses her on the temple, effectively backing down like a good partner. *Wise choice.* I think the conversation is over, but then Truly bends forward and lets out a pained cry.

I jump up and rest a hand on her back. "Are you sure they're Braxton Hicks?"

"No."

"Roch, why don't you time these contractions? Let's see where she's at," I say.

"Look, if you're going to pop that baby out right here in this disgusting clubhouse, I'm out of here," Bexley says.

"She's not having the baby here. If her contractions are close, then I'm sure Roch will take her home so she can deliver the way she wants," Birdie reasons, turning to Truly. "What do you need?"

"I don't know. This feels different." Truly places a hand on her brow. "I think—" Her face goes white, and her eyes go wide.

"What's wrong?" I ask.

"I either just peed my pants, or my water broke."

All eyes go to her feet, where there's a puddle. *Oh, crap.*

"Okay, so those aren't Braxton Hicks," I say, my mind running through everything that needs to happen right now.

"Shit," Roch curses.

"Time to make a decision because there's no way you'll make the ride home. We can either call an ambulance, or you can have the baby right here."

"ER." Roch takes her hand and tugs her toward the door, but she digs in her heels, halting them.

"No. I don't want this baby to come into the world and be poked and prodded at. I want my birth to be natural. If it has to happen right here, then it will."

"Give me your phone." Birdie holds out her hand. "I'll call your midwife."

For the last few months, Birdie has taken all the birthing classes right along with Roch and Truly. With Roch being in the club, there's no guarantee he'd be around or even alive, for that matter. These guys live for today and aren't afraid of tomorrow but prepare for it anyway.

Truly hands her the phone, and she steps into the dining room to make the call.

"Are there any rubber sheets lying around here somewhere?" I ask hopefully. It would be a bizarre question except the clubhouse is full of freaks, and you never know what they get into.

"I'll check," Sissy says, running off to look.

"We need some towels, washcloths, alcohol . . . and not the kind you drink," I say, and Tabitha skitters off. "Do you have a diaper bag packed?"

Another contraction hits Truly, and she doubles over. Roch goes white, a stricken expression on his face. He'll be no help to us. Most first-time dads aren't.

"Roch, need you to sit down, okay?" I point to the sofa. "We don't need you passing out on top of everything else."

He shakes his head and swallows hard. "Fine."

It doesn't surprise me. He's a Royal Bastard, and these men make their women their priority in all things.

"Let's move this party to the casita. You still have a bed in there, right?"

Roch nods, and he gingerly helps her out the back door, snapping his fingers and holding a hand up to his pack of dogs. Their butts instantly hit the ground, stopping them from rushing up to Truly.

"I think I'll wait here," Bexley says, but I see the worry in her eyes. She acts like a hard ass, but when push comes to shove, she always shows up.

"Do you know how to deliver a baby?" Birdie asks.

"Yes, but let's hope the midwife gets here before that happens."

An hour later and five minutes before the midwife makes an appearance, Truly and Roch's baby boy is born. He has a head full of blond fuzz—something he got from his dad—and a deep skin tone from his mom, though that could be because he's brand new. Only time will tell.

I run a hand over his head as he suckles on Truly's breast. "He's beautiful."

Truly beams up at me. "He is, huh?"

The midwife flutters around, doing all the cleanup and making sure Truly's comfortable, while Roch's dumbfounded gaze shifts back and forth from the newborn to his woman. Everyone else left once things got real and Truly was naked from the waist down, legs spread open.

"Now that you've been all up in my business, I think we're best friends." Truly's hand grips mine, giving it a grateful squeeze.

"I think you're right."

"Seriously, Petra. Thank you so much. I don't know what we would've done without you."

"You're welcome. I'll send you my bill." I wink and stand. "I'll let you guys get settled."

Roch stops my departure, putting his big body in my way. He doesn't say anything, but he pulls me in for a back-slapping hug that nearly knocks the wind from me. I look over at Truly, who has a tear in her eye. I guess this is a monumental moment for him but for me, it's really super awkward.

"Thanks," I say and sidestep him, getting out of there as fast as I can.

I'm laughing at how strange the last hour has been when I hear the telltale sound of bikes rumbling. My feet pound the pavement as I run around the clubhouse to the parking lot, ready to welcome my guys home. But I stop short when I see the somber mood they're in as they climb off their bikes.

Sly sees me first. He flicks Moto with his hand and nods in my direction. He turns to face me, his white T-shirt and jeans covered in dark red.

Blood.

I rush to him, looking him up and down, trying to find the source, when I realize there's too much blood for it to belong to him. He's still standing. He rode his bike here. This isn't his.

I turn in a circle, taking inventory of the bikers. Khan, Loki, Coyote, Goblin, plus Moto and Sly. Then it hits me.

"Where's Ford?" I ask and am met with silence. "Where the fuck is Ford? And where's Roxy?"

They glance at the van, and I head that way, only to be stopped by an arm looping around my middle.

"Need to prepare you first because we need your help," Sly says in my ear.

"Is it Roxy?" I ask.

"No, baby. It's Ford. He didn't make it, and Roxy is having a hard time accepting that. You're her best friend, and she needs you."

My eyes blur with tears for both my friend and the man who spent the last month hanging out in a dressing room to protect me.

I wipe my eyes and nod. "Okay."

He releases me, and I slide open the door. There's no way to prepare for what I see, but this is so much worse than I could've imagined. Ford is flat on his back, covered in blood, a knife sticking out of his abdomen. Roxy is combing through his hair, cooing words of comfort, not recognizing he's gone at all.

When daylight hits her face, her attention shifts to me. "Thank God. I need you to put your doctor's hat on. Ford needs you." She climbs out of the van and pulls me closer. "I didn't remove the knife. I watched a show one time, and they said to leave it put. Was that the right thing to do?"

I blink. "Yeah, it was."

When I don't move, she gives me a shove. "Hurry. He's lost a lot of blood."

"Roxy—"

"No. Not you too. I thought of all people, you'd be the one to see reason and help him."

"Roxy," I try again. "It's too late. He lost too much blood. I'm so sorry."

She releases a sob, her battered face contorting as she crumples in on herself. I catch her before she falls to the ground, wrapping my arms around her shaking body.

"Dove, need you to get her cleaned up and safe. We'll take care of the rest," Moto says.

"Come on. Let's go inside."

"No. If you won't help him, I will." She tries to pull away, but I keep a hold of her.

"Roxy, listen to me. He's gone. There's nothing anyone can do." My voice cracks because she's not the only one who lost someone important. While he was my friend, he was Moto and Sly's brother. My heart aches, and I want to comfort them, but it'll have to wait.

"It's not fair," she wails, and I gently ease her toward the clubhouse, taking one last glance back. That's when I notice there was more than one body back there. Behind Ford is Tyler, but unlike Ford, Tyler is alive. He's on his stomach, his mouth duct-taped shut, his hands cuffed behind his back.

What are they going to do with him? And Ford?

I don't know if I want to know the answer to either question.

After helping Roxy shower off the blood, I sit her down and clean up the cuts on her face. She remains silent, allowing me to turn her head this way and that, inspecting each one for signs of infection. I want to ask her what happened but now's not the time. Maybe once she's had time to process Ford's death.

"Okay. All done." I close the first aid kit and tuck it back into the bathroom cabinet. "Let's get you to bed."

She falls asleep almost instantly, thank God. She needs the rest, and I need to see what my guys are up to.

I thought about it the whole time I was taking care of Roxy. If there's one thing I know for sure, it's that they brought Tyler here to kill him, something that would have me calling the police so fast in my previous life. But not now. I've seen and experienced too much.

Prison is too good for him and leaves the door open for him to hurt someone else. Death is the only way to rid the world of his toxicity, and I deserve to be there when it happens.

Chapter
TWENTY-SIX

Sly

"**W**here's the girl who was with Dove?" I ask, circling around him like I'm the predator and he's the prey. After paying our respects to Ford, we sent him away with Duncan, who will take him to be cremated after hours. Most of the time, the bodies we accrue are disposed of in the Great Basin Desert. But sometimes, we use our funeral home hook-up.

Ford deserves to have his ashes sprinkled on the road, and after this shit is all over, we'll find the perfect highway to set him free.

"I don't know," Tyler mutters, his head swaying side to side. Moto's boot did some serious damage to his face. His nose is pushed into his skull, his front teeth are knocked out, and both of his eyes are already black and swollen. I have zero sympathy, and if he keeps playing games, things will get a lot worse for him.

"See, the thing is, I think you do." Moto fists his hair and tugs it back. We have him strapped to a chair in the kill room. It's a completely soundproof, walled-off area hidden from anyone who might stop by.

"There's been a lot of girls."

"But you remembered Petra," I say, that name tasting like acid on my tongue.

"You mean Cameron?" The cocky asshole has the audacity to smirk.

I punch him in his already disfigured nose, and he yelps in response. "Try again."

Blood oozes from his nose, over his mouth, and down his chin. "I sold her, all right? The same way I did to all the others."

"Who did you sell her to?" Moto asks.

"I don't know. You'd have to look in my books."

"Where are your books?" Moto's patience is drying up, and I don't blame him. We've been at this for a half-hour. After the day we've had, we're beyond exhausted and ready to be done with this. But that doesn't mean we're letting him off the hook.

"I'll tell you if you let me go."

I scoff. "What do you think this is? A stay at the Royal Bastard Inn?" Crouching in front of him, I say, "You're not leaving here alive. The only thing you have control over is how long it takes me to kill you. I can keep you alive for weeks, months even, and every day will be worse than the last. Or we can get this over with today, and you can give me all the answers I need."

For the first time, I see true fear. Good. It's finally sinking in.

"It's at my house, in my office, bottom filing cabinet."

I look at Khan, who's standing near the door in case he's needed. He nods and leaves. He'll send someone else if he doesn't go himself, and we'll know soon if he's telling the truth.

"While we wait, why don't we have some fun?" Moto asks, scanning the tray of implements. He picks up a pack of smokes someone left in here. "Take his pants off."

I stand Tyler up, and I'll give him credit; he knows he's about to feel some pain, yet he doesn't whine, cry, or beg. Not yet anyway. We'll see after Moto gets done with him.

"The two men who had Petra liked to leave scars on her

beautiful skin. She's ashamed of those scars now." He lights the cig and blows out a long puff of smoke as though it's a regular vice for him when I know it's not. He actually can't stand the taste.

I undo Tyler's pants, pushing them to his ankles. Sitting him back down, I use rope to tie his ankles to opposite legs of the chair, keeping them spread wide open.

Moto wastes no time pressing the lit cigarette into his thigh. Tyler hisses in pain. Moto doesn't stop there. He lights smoke after smoke, extinguishing each of them all along Tyler's inner thighs until the pack is empty and angry red burns litter his skin.

"I'm next." I pick up a scalpel. It's rusty and old, probably been used on more than a dozen other victims without being sterilized. There's no point since the men we bring down here don't stay alive long enough for infection to set in. "On top of burns, they liked to cut her too. Just for sport."

I press the scalpel in deep enough to hurt, but not so deep I hit his femoral artery, and drag it up his inner thighs. He struggles and cries out, but it's no use. There's nowhere to run. Blood drips down the chair from each cut, reminding me of Ford. Rage surges through me, and I get the urge to end him right here and now.

Instead, I stab the scalpel into his thigh, going through fat and muscle. "You're a piece of shit."

Moto's cell phone rings, and he answers, putting it on speaker. "Yeah?"

"It's here," Khan says.

"Can you look back four years? Would've been in July. Look for Mia or Cameron or maybe even Petra, I don't know."

We hear the sound of pages being flipped through until Khan finally speaks. "Cameron, age twenty-six. Sold to Antoine Bowers. Mia, age twenty-five. Sold to Eli Castillo."

"Any other information on the buyers in there?" Moto asks.

"No. That's it. But bro, there are thousands of women named in this book. Literally thousands."

"Bring it back with you. We'll find a way to get it to the cops and help other families get closure."

"You can't do that," Tyler argues.

"Fuckin' watch us, asshole." I push the scalpel until I feel it hit bone.

Through gritted teeth he says, "You have no idea the men you'll implicate."

"In case you haven't figured it out by now, we don't give a fuck," I say.

"On my way back." Khan hangs up.

With one look my way, Moto knows what I'm thinking. "You want to start digging, don't you?"

"Yeah."

"Let's go. This can wait."

We walk out the door, ignoring Tyler's protests to not leave him there. Like we care what he wants.

I crack my knuckles as my computer boots up. "I hope those names aren't aliases."

"He didn't use an alias for Cameron or Mia." Moto shrugs. It's the first time he's called her by that name. Dove suits her more, but Cameron is a close second.

I start by doing a basic Google search. You'd be surprised how much information is readily available for anyone to find. I want to look for Dove's buyer first, but since she's safe and sound, it makes more sense to start with Eli Castillo, Mia's buyer.

I'm not surprised when hundreds, if not thousands, of Eli Castillos pop up, so I narrow the search by adding 'billionaire.' It's safe to assume the men who purchase human beings are wealthy beyond measure.

I scan the first article. "Eli Castillo, CEO of Castillo Entertainment, owns and operates three of the top-grossing casinos in Vegas."

"So she never left Nevada," Moto mutters.

"She never even left Vegas if she's still with him."

"What else?" Moto sits on my bed, comfortable to let me do the reading and trusting me to relay whatever information I learn.

"He's a piece of shit. A bunch of domestic violence charges, tax evasion, racketeering—all of which his high-powered attorneys got him off on."

"You think he still has her?"

"I don't know, but it's worth looking into."

"Now try Antoine Bowers," he says.

I type the name and add the same qualifier. "Antoine Bowers, CEO of Bowers Electric, produces motors and components for home appliances, smart metering, power tools, security, and a bunch of other shit."

"Sounds boring."

I shoot him a look over my shoulder since this is right up my alley. Ever since I was a boy, I loved taking things apart and figuring out how they work. Even to this day, taking things apart is a stress reducer for me.

"What now?" he asks.

"Now we finish off Tyler. We'll go after Eli next."

"Yay. I've been wanting to take a Vegas vacation."

I roll my eyes. "It's a work trip."

"I'll bet we can find some time to gamble." He climbs off the bed. "Ready?"

A knock sounds on the door, and Loki pops his head in. "You guys might want to get downstairs."

"Shit." I flip off my monitor, and we bolt down the stairs, expecting to find Tyler missing or that he found a way to kill himself. Neither of those was right.

"What's going on?" Moto asks Dove nonchalantly, slowly walking toward her.

She has a switchblade in her hand and a long piece of Tyler's skin in the other. There's a dazed and almost manic expression on her features, and her hair is curtained around her face. It's eerie.

Glancing down, I see Tyler is very much alive but headed toward shock from getting a good portion of his thigh carved off.

"I came looking for you. Instead, I found him," she says, tossing the hunk of thigh to the side.

"I see that." I leisurely step into the room, needing to see where her head is at.

"Is this okay?" she asks.

"Is it okay with you?"

Her face softens. And goddamn, she's beautiful, even covered in the blood of the man who sold her into sex slavery. "Yeah. I think I need this."

"Then it's okay with us."

She grins. "Thanks."

Going back to what she was doing, she lowers to her knees and digs into his other thigh. It's the wrong weapon for the job, but I'm not about to tell her. She saws away at his flesh while he wails at the top of his lungs, tears coming out of his eyes, the chair bouncing up and down from the force of his movements.

Moto leans into me and whispers. "You think she's all right?"

I watch as she hums a happy tune, completely ignoring Tyler's distress and working hard to cut through the layers of skin and fat.

My cock thickens with her crazed look and the indifferent way she mutilates the man who ruined her life. "Are any of us all right?"

"I like what you did here." Dove drags the bloody knife over his inner thighs.

"Payback's a bitch," I say.

She resumes her cutting until another hunk of leg is free. It's gruesome and fucked up, but this is her vengeance, and she deserves every minute of it.

"Are you just going to let her do this?" Tyler cries.

"Yep." Moto lifts up onto the counter.

"He told you where Mia might be?" Dove asks, discarding the flesh.

"He did, and we're looking into it." I approach her and run a hand through her hair, pushing it away to expose her angelic face. "I love you."

"I love you too." She lifts on her toes and kisses me.

"What do you say we forget all this and go upstairs?"

Her eyes narrow. "No. I want him dead."

"Then let me take over, okay?"

What she's done is fucked up already; she doesn't need ending his life on her conscience.

"You'll kill him?"

"I'd do anything for you." I take the knife from her hand. "But this isn't asking much. He deserves to go to Hades."

"Okay. Thanks."

I kiss her long and deep, not caring about her bloody hands snaking under my cut and T-shirt to rub up and down my bare back. Our tongues entwine, tasting each other and reminding me of all the dirty things her wicked tongue can do.

I'm beyond exhausted, body and soul, but she brings me back to life, soothing my heavy heart from Ford's death. I want her. I want my man too. But first, I need to take care of this whiny bitch next to us.

"Go sit with Moto," I say.

"Okay." She leaves me, and I immediately miss the absence of her warmth.

"Come here." Still sitting on the counter, Moto spreads his legs wide to make room. Just like she did with me, she slips her hands under his shirt and hugs him tight. My sexy, strong man holds her to him, kissing the top of her head before turning her around so she can watch my next moves.

He massages her shoulders, and her head falls forward for

a minute while she relaxes into his touch. I can't take my eyes off them. The level of comfort we've reached with each other is phenomenal, and I've never felt at home more than I do now. I've found my people.

"Get on with it," Moto urges.

"Slow or fast?" I ask.

"Slow," Dove says with an icy tone I've never heard from her.

"As you wish."

Tyler's body shakes, and he's a grotesque disaster. His face is covered in dried blood, his nose is crooked beyond repair, his legs are tied open on the chair, muscle and flesh are exposed on each thigh, and his groin is covered in cuts and burns. His lips move, but no sound comes out, probably praying for death.

I grab a hemostat and lift his dangling hand. Wedging the scissor-like blades under his thumbnail, I separate the nail from the nail bed, then grip the nail and pull. Tyler makes a pained grunt, his head falling forward on his shoulders and swaying side to side.

I work my way through his whole left hand before he passes out cold. Kind of disappointing.

"What now?" I turn to ask Dove and am surprised to find Moto's massage has moved down to her tits. Her pupils are blown, and her plump lips are parted. She's turned on.

We're all three fucked up beyond measure. But at least we're in good company.

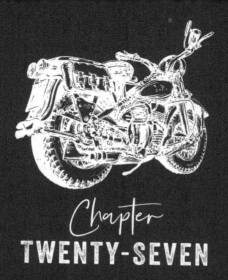

Chapter
TWENTY-SEVEN

Moto

"**C**old water," I say casually, like I'm not feeling up our girl. Sly nods and moves to the industrial sink. He pours a cup of water and pulls Tyler's head back before tossing it in his face. Tyler stirs, muttering deliriously.

I wrap a hand around the base of Dove's throat with my thumb and first finger, cradling her chin and turning her head as I bend forward to kiss her. It's a teasing kiss where I lick the seam of her mouth before nipping at her lower lip. Then my mouth is on hers, devouring her like I'd die if I couldn't have this moment with her.

Not wanting to keep her from watching Tyler die, I pull away and turn her head back around, not missing the cute little whimper she lets out.

"Don't worry. I'll take care of you both once this is over." I ease her forward and hop down from the counter but stay positioned behind her. There's no harm in teasing her more, so I slip a hand down the front of her sweats to find her soaked. "Does it turn you on to watch him suffer?"

"Does that make me a bad person?" she whispers, gripping my forearm, keeping me in place.

"No, it makes you a survivor." I rub her clit firmly but slowly, not trying to make her come just yet.

Sly's moved onto Tyler's other hand but has to take breaks to rouse him with cold water. Eventually, he wises up and turns on the hose we use to clean this room once we're done torturing our victims. It's high pressure, so the force blows Tyler's head up before he comes to.

"Stay with me," Sly says. "Almost done."

He unties his ankles and the rope wrapped around his torso holding him up. Tyler falls to the hard ground in a heap. Sly huffs and puffs as he works to set Tyler back on the chair, but this time, his stomach is resting on the seat, his head flopping over the edge, and his boxer-covered ass on display.

Dove leans back into me, my erection pressing into her back. "Is he . . ."

"I think he is."

Sly yanks down Tyler's boxers before reaching for a knife with deep serrations down the side. I clench my butt cheeks in response because, goddamn. Ouch.

He pulls one of Tyler's butt cheeks to the side, exposing his hairy, puckered hole. He rears back with the knife, then swings forward, shoving it up his ass. Tyler's head flies up, but then he's gone—dead or passed out.

"That felt good." Sly stands to full height, his torso covered in blood spray. He licks his lips when he sees what I'm doing and stalks toward us. Attacking me with a wild kiss, his hand goes under Dove's shirt to play with her tit. She grinds against my fingers, her aroused frenzy intensifying.

"More," she whispers, and I slip two fingers inside her wet cunt, hooking them so I stroke against her G-spot. "Oh God."

Sly breaks free from me and lifts the hem of her shirt. I remove my hand so he can pull it off and take the opportunity to strip off my cut, shirt, boots, and pants, then I'm back inside her panties, rubbing slow circles against her clit.

If anyone walked in right now, they'd be horrified by how fucked up this is. Except maybe Khan; that fucker is into shit like this. There's a dead man no more than six feet away, and we're covered in his blood and turned on by it.

Sly dips down to bite and suck on her nipples while shoving her pants and panties down. "This cunt is ours. Say it, Dove. I want to hear you say it."

"It belongs to you and Moto," she moans out.

"Good. Now spread these legs so I can worship my pussy." He gets down on his knees, removing his cut and shirt.

I pull my hand away, but he grabs my wrist, stopping me. Sucking my fingers into his mouth, he cleans them of her arousal. His tongue feels so good, twisting around each one, making me think of how good it would feel for him to be sucking my cock.

Once finished with that, he lets me go and throws one of Dove's legs over his shoulder before diving between her legs. Dove palms my cock while writhing in pleasure, and I give her tits my full attention. It takes seconds before she screams her release.

Thank fuck this room is soundproof.

"Tell me how you want it, Dove," I say once she comes down.

"I want both of you. Please."

"You got it." I bite her earlobe and give it a tug.

Sly stands and kicks off his boots before shoving his pants down. Grabbing her by the back of the thighs, he lifts her up, her legs wrapping around him. Not having a bed will make things challenging, but not impossible.

I grip Sly's cock at the base and help ease him inside her pussy. He lets out a pleasured moan once he's fully seated inside her.

"There's no lube," I say, immediately pissed off that I might not be able to make her wish come true.

"Look in the cabinets for something," Sly says, pushing Dove against the wall so he can fuck her. Lucky bastard.

I pull open each cabinet, frantically searching for anything I know won't hurt Dove. That's when I see it. A jar of petroleum jelly. No idea why it's here, but it doesn't matter right now. I smear the goop all over my hard cock and scoop a fingerful before returning to my partners.

Dove's bloody hands are pressed against the wall while Sly pounds into her, his tight ass muscles working with every thrust. I take my non-lubed hand and squeeze one of his round globes, feeling the power he's giving Dove. He looks over his shoulder, and I sneak a kiss in.

When I pull away, he adjusts his hold on Dove and turns to give me access, backing up against the wall to give himself a little break from holding her up. I smear her back hole with the jelly before pumping two fingers inside her tight heat. I scissor her open, careful to prepare her properly. She puts so much trust in us when she has no reason to trust anyone ever again. I make sure to never give her a reason to regret that.

Once she's stretched enough to take me, Sly pushes off the wall. Gripping myself at the base, I work my cock inside slowly, trying not to embarrass myself because this is my first time inside her this way, and fuckin' hell, it feels so good.

"Do it, Moto. Please," she begs.

I push the rest of the way in and blow out a breath. Nothing has ever been this tight or this good, and knowing all three of us are joined and feeling the same level of pleasure only adds to it.

"Hang on, baby." Sly weaves his arms under her thighs so he can bounce her up and down. It takes a minute to get a rhythm, but once we're there, it's fuckin' heaven.

"Fuck," I say, helping hold her up by cradling her under her ass. We fuck her good and hard until she breaks apart, shouting her release. She bears down, squeezing the life out of my cock in the best way possible.

I can't do it. I can't hold it in any longer. My balls draw up, and orgasmic pleasure overtakes me. My vision narrows, and my body comes apart at the seams. I fill her up with so much cum, it dribbles out and down my balls.

Feeling like every ounce of energy is gone, I pull out and step back until my ass hits the counter.

Sly's still going, though, and like a machine, he continues to fuck her senseless. His biceps bulge, a sheen of sweat covers his body, and his eyes meet mine. I might be out for the count, but he keeps me right there with them.

Goddamn, I love this man.

He bites his lower lip, a telltale sign he's about to come. Dove's nails dig into his shoulders as she holds on for dear life, her tits bouncing and her hair swinging. My cock twitches, but I'm so wrung out, that's all it can do.

"This pussy is so good," he grits out. "Gonna make me come. You ready for me to fill you up, baby?"

"God, yes. Please," she says.

He flips around, slamming her into the wall roughly, and I get a magnificent view of his ass as he pumps his seed deep inside.

Today was a rough one, and there'll be plenty more where that came from, but as long as they end like this, we'll be okay.

Sly lowers her on wobbly legs but hangs on until she's steady. We take in the bloody scene as if coming out of a trance. Tyler's dead body, a knife shoved up his ass and blood everywhere, and Dove with our combined cream dripping down her thighs.

"What do we do now?" she asks.

"I'll have Ford . . ." Sly's head lowers. "Shit. I forgot."

"I'll get Miles and Duncan down here. They'll handle everything." I wet some paper towels and get down on my knees to clean Dove up.

"I can do that," she protests.

"No. For some unknown reason, you let two dirty assholes like us fuck you and come inside your beautiful body, so you won't be the one cleaning up."

She smiles as if what I just said was sweet and runs a hand through my hair. "I love you."

"Love you too, Dove."

"Hey, I heard you delivered a baby today," Sly says, helping her into her clothes. They'll have to be burned later, but she's sure as shit not walking upstairs naked. Even me and Sly have limits, and a hard one for us is anyone else seeing her perfect pussy.

"I did." She beams.

"Did you hear what they named the kid?" I ask.

"No, I didn't ask."

"Ford," I say through a lump in my throat.

Dove's eyes well up. "Really?"

"Yeah. They were worried it was too soon, but we thought it was a fitting tribute."

"It is," she agrees. "One perfect life gone, another perfect, new life beginning."

"Couldn't have said it better myself, baby. Thanks for taking good care of them. Roch didn't say shit about what happened but Truly filled Loki in, and she said she couldn't have done it without you," Sly says.

"It was amazing to bring him into this world, but it didn't change my mind about OB."

"You don't want to be a baby doc?"

"Definitely not. I prefer trauma."

I glance at the hacked-up body. "Causing trauma or fixing it?"

"Fixing it, though I guess I'm good at causing it too." She frowns, and I wish I hadn't said shit about it.

"He deserved to go to Hades. You know that, right?"

"Yeah. I know."

"And he deserved to suffer all the way down." I lift her into my arms. "Let's get you showered and into bed."

Her head rests on my shoulders, her arms looped around my neck. "Yes, please. It's been a long day."

Chapter
TWENTY-EIGHT

Petra

I wanted to go to Vegas with my guys, but it's been a week since Tyler killed Ford, and Roxy still isn't doing well, so I stayed behind to take care of her. It felt a little like I was choosing a new friend over an old one. If Mia's still alive and with that sick freak, she'll need someone too.

Sly had a different take. He doesn't think Mia's still with him, and it'd get my hopes up if I went with them. Too bad I already have my hopes up.

"When are they going to talk to him?" Roxy pulls the covers up to her chin.

She's been staying in my room at the clubhouse, and I've been sleeping in Sly's room with my guys this last week. We thought it was better since Roxy lives in an apartment alone. No one should have to lose someone and go home to an empty house.

"Tomorrow. They wanted to take their time riding to Vegas."

"Did they do it?" she asks, and I know exactly what *it* she's referring to.

"Yeah. They found a deserted highway, and Loki spread his ashes in the wind."

Tears well in her eyes. "I should've stopped him. After he got me in the van. I should've stopped him."

"You can't tell a biker what to do. Take it from me. They have this alpha caveman thing when it comes to their women, and if there's a threat, they will stop at nothing to protect us." I sit down next to her on the bed.

"I didn't love him, but I wish I did. He deserved to have a woman's love before he died." Her voice cracks, and liquid sadness rolls down her cheeks.

"Did you fuck him before you were taken?" I ask, shocking her into a fit of laughter.

"I gave him a blowjob while you were on stage that night."

"Then I'm sure he was fine." I nudge her with my shoulder.

"He deserved a full heart *and* empty balls."

"I don't know. He was pretty smitten with you. I think that counts." I sigh, not knowing what else to say. "So, what now?"

"I don't know. I need to go back to work at some point. Coyote gave me a paid week off and told me to take as much time I need, but I'm not a saver, so I don't have much to fall back on."

"Well, you're more than welcome to move in here. I've already cleared it. The guys like having you around."

"That's sweet, but I think I need to get back to my life."

"I get that."

"Do you?" she asks.

"What do you mean?"

"You had a life, and you haven't even considered going back to it."

She's right, of course. I did have a life, and I should go back. At the very least, tell Mom and Mama—as I affectionately called my moms—that I'm alive. But the thought is overwhelming. They'll have questions I don't want to answer and expectations

I'm not sure I could meet. They'll want me to move home, spend every waking hour with me, and get back to my career.

It's exhausting just thinking about it, let alone doing it.

"Maybe I will someday. I just don't think I'm ready."

"Why?"

"I don't know. I'm not the same person I used to be. They might not like this version," I admit.

"How could they not? You went through something horrific, and you're still here, living life. You met two amazing men who worship you, and you're doing something you love."

"I'm not sure they'll see going from a doctor to a stripper as a positive step. And I'm fairly certain they won't understand my relationship with Sly and Moto."

"They might. You'll never know until you try."

"I guess." I sigh. "So, you want to go home?"

"Yes, but is it all right if I stay one more night?"

"Of course. You're always welcome."

"Thanks." She snuggles down into the mattress. "Wanna sleep with me tonight since Sly and Moto are gone?"

"No, it's okay." I don't tell her why because it's embarrassing. My bed smells like Roxy, while Sly's bed smells like them, and I want to be wrapped up in their scent while I sleep. "Goodnight."

"Goodnight, Petra. And thank you for everything."

"Of course. I'm here for you, girl."

My phone rings as I walk into the front door of the clubhouse after Duncan and I took Roxy home. I offered to stay with her, but she declined, saying she wanted some time alone before starting back at work tomorrow.

"Hello?" I answer.

"Cam?"

I freeze mid-step, recognizing the voice instantly. "Mia?"

"Oh my God, it's you," she cries. "I can't believe it."

"Mia, where are you?"

A rush of emotion overwhelms me, and tears spill from my eyes. I can't believe it's really her. I already convinced myself that this was a fool's mission and they wouldn't find her. My past comes rushing back to me in a whole new way. I could pretend they weren't real when it was just my memories. But after hearing Mia's voice, there's no denying it.

"I'm with some really scary-looking men who claim to be your boyfriends. Please tell me it's true, and this isn't a trick."

"Is one a sexy Japanese man built like a brick house?"

"Yeah."

"Is the other stupidly handsome and a little goofy?"

"Yeah." She giggles, but it's snotty and wet from crying.

"Then yes. They belong to me."

I try to make out her next words, but she's sobbing too hard. The phone jostles, and then Sly's voice is on the line.

"Hey, baby."

"How is she?"

"She's alive. That's about all I can say for now. We're taking her to the hospital now."

I gasp. "Why? Is she hurt?"

"I don't know, but I think she should go. She wants to talk to the cops and report it all."

"Oh." I hear his unspoken words. If she does that, then they'll know I'm alive too. They'll tell Mom and Mama, and I'll be forced to talk to them. I can't hide any longer.

"Wanted to give you a heads up so you can decide how you want this to go. Maybe we can talk to her about holding—"

"No. She deserves that closure if that's what she wants." My stomach sinks, but I know it's the right choice. The best thing the Royal Bastards did for me when I got out was let me make decisions. It gave me power after not having any for so long. "I guess that means you aren't giving that guy the same treatment as Tyler?"

"No. He's too high profile anyway."

"Okay."

"I think you should fly out here."

My stomach sinks. I wasn't prepared for any of this, and I don't know if I'm strong enough.

"You're ready, Dove," he says, reading my mind. "I'll book the soonest flight I can. Duncan can take you to the airport."

"You'll stay with me?"

"We both will."

"Okay." I sniffle.

"Love you, and we'll see you soon. I'll text your flight details."

"Love you too." I end the call and rub my phone back and forth in my palms as I pace the dining room.

This is happening whether I want it to or not.

I run through baggage claim full speed toward my guys. Moto catches me first, one hand wrapping around my waist and the other settling on the back of my head while I cry. I don't even know why I am.

"Shh, Dove. We got you."

He sets me back on my feet, and I immediately go to Sly's open arms. It's only been two days since I saw them last, but I missed them so much. I've been feeling too many emotions, and without them there to ground me, I'm spiraling.

"It's okay, baby," Sly says.

After collecting my suitcase, they lead me outside where a blacked-out car waits, complete with a driver.

"Where are your bikes?" I ask.

"Back at the hotel. We figured you'd have luggage," Sly says. "Right."

We slide onto the expensive leather, all three of us choosing to sit in the back seat. I think they missed me as much as I missed them.

"Where are we going?" I ask.

"That's up to you. Mia gave her report to the cops late last night after she was checked over—"

"Is she okay?" I interrupt.

"She will be. She had a broken shoulder that wasn't set properly and some internal scarring, but there's nothing the doctors can do about that. It's mostly mental stuff, you know?"

I frown. "Yeah. I know."

"Anyway, the cops arrested Eli Castillo this morning, and they also paid a visit to your moms. They want to talk to you next."

"Did you have to talk to them too?" I ask.

"No. Mia agreed to leave our names out of it. She told the cops she saw a chance to escape and took it. She's been keeping us in the loop through texts."

"That's good."

"Dove," Moto starts.

"What?"

"Your moms spoke to Mia. They're pretty desperate to see you."

"I know. But I think I want to see Mia first. Is that okay?"

"Sure." Moto leans forward to speak to the driver. "Take us to UMC, please."

"You got it."

The ride to the hospital is quiet, my guys trying to make small talk with me, but my heart isn't in it. Today will be a long day, and I need to preserve all my energy.

Apparently, they hired the driver for the whole day, so he drops us off at the entrance and then parks, waiting for further instruction. I hold both their hands as we take the elevator to Mia's room. Sly told me the doctors are keeping her here for a couple days but only for observation.

I take a deep breath before I step inside the room. I'm uncomfortable in the outfit I chose. If I had it my way, I'd have worn Sly's sweatpants and Moto's RBMC tee, but I figured it wasn't appropriate, so I opted for a pair of flare jeans and a cropped black tank with the RBMC logo on it. I look every bit the biker babe I'm becoming.

"You can do this," Sly urges.

"We'll be right there with you," Moto says.

"Okay." I step inside the sterile room, the scent of alcohol singeing my nostrils. Then I see her. She looks both the same and different. She still has her curly red hair and grass-green eyes, but she's much thinner and looks sickly. "Mia?"

"Cameron." She holds her arms open, and I quickly move into them, careful not to kink any of the tubes and wires coming off her body. "Oh my God, I missed you so much."

"I missed you too. Are you okay?"

"I am now. Thanks to Moto and Sly."

Last night on the phone, Moto and Sly detailed how they found her. It was much easier than any of us thought it would be. They knocked on the door, and when the maid answered, they put a gun in her face and told her to lead them to the girl.

The maid knew exactly who they were there for and led them to the cellar where Mia was kept. There was a mattress on the floor for her and a bucket in the corner. That's it. That was her room for over four years. She was only allowed out when that sick bastard wanted to play with her. Moto and Sly didn't ask for specifics. It wasn't their place.

Maybe someday she and I can trade war stories, but none of that is important now. The only thing that matters is getting Mia healthy again.

"I missed you so much," I choke out, emotion clogging my throat.

"I missed you too. Every single day."

A wave of guilt hits me because, for the last seven or eight months, I've been living a dream while she was still stuck in a nightmare.

"Cameron," a woman says from the corner. I hadn't even noticed her parents.

"Mr. and Mrs. Garcia." I extract myself from Mia and give them each a hug. Before all this happened, our families were close. The six of us vacationed and celebrated holidays together and had become somewhat of a forced family because Mia and I were inseparable.

"It's so good to see you," Mrs. Garcia says through tears. "Your moms have been beside themselves with worry."

"I know." I don't need confirmation from anyone to know without a doubt that's true.

"Let me give them a call, get them down here." Mr. Garcia pulls his phone from his pocket.

"No." I stop him. "I'm headed there now. Just wanted to see Mia first."

"They tell me you live in Reno now," Mia says, eyeing Moto and Sly, who are standing near the door, no doubt in case they need to make a quick exit.

"I am. They saved me and nursed me back to health."

"That's what I don't understand. Why didn't you tell anyone?" Mia asks.

Isn't that the million-dollar question? I don't think I can make anyone understand why I did the things I did, so I shrug. "I only recently got my memory back, and then it became more important to find you."

"Thank you. Two stupid words that aren't nearly strong enough for what I want to say, but it's all I got."

"I get it. That's how I feel about them." I hook a thumb over to my guys.

"I have so many questions."

"There'll be time. Now that we're both safe, we have all the time in the world," I say.

"You're right about that." She rests back into the bed, her eyes growing sleepier by the minute. I know that feeling. She's spent the last four years on high alert, but now that the danger is gone, she can truly rest.

"I'll come see you when you get out of here, okay?" I give her another hug.

"Promise?"

"I promise." I turn to her parents. "Please don't tell my moms I'm coming."

"Sure, sweetie." Mrs. Garcia gives me a watery smile.

"Talk soon." I wave my goodbye.

My hands are quickly snagged up by Moto and Sly in the hall.

"Where too now?" Moto asks.

"Home."

Chapter
TWENTY-NINE

Sly

We pull up to a two-story stucco home in one of those housing complexes where every house looks identical and is spaced only a few feet apart. I try to imagine Dove growing up here, but it's so plain, and she's so vibrant. She doesn't fit.

Maybe she did four years ago.

It's hard to imagine she's a whole different person than she was back then, but she's been through hell and back, so maybe.

We sit parked in front of the house for long minutes, none of us moving. This is so far out of my and Moto's comfort zone. We're not the "meet the parents" kind of guys. Matter of fact, her moms probably wouldn't even answer the door if we were standing at it.

We did our best to look presentable today, leaving our cuts back at the hotel and putting on jeans that weren't stained with grease and worn with holes. But we can't hide the tattoos on our forearms or the hard edge to our eyes that living as an outlaw gives us.

"Want us to wait here?" I ask, prepared for her to say yes and trying like hell to not take offense.

"No," she scoffs. "You said you'd be there for me."

"We will." I take her hand and rest it on my life. "Whatever you need, Dove. We got you."

"Good." She stares up at the house. "I'm not Cameron anymore, and I'm worried they won't like Petra."

"They can get to know the new you," I say.

"They're not expecting a new me."

"You won't know until you go in there." Moto rubs circles on her back.

"What if they don't accept us?"

"I don't know. You can decide that after you go in there," I say, putting a little force in my tone. All this waiting has me feeling some sort of way, and I'm eager to get it over with.

"Okay."

"You ready?" Moto asks, opening the car door.

"As I'll ever be." We let her lead us to the front door, where she freezes again. "Do I knock?"

"I think that's best," I say.

Her knuckles rap on the door, and a minute later, a woman answers. She looks like Dove with long black hair, but hers is streaked with silver. She's short like Dove, too but has some extra weight around her middle.

Her eyes scan from me to Moto before finally landing on Dove.

Her hand flies up to cover her mouth, and her eyes glisten with tears. "Cameron?"

"Mom," Dove croaks.

The two women slam into each other, painful sobs echoing down the street. Another woman appears, no doubt hearing the commotion. This one is tall and lanky with cropped hair that's curly on top. She does the same thing as the first, spotting me and Moto before realizing what's in front of her.

"Oh my God. Cameron. You're home." She doesn't cry but wraps her arms around the two still wrapped up in each other.

"Mama," Dove sobs.

This lasts for a long time while Moto and I stand here, hands tucked in our pockets, trying not to look out of place and failing.

"Come inside," the second woman says, and they break apart.

Dove wipes snot from her nose and stands up straight. "I want you to meet the men who saved me first."

The two women look at us, suspicion in their gaze. I don't blame them.

"This is Moto and Sly." She points to each of us. "And these are my moms, Lori and Savannah." She giggles nervously.

"Hi." I hold out my hand, and Moto does the same.

"Nice to meet you," Lori, the one who looks like Dove, says and shakes our hands.

"It's a pleasure," Savannah says, keeping her hands to herself.

We follow them inside a spacious home decorated in chili peppers. Seriously. Every flat surface has some form of chili pepper on it, and the walls are decorated with chili pepper art. It's not at all what I was expecting.

"You have a lovely home," Moto says, not sounding like himself. *Who is this proper man?* Then I remember how he grew up. Respect, especially for elders, was instilled in him long before he could even talk.

"Thank you," Savannah says. "Lori has a thing for peppers."

"I see that," I mutter, earning me a slap to the gut and a glare from Moto. Apparently, I'm the only one who isn't good with parents.

"Where have you been, sweet girl?" Lori coos, sitting Dove down on a large leather sectional in the living room.

"It's a long story."

"We have nothing but time now that you're home."

That's the second mention of this place being Dove's home. It pisses me the fuck off. This isn't her home. She lives with us. If she wants a place like this, I'll buy it for her. But it'll be in Reno, where she belongs.

Dove's lips purse as she thinks about where to start. Then she tells them everything leading up to us rescuing her. She doesn't mince words, describing how she was taken, the abuse she endured, when she was given to Anthony, the drug and alcohol addiction, and finally, the day we stole her from Anthony's mansion.

To give Lori and Savannah credit, they hold it together and don't interrupt. But the horrified expression on both their faces couldn't be masked.

"My God," Savannah says. "It's a miracle you survived."

"It was."

"Why didn't you come home right then?" Lori asks.

"I was diagnosed with dissociative amnesia. For months, I couldn't remember who I was. I only recently got my memory back, and I wanted to find Mia before I came home."

"You could've called." Savannah doesn't hide the hurt in her tone.

"I don't know how to make you understand. It wasn't because I didn't want to, per se. It was more that I didn't know how."

"You let us worry for months when we didn't have to. Your mom"—she pauses to collect herself—"was depressed to the point of being hospitalized."

Dove's eyes fall to her hands that are fisted together. Hell, no. They aren't going to put more guilt on her than she's already been feeling.

"I don't think you can judge her for what she's done to survive and get healthy. Dove's been through hell. She was hospitalized too after leaving her nightmare. She was dependent on drugs and alcohol just to get through the day," I say, my voice too loud and too angry.

"Dove?" Lori asks.

"It's a nickname," I growl.

Savannah stands. "I think it's time we were alone with our daughter."

Fuck that.

"I think we should let Dove decide," I say.

All eyes go to our woman, who has pulled her hair around her face, her shoulders sagging, looking every bit the woman we rescued so long ago.

"Maybe it's best if I spend some time here alone while I explain it all."

Well, shit. That hurts.

Lori and Savannah sit up straighter, pleased as fuckin' punch with themselves.

"If that's what you want." I stand, along with Moto. "Just shoot me a text when you want to be picked up."

"I will." She gets up and hugs us both. "Thank you."

"Anything for you," I reiterate, glaring at her moms over her shoulder. It's not a smart thing to do. Someday, they'll be our in-laws and want to be a part of their grandkids' lives. We'll need to make nice. But that's not right now, so I choose petty.

Moto and I walk out, feeling like kicked puppies, and head back to the hotel.

"You think she's okay?" I ask, lying flat on the king-size bed in the suite we rented.

"I'm sure she is." Moto turns on his side to face me.

We haven't moved from this spot all day, slowly watching the sun go down through the floor-to-ceiling window overlooking the Vegas strip. We sprung for this suite thinking it could be a mini-vacation with our woman. It's on the top floor and so big that she could scream as loud as she wanted without disturbing our neighbors.

But it's dark out now, and she still hasn't texted.

"Did you see how they looked when Dove said we should go?" I huff.

Moto rolls his eyes because it's the tenth time he's heard me say that. "She needed some time, and having us there made her moms uneasy. It wasn't a slight toward us."

"Sure felt like it." My phone buzzes, and I scramble to grab it off the nightstand where I've kept it plugged in all day, just in case.

Moto looks over my shoulder as I read.

Dove: If it's okay, I think I'll stay the night here. My moms are a bit wigged out and I think it'll make them feel better.

"I fuckin' knew this would happen," I say.

"Knew what, bro? That she'd want to stay in her childhood home after being gone for four years? Because that's all this is. She loves us. She said it herself."

"She thought she did, but now that she's back in her real life, she'll shove us aside and get back to her important work as a doctor. All we ever gave her was a biker clubhouse and a job as a stripper."

"We gave her a lot more than that, and you know it." He places his arm over my chest, bringing his face close to mine. "She loves us the same way we love each other."

This role reversal is weird. He's usually the one with a negative outlook on shit, and I'm the one pumping him full of fuckin' rainbows and sunshine. It makes me love him even more for holding himself together while I come apart.

I meet his dark brown eyes full of all that love he's talking about. "I hope you're right."

"I am. Now text her back and tell her it's okay. And don't be a dick."

I scowl as I type.

Me: I've said it before, and I'll say it again. Whatever you need, Dove.

Dove: Thank you for understanding. I'll text you in the morning. Love you both.

Me: We love you too.

I toss my phone back onto the nightstand. It sails over the top and lands on the ground, but I couldn't care less.

"Guess it's just me and you tonight. Want to order room service or go out?" Moto asks, resting his head on my chest. I'm so fuckin' grateful I have him. I couldn't suffer this alone.

"Order in. I'm not in the mood to be around people."

We're scarfing down burgers in bed a half-hour later while an old western plays on the TV. Neither of us is paying much attention, too lost in our own thoughts.

"What do we do if she decides to stay?" Moto asks.

It's the same thought that's been spinning around in my head over and over.

I blow out a breath. "I don't know. I guess we let her."

"Fuck that. We should drag her back to Reno and make her remember why she chose us in the first place."

"We could. But I think she's had enough choices taken away from her."

"So, we do what? Go back to fuckin' random pussy?"

That doesn't sit right with me. Not after experiencing the magic we had with Dove. Anything less than that feels wrong.

"I don't think I can," I admit.

"Me neither." He piles our plates and sets them on the room service cart the guy left behind.

"I guess it's just us then."

"*If* that's what she decides." He flops onto his belly, holding his head up with a hand.

"Wouldn't be so bad." I run my hand through his long, dark hair, loving how silky it is.

"No. It wouldn't," he says, but I don't miss the doubt in his eyes. And I don't take offense because I feel it too. We were good before Dove, great, even. But there was always a niggle of something missing. Until we saw her. I don't believe in love at first sight or any of that bullshit, but there was definitely something with her.

"We've been through some serious shit together, and we're still us. That's enough for me."

"Me too." He crawls up my prone body and leaves a bruising kiss on my lips. "Why don't you let me make you feel good and forget about everything for a while?"

"If you're offering, I'm not turning it down." I smirk.

"Didn't think you would." He lifts my shirt off and kisses his way down my body before giving me a blow job that did make me forget. At least for a while.

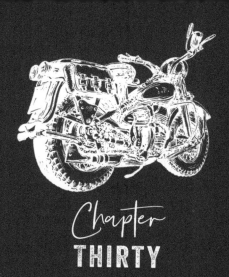

Chapter
THIRTY

Moto

The next morning, we wake to a text from Dove. I rub the
sleep from my eye as I open it up.

**Dove: My moms want to take me shopping today. Can
we meet up later?**

Me: Shopping for what?

I can't help but take offense because we've made sure that
girl has everything she could ever want and more. It's a little
stalkerish, but Sly monitors her online activity, and if she stops
at a website to look at anything, we buy it. She has a closet full
of clothes, a shit ton of makeup and whatever other girly shit she
wants, and her room is decorated in that muted decor she likes.

**Dove: Clothes and stuff. I don't think they like my biker
chick look.**

**Me: They'd be even more disappointed in your usual
outfit of oversized sweats.**

Dove: LOL. Probably. So, is that okay? Or should I tell them no?

Me: It's fine, Dove. Whatever you want to do.

Dove: Why don't you come by the house around six for dinner? Now that I've filled them in on everything, I want them to meet you properly.

Me: How did they take it?

Dove: I don't know. Not well, I guess.

Me: You need anything?

Dove: No, I'm okay.

Me: Then we'll see you at six.

"Sounds to me like they're trying to erase who she's become," Sly says.

"Me too."

"I don't have a good feeling about this."

Sly and I walk around The Strip for a while, grabbing lunch and seeing the sights. We get a lot of sideways glances and gain attention from a lot of women. Last year, we would've had our fill of all the ladies. Now, we ignore them and go about our business.

When six rolls around, we're at her door, knocking. We decided we shouldn't try and sugarcoat who we are anymore, so I'm in a pair of black jeans with holes in the knees, a fitted black tee, my boots, and my cut. Sly looks like a sex god in his black leather pants, worn RBMC tee, boots, and cut.

The door opens, and Savannah answers. "Welcome. Come on in."

I thought Dove would be waiting, but she's nowhere to be found as Savannah leads us into the living room and tells us to have a seat. Lori is already here, perched on the edge of a leather chair, a glass of wine in her hand.

"Cameron will be right down. But I thought we could have a talk before she does," Savannah says.

Fuck. Here we go.

"We wanted to apologize for yesterday," she says, and my jaw drops. It's not at all what I thought she was going to say. "We were being protective and directing it at the wrong people."

"Understandable." Sly leans forward, resting his forearms on his thighs.

"It is, but it doesn't make it right."

"We're just so grateful for you." Lori's eyes well with tears, and I get the urge to hug the woman I was convinced was stealing our Dove away five minutes ago.

"We're glad we were in the right place at the right time. She means a lot to us too," Sly says. I'm glad he's the one talking because even though they're being nice, I'm still suspicious of their motives.

Yesterday, the manners I was taught as a kid kicked in, and I had no choice but to be polite. Sly was the one playing the role of asshole. But today, I have my walls up.

"She told us the same about you," Lori says.

"Did you guys make my mom cry?" Dove says, breezing in. I do a double-take because she doesn't look like herself. She's wearing wide-leg white jeans and an olive-colored top with little white daisies embroidered on it. She has on makeup, something she only did at the club, but it's light and fresh. Her hair is different too. I think she colored it, and instead of it being parted in the center so she can hide behind it when she wants, it's split on the side and curled.

"Baby, you look beautiful." Sly stands and gives her a hug.

"You like? I got highlights."

"Why?" I ask, earning a frown from both.

261

"I thought it looked nice." She combs her fingers through the curls.

"Don't be a dick," Sly says under his breath, reminding me for the millionth time.

"I didn't mean it like that. You look hot as hell." I stand and open my arms.

"You mean it?" She falls into me, and for the first time since I walked through the door, I feel like I can fuckin' breathe.

"Yeah, Dove. Just different, is all."

"Well, I think dinner is done. I made Cameron's favorite, sweet potatoes stuffed with veggies and vegan cheese." Savannah guides us to the formal dining room decorated like the rest of the house, in fuckin' chili peppers. This time, it's in the form of a wallpaper border around the top of the room.

"Are you a vegan?" I ask because while she was with us, she ate meat. Sissy and Tabitha would've had a riot on their hands if they had tried to prepare stuffed sweet potatoes for us.

"I was," she whispers, taking the seat between me and Sly with her moms on the other side of the table.

"You aren't anymore?" Savannah asks. It's not judgmental; she sounds genuinely curious.

"I didn't remember who I was, then once I did, it didn't seem important."

There's a flash of pain behind Savannah's eyes, and I can tell her daughter's disappearance weighed heavy on her. I get it. If Dove vanished from our lives, I'd lose my fuckin' mind. The difference is, they let the cops handle it and trusted them when they said they were looking. I would've bypassed law enforcement and burned the fuckin' world to ash in order to find her.

Lori walks around the table, placing a baked sweet potato loaded up with beans, peas, greens, and onions, topped with something that looks like cheese but didn't melt completely in the oven. My lip curls. It's a side dish. Where's the steak? Or hell, I'd take a chicken breast.

I inspect it with my fork, then glance over at Sly, who's doing the same thing.

"Just try it," Dove urges.

"I should've known grown men like you would need something more," Savannah says.

"No, it looks . . . good." Sly takes a big forkful and shoves it in his mouth. The face he pulls is comical. Dove and I bust out into a fit of laughter.

"Well, I love it." Dove takes an even bigger bite, but apparently, her tastebuds have changed, and her face contorts in disgust.

Instead of being offended, Savannah and Lori join in our laughter, spurring us on even more. By the time we compose ourselves, Dove has tears leaking from her eyes.

"I think this calls for pizza." Lori places a finger on her bottom lip. "I'm thinking a meat lovers for you boys."

"Thank you," Sly says, pushing his plate away.

The rest of the night is surprisingly fun, and slowly, my defenses go down. Her moms tell us comical stories from Dove's childhood, and I can feel the love they have for their daughter. Someday these women will be my in-laws, and being part of their family doesn't seem so bad.

We've never talked about marriage with Dove, but Sly and I have already planned it out. It's not legal for the three of us to marry, so it's a good thing we're outlaws. We'll have a ceremony, and though it won't be filed through the courthouse, it won't matter to us.

"It's getting late. We should head out," Sly says, standing. We congregated in the backyard after we ate pizza. They have an awesome setup with cushiony chairs and a fire pit.

"Do you have to?" Lori says, but it's directed at Dove.

"Um." Dove looks to Sly and then to me. She's conflicted.

"You want to stay here again tonight?" I ask.

"Only if you don't mind."

"We don't mind, baby," Sly says. "I'm glad you're enjoying your time with your moms."

She beams up at him. "I really am."

Walking us outside to our bikes, she holds our hands, happily swinging them back and forth. I haven't ever seen her this carefree. Even in the best of times—when I knew she was happy—it doesn't compare. It makes me feel all kinds of guilty for not making her do this sooner.

"I'll see you guys tomorrow?" she asks.

"You know it." Sly takes her in his arms, giving her a kiss.

They break apart, and she comes to me next. "How long can we stay?"

"How long do you want to stay?" I ask.

"I don't know. I just know I'm not ready to say goodbye again. Mia's being released tomorrow and invited me over. It'll be a rough day. I can already feel it. We have so much to talk about."

"If you need us to be with you, we will," I offer.

"No, I think it's something I need to do alone."

"Okay, so we can plan to leave the day after tomorrow?" I ask hopefully. I'm glad she did this and has reconnected with her past, but I'm anxious to get home.

She looks hesitant. "My moms got me a meeting with the head of my department at UMC. They think if I explain what happened, they might work something out with me."

My gaze flips to Sly, who looks like he just got punched in the gut. "You want to stay here?"

"No, but if I want to be an ER doctor, I need to finish my residency. I might need to live here long enough to finish my fourth year. I can maybe finish in Reno, but matching with another program sounds like a nightmare. I already have a medical license, though I wasn't around to renew it two years ago, so I need to figure that out too." She sighs. "There's just a lot to do."

"We'll figure it out," I say, but I don't fuckin' know anything about medical licenses or residencies. I barely scraped through college, earning a mechanical engineering degree before I peaced out of California and landed in Reno.

The differences in our lives before all this shit happened are becoming glaringly obvious. Petra was on our level. She saw some dark shit and, because of that, was jaded. But Cameron is optimistic and full of sunshine.

The woman in front of me right now would never cut the flesh off a man and then have sex three feet from his dead body, but Petra did. I'm starting to see that there's no future for us if this is who she wants to be.

"I'll call you after I get back from Mia's, and maybe we can go out or something," she says, looping her arms around my neck.

"Sure." I cradle her face in my hands and kiss her, pouring every ounce of emotion that I can into it.

"Love you."

"Love you too. Always will."

She watches as we start our bikes, the loud rumble filling the neighborhood and making her neighbors take a peek through their windows.

My mind races the whole drive back to the hotel, trying to find a way for us all to get what we want and be happy while doing it. I couldn't take being separated from Dove for an entire year or more. And by the time she's done, she'll have a whole life here with friends and coworkers. She won't want to come back to Reno to do what? Live in a dingy biker clubhouse where tomorrow isn't promised to us?

Only one thing makes sense. We need to let her go.

Chapter
THIRTY-ONE

Petra

My eyes are swollen and red after talking to Mia for four hours. I'm exhausted, and though I want to spend more time with Mom and Mama, I really need my guys. I need them to hold me and make me feel good, sleep nestled between them, and wake up to lazy morning sex.

The second Mom pulls into the driveway, I'm running upstairs to call them and see if they'll come get me. I bring up Sly's contact and hit the call button. It rings and rings, no answer. Maybe he's napping or in the shower. I dial Moto next, not getting an answer from him either.

Maybe they're *indisposed*. My pussy clenches at the thought. I want to be there with them.

"Mom, can you take me to the hotel Moto and Sly are staying at?" I call out as I dash back down the stairs.

"Why don't you take my car? I don't need it for the rest of the night."

"Are you sure?"

"Of course. Tell the guys I said hi." She smiles, and oh, God, it's so good to see that smile again. I hug her tight, rocking us back and forth. "I love you."

"I love you too. Be safe."

I can't imagine how hard it is for her to let me walk out the door alone. The dangers of the world are very real now.

I drive to the hotel without using GPS. Though my memory has returned, it's still a little broad and fuzzy. But the second I landed at the Vegas airport, it became crystal clear. I remember where things are and how to get there, and I remember my favorite restaurants and the best place for a cup of coffee.

I valet the car so I don't have to navigate the parking garage and walk with purpose to the elevator.

Sly told me their room number in case I wanted to be dropped off at the hotel, so I press the button for the top level and wait, tapping my toe. I hope I find them naked and doing dirty things that make me blush.

I find their room and knock on the door. There's a rustle on the other side, and a smile creeps onto my face in anticipation. Except the person who answers isn't either of the two I expected. It's a pretty woman in a fuzzy white robe.

"Hi," she says.

"I'm sorry, I think I have the wrong room."

"Oh, no problem. Have a nice day." The door shuts, and I glance at the plaque with the room number engraved on it. I'm certain this is where they said they'd be.

Deflated, I check with the front desk. Maybe I'm wrong, or maybe they moved rooms without telling me. I wait in line, shooting a quick text to Sly, telling him I'm here. But there's no response.

"Checking in?" a professional-looking woman behind the desk asks.

"Actually, I was hoping you could see if my"—I pause, not wanting to say boyfriends and earn a strange look—"friends moved rooms."

"What are the names registered? I can't give you the room number, but I can call up and let them know you're down here."

"Perfect. Thank you. It could be under—" My mouth clamps shut. They wouldn't register the room under Sly or Moto, but I've never asked their real names. How have I never asked them their real names? "Actually, never mind. They just texted." I hold up my phone like it's some kind of proof.

She smiles politely and moves on to the next customer.

I take a seat in the lobby, a weird feeling stirring in my gut. For as close as we are, I suddenly feel like I don't know them at all. There's not a lot of talk about who they were before the club. Sure, they each gave me small tidbits about their childhood, but they know everything about me. Every detail.

Am I that selfish that I didn't even think to ask them basic questions like their real names?

Pushing that aside for now, I text Moto this time.

Me: Where are you? I need to see you.

It's left on delivered. He doesn't even read it. Something's going on, and though I don't want to believe it, I think they left me.

Days. It's been days, and I haven't received so much as a text from either of my guys. The first day, I gave them the benefit of the doubt. Maybe something came up with the club, and they had to leave in a hurry. But four days later, there's no doubt left.

They abandoned me without so much as a goodbye. How could they do that to me? We were three peas in a pod. We spent every possible minute together for months. They took care of me, made sure I got better and were patient with me.

We killed a man together. Does that not mean anything to them? Though that woman—the one cutting a man to pieces—doesn't feel like me anymore. Not in this place where my moms live and where I went to college and medical school. That woman didn't get on the plane with me.

I haven't tried to call anyone else yet. I don't want to come off as an obsessed loon. I arbitrarily decided four days was a decent amount of time for Sly or Moto to get ahold of me and tell me the club was under attack, and that's why they had to rush out. Or Loki needed them for a run, so they thought they'd let me spend more time with my moms while they went.

Something. Anything.

But today is day four, and though I was up at the crack of dawn, I forced myself to wait until ten. That's late enough for a phone call, right?

I bring up Birdie's number first, not wanting to disturb Truly. She no doubt has her hands full with a new baby.

Birdie's chipper voice comes over the line. "Petra! Where you been, girl?"

"I'm in Vegas. I reunited with my moms and have been spending some time here. How are you?"

"I'm good. What's up?"

"Have you seen Sly or Moto lately?" I ask.

"Yeah, I saw them last night when I brought some food to the clubhouse."

So, they did go home. Somehow that hurts worse than if she said they were missing. At least then, an action plan could be made. The guys would rally, and we'd find them. Knowing they left and are ignoring me is so much worse. It leaves me with no control over the situation.

"Oh."

"Are they not answering their phones? I swear, these men. What would they do without us, am I right?"

"Yeah. What would they do?" My voice cracks, and I swallow back the emotion.

"You okay? Are you crying?"

I wasn't, but now that she asks, the tears spring free.

"They left me here and aren't returning my calls or texts and I don't know why."

"What happened? There had to be something. Did you get into a fight?"

"No, there was no fight. They just left."

"Think hard, girl. Men like ours don't leave for no reason. Especially when they're as in love as those two are with you."

I pull my covers up to my chin, wishing I had my weighted blanket. Sly got it for me after reading an article about how it suppresses the nervous system and eases anxiety. He was right. It worked.

"They came to dinner at my moms' house, and we had fun. I told them I wanted to stay the night there because I was visiting a friend the next day. I walked them to their bikes and told them how I had a meeting about returning to UMC to finish my residency. We kissed, and they said they'd see me the next day."

She lets out a knowing sigh.

"What?" I demand.

"Look at it from their eyes, babe. You're this smart woman with so much potential. I don't think they want to hold you back."

"Bullshit," I spit out, but it's not her I'm angry with, so I soften my tone. "I told them we'd work it out. We might have to be separated for a bit, but I'd only be an hour plane ride away."

"An hour plane ride is too far for men like ours. They need to have eyes on us, be there for everything we do. It's who they are. If you're clear 'cross the state, they can't do that. Plus, I'm sure they feel like you're too good for them. Doctors don't

typically hang out with a 1%er biker gang. This is all specula-
tion, but I've been around them long enough to follow their
thought processes.

"Loki had the same issue with me. I grew up in a mansion, attended private schools, drove a freakin' Range Rover.
He thought I was too good for him. It took a lot for me to
convince him otherwise."

"Oh, God," I cry. "I think I messed this whole thing up."

"No, you didn't. It's all them and their fucked up codes.
They're just trying to earn their sacrifice patch like the boy
scouts they are." I can practically hear her eyes roll.

"So, what do I do?"

"Go get your men, babe. But if you do, make sure it's what
you want."

"It is what I want. They're all I want."

"Good. Because men like them deserve the whole heart of
a woman, and when they get it? Fireworks. All the time."

"I know."

"Hate to cut this short, but I gotta run."

"Of course. Thanks for talking me through this."

"Anytime. And listen, when you get back to town, we need
to plan a girls' night."

"Okay. I'd like that."

Birdie has always been nice, but I think she was hesitant to accept me into the ol' ladies club. I don't blame her. So
much of my life was up in the air. But with that one invitation,
I know she liked what she heard from me today and is opening the door. I love how that feels.

"Good. Talk soon. Bye."

I disconnect the call and sit up. She's right. I need to know
exactly what I want and how I'm going to get it before I go
back home. I can't show up with some long-distance plan. And
now that I think about it, I don't want to be away from them
for an entire year. Somehow, I got caught up with everything

Mom and Mama were saying and all the plans they had for me.

I'm not Cameron, but I'm also not Petra. There must be a way for me to merge the two and get everything I want. My career, my guys, and the happy ever after I deserve.

It's time to clean up my mess.

"Thank you," I say, checking off the next item on my list.

"It's a pleasure. We're looking forward to having you on board," Mr. Mott says.

I hang up, feeling accomplished. I got a lot done in a week. After checking the Residency and Fellowship Database, I found a position open at a new hospital in Reno. I applied, and after meeting with the director of my program at UMC, he agreed to recommend the move.

I also managed to get my license renewed after explaining my situation and providing documentation. I have to be cleared by a psychologist and a doctor before issuing the renewal, but that'll be easy.

Mom and Mama are reluctant to let me go, but their parents weren't supportive of their relationship, and they vowed to never do that to me. So, they're standing behind my decisions and trusting me to make good ones.

There are things I can't fix. At least not until I get back to Reno next week. It won't be as easy as figuring out my career because there's no application to prove that just because I'm a doctor, I don't belong with bikers. That's a realization they'll have to come to on their own, but I'm hoping once they see everything I'm working through to be with them, that'll come on its own.

There's a chance I'm doing all of this, and they'll still reject me. It's a very real possibility, but there's no turning back. For this position, I have to live in Reno for at least a year, and I know I run the risk of seeing them every time I go out into the world.

That thought alone devastates me, but I need to have faith. Faith that what we had was special and worth fighting for.

Mom sets a cup of tea on the dining room table where I've spread out papers and files. "You look like you could use this."

"Thanks." I inhale the scent of my favorite tea that still takes me back to when I drank it long before living in Reno.

"Did you get everything squared away?" she asks.

"Yep. Only one thing left to do."

"What's that?"

"Go get my guys."

Chapter
THIRTY-TWO

Sly

"**W**as it the right choice, though?" I ask, resting against the carport post, arms folded.

"Yes," Moto huffs from where he's installing a custom timing cover on his new bike. It's a badass Royal Bastards logo, and I'm slightly jealous.

"What do you think she's doing right now?"

"She's probably already working for UMC."

"Yeah. Probably." I kick a rock that escaped from the gravel parking lot. "I miss her."

Moto sighs. "Yeah. Me too."

Leaving after having a chill night with her moms was the hardest thing I've ever done. Ignoring her calls and texts was the second hardest. The third? Not jumping on my bike right this fuckin' second and bringing her home.

"So, was it the right choice?" I press.

He shakes his head. "I don't know. Probably not."

It's the first time he's cracked. He knows we made a bad decision, but the asshole is stubborn as fuck. Since I can't go back and get her without him, I've been annoying him daily, waiting for this moment.

"Then let's go." I push off the pillar.

"We can't. She has a life."

"Correction, she had a life. One she loved. You know it, I know it, and she sure as shit knows it. We always said we wanted her to have all the power, but by leaving without even talking to her, we made her choice, and it wasn't right, bro. We gotta go back."

In the moment, I thought it was in her best interest. Then we got home, and I had more time to think. Maybe Cameron would've been happy living her perfect life in Vegas, but Petra wouldn't. She's seen too much, been through too much. Now she lives on the dark side, with us. I'm positive of it.

Moto brings his knees up, resting his forearms on them. He has his serious thinking face on, the one where his brows knit together and his jaw ticks. He looks broody and sexy. I shake my head.

Not now. Focus on getting Dove back.

"How about this? We go to Vegas, apologize for ghosting, be the grown men we are, and just fuckin' ask her what she wants. There's no harm in that, right?" I prod.

He stands up, and I think he's going to shut me down, but then he grins conspiratorially. "Fuck that asking shit. She belongs here with us."

"There's my man," I say, then give him a lip-smacking kiss.

Seven grueling hours later, we pull into the same hotel where we rent the same suite. Dove never had a chance to enjoy the amenities. Like the huge ass bathtub or the detachable shower head with a million different settings. I had big plans to see how many orgasms we could get out of her in one night.

The ride exhausted us, but the second we reach the room, we're buzzing with anticipation.

"Blow job or go get Dove?" I ask.

"Huh?" One dark brow quirks up in confusion.

"You won't sleep tonight if you're all antsy like this. So, I can give you a BJ, or we can go get our girl right now."

"Her moms will probably call the cops if we pound on her door at midnight."

"So, blowjob?"

"No. Let's go get her."

I chuckle and head for the door.

Riding at night is my favorite. There's a different vibe on the roads. It's more relaxed and chill. And I can turn on the purple LEDs on my bike that look badass.

Moto isn't a purple LED kind of guy. He's less talk and more action. It's what I love about him. He's the calm and balance to my crazy.

People honk and wave as we make our way down the strip. Everyone's fat and happy, drunk off indulgence and alcohol. It's like Reno, but on a heavy dose of steroids.

Once we hit the freeway, I open her up and cruise past the steady stream of cars. The anxious part of me wants to get there and get this over with; the rational part of me wants to delay in fear she'll turn us away. Or at least try to because if that happens, I'm not above using force.

Dove is ours. Maybe she got caught up in the safety of normality. Once we get her back, she'll be reminded that security isn't the same as happiness. How can you appreciate your life if you have nothing to lose?

We pull up to her house. The porch light is on, but everything else is dark, meaning she's asleep. We can't even pull some *knights in shining armor* bullshit and chuck rocks at her window because we don't know which one it is.

"Guess we knock," I say and pound my fist on the door, loud enough to wake the whole house.

Moto tugs on my wallet chain and grins in a boyish way that tells me how excited he is to see our girl. It's fuckin' cute.

Lights turn on inside, starting with upstairs where the bedrooms are, before slowly popping on downstairs. There's a moment of silence, probably looking through the peephole, then the lock disengages, and the door opens.

"What—"

That's the only word she gets out before I lift her off her feet and kiss her. She tastes like mint, telling me she hasn't been in bed for very long. Her feet barely touch the ground before Moto has her in his arms, giving her the same treatment.

Her eyes are wide when he sets her down. She has on the sexiest little sleep set. The tiniest pair of white sleep shorts barely cover her ass, and the matching tank is sheer enough that even with the dim lighting, I can see her puckered nipples. Goddamn, I can't wait to get them in my mouth and between my teeth.

"What are you doing here?" she asks.

"We came to get our woman," I say simply.

"But you left me." Her brow wrinkles, and the hurt we caused is written all over her face.

"We're sorry about that. We thought we were doing the right thing." Moto tucks his hands in his pockets.

"Well, you weren't. You didn't even tell me why, or hell, even say goodbye." She wraps her arms around herself protectively and fuck me. I hate that she feels like she has to do that with us. I deserve the shame it makes me feel.

"You had all these plans, and we didn't fit in them. There was no way we were gonna stop you from living your dreams, Dove," I say.

"I hadn't figured anything out. I was just excited about getting back into the program and was throwing ideas out." When she looks up, she has tears in her eyes. "Do you have any idea how badly it hurt when you abandoned me? The two men who swore they'd be there for me no matter what and then to find out it was all a lie."

It hits me that we might lose her. We fucked up, and realizing our mistake might not be enough to get her back.

No. I can't let that happen.

"It wasn't a lie, Dove. We're nothing without you. Fuckin' nothing. You're the air I breathe, and I'll fuckin' suffocate if you don't forgive us. Please give us the chance to make this right."

"I don't know what else to say except that we're sorry. We've been miserable without you. We royally fucked up like the bastards we are," Moto pleads.

"Yeah. You really did." She scowls at us while I try and come up with something else to say that'll get her back. I'm about to try again when a slow smile crosses her lips. "I got a new job."

My heart sinks to the ground. She's already moved on. We're too late.

"Oh yeah? Did you get back into your program?" I try to sound happy for her, but it falls flat. This could complicate things.

"No. It's a new program. You know that brand new hospital that opened up off Longley?"

She says it like I know Vegas well enough to know street names. The only Longley I know is in Reno.

In Reno.

My brows raise. "Really?"

"Really. I start in two weeks." She moves to the side and motions to the pile of boxes and suitcases sitting near the door. "My moms are driving me back to Reno tomorrow. I was hoping I could have my old room back. But I can always find an apartm—"

Moto has her back in his arms before she can finish, spinning her around on the porch. "Hell yeah, but you can't have your room back."

He sets her on the ground, and she flashes him a pouty scowl. "Why not?"

"Because we're all moving into Sly's room. His bed is bigger, and I can't take another night without you tucked between us."

"I like this plan," she says.

"You wanna be in my bed, baby?" I smirk, stepping between them so I can grab her ass and give her a kiss.

"Every night," she says against my lips.

Fuck me, she's perfect.

I bring a tray of two coffees and a tea to my room. It's nearly noon, but we just woke up. We're wiped out after the last few days.

Lori and Savannah followed us back to Reno. Dove took turns riding on the back of our bikes, much to her moms' dismay. It was stressful to have them driving behind us. I followed all traffic laws, including going the speed limit, and I hated every second of it. But having Dove's arms wrapped around me for half the ride made it better.

It was especially nice when she slipped her hand under my shirt and rubbed up and down my chest and abs.

Having her moms at the clubhouse was a whole new level of stress. I've never wanted to impress anyone but fuck if I didn't make sure everyone minded their manners while those two women were in our space.

I set the tray down on the bed and hand Dove her tea before giving Moto his coffee. They both give me appreciative smiles before taking a sip.

"I love my moms, but I'm so glad they're gone. I'm exhausted." Dove adjusts the sheet covering her naked body.

"What did they think of everything?" I ask, plopping down on the bed.

"I think they're okay with it. I'm glad we showed them

around Reno and got a tour of the hospital. I'm sure they were nervous, but they love you guys and trust you'll take care of me."

"They'd be happy to know we took real care of you last night." Moto slips a finger between her breasts and tugs the sheet down, putting her tits—tits covered in little red marks from all the love bites and hickies we left behind—on full display.

"I think we took pretty good care of each other." She yanks on the sheet covering him and exposes his thick cock already at half-mast.

I guess last night wasn't enough to satisfy them. Good, because I'm not done either. I move the tray to the dresser and push down my boxers. Both Dove and Moto stare as I walk over, my hard dick bobbing with each step.

"Get on your back, Moto. Dove, show me what a good girl you are and suck his fat cock," I say, stroking myself.

Moto lies flat, and Dove crawls seductively between his legs. Every time we're together, she shows more and more of her freaky side. It's a fuckin' honor to watch her own her sexuality.

She takes him in her mouth, her ass perched high up in the air, exactly as I envisioned. Moto gathers her hair into a ponytail and guides her up and down his length. She makes sloppy, wet sounds that are so fuckin' erotic.

I take my place behind her, standing at the edge of the bed. Her puckered hole and pink pussy are on display, and I debate which one I want to fuck. Maybe both.

I drag a finger up her slit, gathering moisture, and bring it to her cute little asshole. Her pussy's so wet and inviting that I make the split decision to guide my cock there. She moans in pleasure as I work myself inside. I don't care how many times I've been inside her; it never feels anything less than incredible.

I palm her ass cheeks roughly before giving one a smack. I'm an ass man, so seeing the way it bounces turns me on. I do it again and again until it's a vibrant red shade. She must like it too because she's drenching my cock in her arousal.

I glance up and see Moto's head off the pillow, his face scrunched and his bottom lip between his teeth. I fuckin' love watching him receive pleasure from our girl.

I bend over her body and hold out my thumb. His mouth opens, knowing what I want. Twirling his tongue around it, he gets it nice and wet before releasing it. I straighten and work my thumb inside her back entrance. She pops off Moto's cock and lets out a gasp.

Our girl loves having both holes filled up, which works out well for us. I hook my thumb in and fuck her harder, the loud slapping filling the room. Dove gets back to work on Moto, taking him deep enough she chokes, and oh, fuck. The sound it makes.

Lucky bastard. Not that I'm complaining because her tight heat is wrapped around me like a vice.

"Want me to come on your tits or down your throat?" he asks.

Dove doesn't answer so much as she releases his cock and arches her back. I wish I could see it, but from where I'm standing, all I see are her arms moving up and down as she jacks him. She doesn't have an aversion to swallowing, but I've noticed she does prefer to have us mark her.

Low, guttural grunts erupt from Moto before he's gasping for air. Watching him come has my balls tightening and my own orgasm cresting. I pull out and walk to the side of the bed.

"I want to come all over those tits too." I jack myself off, using her arousal for lubrication.

It takes seconds for my release to wash over me like a fuckin' tidal wave. Dove turns, fondling her cum coating tits, offering herself up for more. White ropes of cum shoot from my tip, landing on her breasts and stomach.

Fuck me, that was good. But our Dove was so focused on pleasuring us that she was left hanging. That won't do.

"Lie back, baby. Let us take care of you," I say.

She grins, knowing that when she has both our attention, she comes and comes hard.

I place my hands on her knees and spread her open before diving between her legs. Flicking her clit with my tongue, I finger her hole, making sure to stroke along her G-spot. I lap at her juices, savoring everything she gives me.

Glancing up, I'm stunned stupid to see Moto licking our mutual cum off her tits before giving her a raunchy kiss full of tongue. My cock twitches in response. There's no end to the amount of pleasure these two bring me.

I know she's about to come when she clenches down on my fingers. I suck on her little clit as she grinds her pelvis against my face. This is my favorite part. Watching her lose herself and chase her own release.

She screams our names before collapsing to the bed, her chest heaving with exertion.

We crawl back under the covers, not caring that we're a sweaty, sticky mess. We go through sheets like underwear, but Dove changes them each time with a shit-eating grin on her face as she mentally recounts how the sheets got dirty in the first place.

"I'm so fuckin' glad you're back," I say, kissing the top of her head.

"Me too."

Moto brushes the hair off her neck and plants a kiss behind her ear. "Me three."

"I have something important to ask you both." Dove worries her lower lip.

"Shoot," I say.

"What are your names? Your real names."

"Mark Watanabe," Moto says.

"Chris Buckley. Why do you want to know?"

"I went to the front desk at the hotel and didn't even have your real names to ask if you had moved rooms. It was embarrassing." The sadness over our brief breakup drips from her voice, stabbing me in the heart.

"I'm sorry about that, baby." I kiss her crown. "But the fact you didn't know those names means fuck all. You know everything about us that really matters. You know that, right?"

"I do. I just don't want to ever be in that position again."

"Sly's right. It means fuck all. Especially because we checked in under Butch Cassidy." Moto chuckles.

Dove turns on her belly and lifts her head up. "You two liken yourselves to cowboys, huh?"

"Only the outlaw ones." I grin, and Dove returns it.

"You two are too sweet to be outlaw cowboys."

I climb over the top of her and tickle her sides. My cock nestles between her ass cheeks and instantly hardens, making her fit of giggles end abruptly.

"Maybe we need to remind you how bad we can be," I growl into her ear, pushing my erection into her.

She moans and whispers, "Maybe you should."

Chapter
THIRTY-THREE

Moto

"Is it done?" I ask, walking into Sly's room.

He has four monitors on, each showing a different screen. I don't understand any of it.

"Yep. Our boy Antoine should be behind bars by tonight."

We could've captured the fucker, brought him to our kill room, and taken care of him that way. He would've deserved it. But he's high profile, and the risk was too great. Sly had a better idea. If he was fucked up enough to buy women and keep them as captives, he was surely up to some other shit.

We were right. He was inflating profits, which drove stock prices he benefitted from. He also bribed top executives in the company to hide his scam. Sly exposed all of this by hacking the Bowers Electric website and posting it all there for everyone to see. He also locked Antoine's web team out so they can't take it down.

The accounting fraud, racketeering, bribery, and illegal trading will probably only land him an eight-year sentence with a hefty fine that might bankrupt him. He deserves it, but it's not a big enough punishment for what he's done. Sly hacked his offshore bank accounts, siphoned off every penny, and donated it anonymously to a charity that works to end sex trafficking.

We also took Tyler's book and gave it to our buddy, Ryker, who works for the Reno Police Department. He promised to get it in the right hands.

Mia's testimony exposing what Eli Castillo did to her will authenticate the book, and with any luck, more women will be found. Antoine's name is in there—we made sure to black out Dove's name—so he'll be publicly exposed, even if they can't prove he was involved. All in all, Antoine's life as he knows it is destroyed.

We still might send him to Hades later on down the road when he's a penniless fuck living on the streets, but we'll decide on that when the time comes.

Franco Corsetti is another loose end we might have to tie up in the future. The news of Tyler's untimely death will reach him soon, and it won't take much for him to figure out it was us who delivered him to Hades. Again, we'll worry about that when the time comes.

"I completed my mission today; did you complete yours?" Sly asks.

I lift my chin. "Yup."

"Good. Let's go." We set off down the hall to find our girl.

Dove's been back at the house with us for a month now. It's been an adjustment to have her working. We used to have her full attention, but now her time is split between the hospital and us.

She's happy, though, so we can't complain. She still works one night a week at the strip club, though she now wears a mask around her eyes, not wanting to show her goods to a potential patient.

We tried to talk her into quitting, but she loves it too much. It's her release after a long week at the hospital. I can't complain.

I fuckin' love the exhilaration I get when I see all the people in the club lusting over what's ours.

We finally find her in the kitchen with Birdie. The two have become fast friends. Apparently, Birdie's the one Dove called when she wanted to know why we disappeared. Birdie saw how dedicated she is to us and let her into the ol' ladies club she shares with Truly, Bexley, and Riley.

"Smells good," I say, inhaling the scent of onion, garlic, and something else I can't place. "What are you making?"

"It's called moussaka. It's a Greek dish with lamb, eggplant, potato, and seasonings, topped with a béchamel and cheese." Birdie's in culinary school and always tries new things out on us.

"When will it be ready?" Sly asks, moving to stand behind Dove so he can feel her up while she works.

"It's ready now. Just waiting for the parsley Cameron is chopping up."

Dove asked everyone to start calling her by her given name, only using Petra when she's on stage. I'd be happy to lose that name completely, but she's taken ownership of it and turned it into something positive.

"Good timing. Come on." Sly takes the knife out of her hand and leads her to the backyard, where the whole club is already sitting around a few picnic tables we lined up.

She thinks she was helping Birdie with a new recipe, but we were just keeping her busy while Moto put together a little something.

Riley helped us decorate the picnic tables with tablecloths and fancy floral centerpieces. But it's still a biker club, so the tablecloths are black, the flowers are blood red, and the frilly stuff around the vases is black.

It's been a hell of a year, and we have a lot to celebrate. Birdie and Loki getting married, Truly and Roch having a baby, Coyote patching in, Goblin finding out he's Riley's dad and reuniting with her mom, and now me and Sly claiming Dove. Things feel settled. I'm sure this doesn't mean there aren't any storms to weather in the future, but it sure as shit gives us a reason to party.

"What's all this?" Dove whispers.

"It's a surprise," Sly whispers back, holding a chair out at the head of the table for her.

She looks uneasy as she sits down, but we like keeping her on her toes, so we give nothing away. Sly and I sit across from each other next to her while Loki and Birdie bring out two huge glass dishes of moussaka.

Once everyone has food on their plates, I flick my fork against my glass goblet of wine and stand. Dove's gaze latches onto me as she twirls a piece of her hair.

"I'm not one for flowery fuckin' words, but I wanted to say thank you. You all threw down for us when we needed you, and that meant the fuckin' world to us. It wasn't without casualty, and Ford'll never be forgotten for making the ultimate sacrifice. Let's raise a glass for him."

Everyone lets off a round of cheers and takes a minute to remember our fallen brother.

Sly stands, joining me. "The second toast goes to our girl, Dove. You've been through hell and back, but you rose from the ashes to become the woman you are now. You fought hard to be here, and we're so damn proud."

I fish the box out of my pocket, my hand shaking like a fuckin' pussy. We're not proposing just to her; we're proposing to each other, so no one gets down on a knee. Instead, we pull Dove to standing.

I take Dove's hand first. "Love was never what we were after. But the second we laid eyes on you, that's exactly what we found. We want to spend our lives making you smile, making you happy, and making you come hard."

My brothers hoot and holler, pounding on the wooden tables and making the glass dishes clank. Dove beams, her brown eyes sparkling.

I turn to Sly next. "This is as much for us as it is for Dove. We're brothers in arms, best friends, fuckin' lovers, and now we want to be your forever."

Sly smirks, managing to keep his biker reputation in check. But I know him well, and the look in his eyes is nothing but love.

"So, can we make this thing official?" I ask.

"Hell yeah," Sly shouts while Dove just nods, a hand over her mouth and tears running down her eyes.

I open the box, revealing three rings. All three are black gold. Mine and Sly's have three rubies embedded into the thick band, while Dove's is different, special. There's a giant ruby in the center and two smaller diamonds on either side, signifying the three of us. Wrapped around the engagement ring are two engagement bands in a woven pattern.

They're perfect.

Removing Sly's first, I place it on his finger before doing the same to Dove. Both of them remove the third ring and put it on my finger. My smile is so big my cheeks hurt. I fuckin' love seeing that hunk of gold on our hands.

Dove places a hand on Sly's cheek, then my own. "I love you."

"Love you too," Sly says.

We've never done this before, but the three of us lean in for a kiss. It's messy and uncoordinated, but it's fuckin' ours. No one needs to understand why we work the way we do; it's not their business. We found something special, something that can't be broken, no matter what.

And we'd die to protect it.

"Cheers to Cameron, Moto, and Sly. May your life be long, your club withstanding, your heart full of love, and your balls always empty," Loki calls out.

Laughter bubbles free and glasses clink while Dove admires the rings. "I can't believe you guys did this."

"Baby, we commissioned those rings to be made while you were in rehab," Sly says.

"Really?" Her ringed hand flies to her chest.

"Really." I stroke a thumb over her cheek.

The women move in, wanting to get a look at the ring, while our brothers crowd around us for back-slapping hugs. Once all the fanfare is over, we return to our seats, our food cold, but no one cares.

Looking around, it's hard to believe how different things are from even last year. We were once a rowdy, horny, lawless group of selfish assholes. Now we're a family, tighter than ever. Wouldn't change shit even if I could. We're better men now that we have love.

And doesn't that make me the luckiest bastard of them all because I have the hearts of two people?

My biker and my dove. My earth and my air. My fuckin' forever.

THE FUCKIN' END

ABOUT THE AUTHOR

 Misty Walker is a *USA Today* Bestselling contemporary romance author. Her books have been translated to Hebrew and adapted into audiobooks.

Her novels range between sweet and steamy to dark and delicious. Representation is important in her writing, so readers can expect a range of ethnicities and sexualities.

Misty currently resides in the high desert of Reno, NV with her husband, two daughters, and two dogs. She enjoys camping in her comfy travel trailer, reading, and writing. She loves connecting with readers, so her email and DMs are always open.

If you'd like to keep up to date on all her future releases, please sign up for her newsletter on her website. You can also order a signed paperback of this book, or any of her releases, there.

Connect with Misty:

www.authormistywalker.com
authormistywalker@gmail.com

Turn the page for a list of all of Misty Walker's books.

ALSO BY MISTY WALKER

Standalones:
Vindicated
Conversion (also available on audio)
Cop-Out
Crow's Scorn: Diamond Kings MC

Royal Bastards: Reno, NV:
Birdie's Biker (also available on audio)
Truly's Biker
Bexley's Biker
Riley's Biker
Petra's Bikers

Brigs Ferry Bay Series:
Kian's Focus (also available on audio)
Adler's Hart
Leif's Serenity
Doctor Daddy
Brigs Ferry Bay Omnibus

You can purchase signed paperbacks on my website:
www.authormistywalker.com

ACKNOWLEDGMENTS

Kristi, I love that as we grow, we grow together.

Ty-bot, thank you for being my safe place to land.

Ariadna, Sarah, Sara, Elizabeth, Lauren, and Jayce, thank you for being my beta team. I'm equally grateful and mortified that you see me in my rawest form and continue to stay!

Diana, you're the bestest alpha reader ever. Thank you!

Sarah Goodman, I wouldn't have confidence without your comments. You hype me up in a way no one else can!

Molly Whitman, you make me a better writer and I'm forever thankful for you. Plus, you're an incredible artist. If this editing thing doesn't work out, I see a future in pornographic drawing for you.

Stacey Blake, thank you for making the pages of this book as badass as the bikers themselves.

Mom, you are stronger than you'll ever know and tougher than any heroine I could ever write.

To my readers & my reader group, Misty Walker's Thirsty Readers, thank you the most! You guys rock my world and motivate me to keep writing. I love nothing more than to get your messages and read your reviews. It's a great big book world, but you choose to read my books, and that means everything.

Lorelai and Mabel, this is another book I don't want you to ever read, mmkay? ILY.